SPECTRED ISLE

GREEN MEN · BOOK ONE

KJ Charles

Published by KJC Books

Cover by Lexiconic Design
Interior design by eB Format
Green Man by Lexiconic Design

Print ISBN 978-1-9997846-6-9

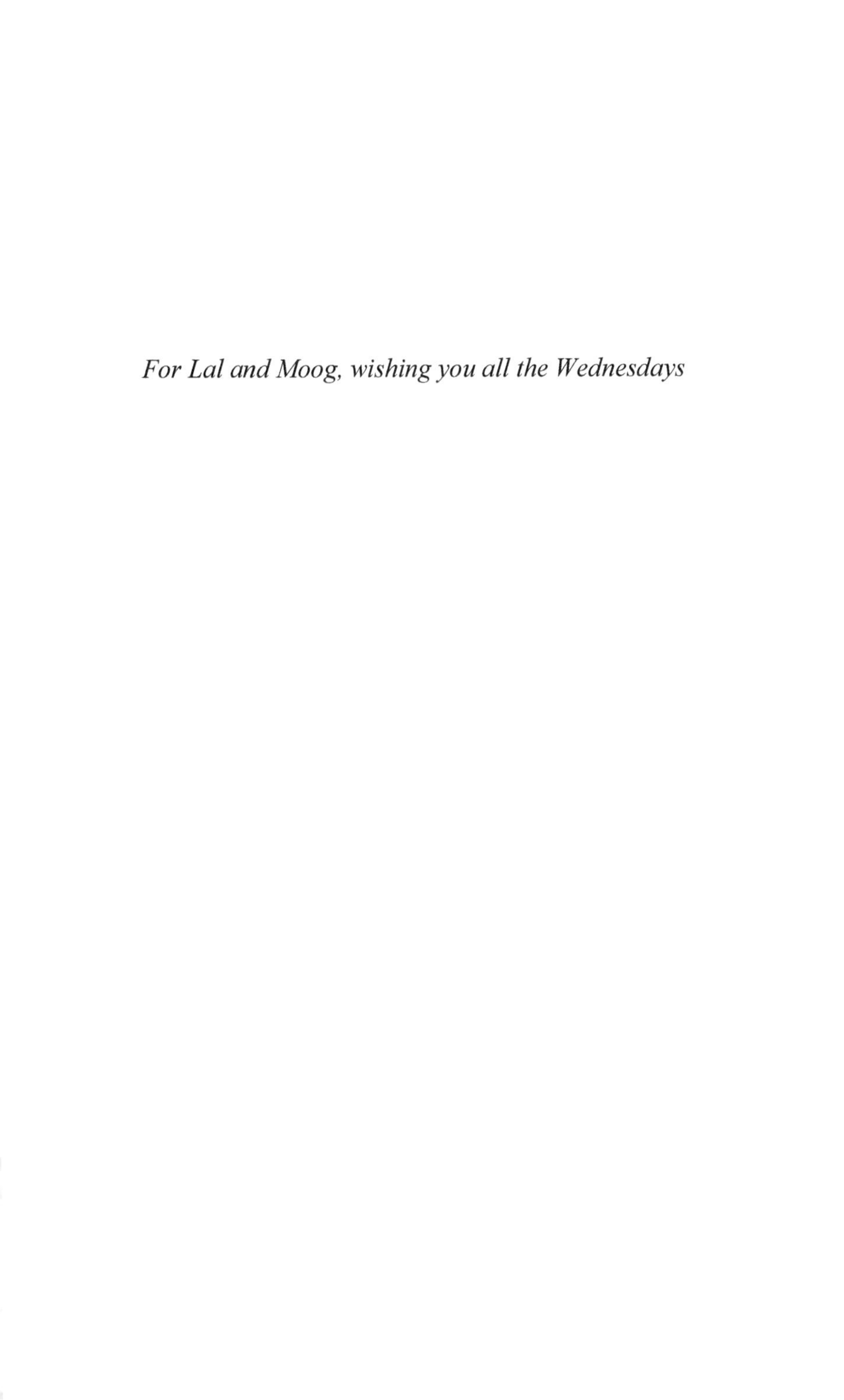

For Lal and Moog, wishing you all the Wednesdays

CHAPTER ONE

London, April 1923

It was a beautiful day for an outing.

Saul Lazenby felt an unaccustomed contentment as he hopped off the train at Oakleigh Park station, up in the wild suburban highlands of Barnet, North London. It was pleasant to stroll in the spring sunshine, particularly because he was doing so alone. He was deeply grateful to his employer, who had taken him on when nobody else would, but that didn't make Major Peabody's endless lectures about his ridiculous theories easier to bear. Saul had no right to complain in the circumstances, and no intention of doing so, but it was undeniably pleasant to have a little time to himself, and to be paid for, literally, a walk in the park.

That was his destination: Oak Hill Park, still a wild expanse of heath despite London's unstoppable crawl outward over the towns and villages in its path. The green space was untouched as yet, dotted with bushes and beech stands and, naturally, oaks. Trees were ever a comfort to Saul. He'd loved the harsh desert landscapes of Mesopotamia and the unforgiving sun; he loved dry bricks and ancient stone and the feel of millennia-old earth on his fingers; but there was something profoundly soothing about an English oak, quietly standing in the green. He inhaled the clean air with satisfaction and turned his back on the city that squatted low in the Thames valley under a sullen grey haze.

Perhaps he should leave after all. He'd come to London because it didn't care; he'd feared, if he moved to some small town, that his reputation would follow him, that new friends and neighbours would turn from him with disgust. Some former friends had suggested he change his name and start afresh, but that seemed like dodging punishment. He deserved to shoulder the consequences of his actions.

He pushed the thought aside, as far as it would ever go, and set off down the path through the park.

If my theory is correct, there will be a site on the west side of Oak Hill Park, Major Peabody had said. *A burial, a standing stone, a sacred grove. A historical artefact or a local legend. Explore for me and see what your professional instincts can discover.*

Saul's professional instincts were shaped by his doctorate in archaeology from Oxford and two years working on excavations in Mesopotamia. Major Peabody believed that if the ravens left the Tower of London, the city would fall. It was not a match made in heaven, but Saul gave the Major the best work he could and strove to be respectful without losing what little self-esteem he still had.

There was no sign of any sacred Druidic grove or whatever bee was in the Major's bonnet this time, but there was a truly magnificent oak dominating the landscape not far ahead. Saul took another step towards it, admiring the gnarled branches and the bright light green of its fresh new foliage, and it burst into flame.

The fire erupted so violently that Saul heard a faint whoomph of air, like an explosion, and his immediate war-trained thought was, *Mortar.* He could see all around the heath, though, and there was no engine of war, no gun, no people, even, except for one man some way down the path who was running towards the tree with such urgency that Saul found himself jog-trotting, then sprinting, to meet him.

By the time Saul reached the tree, it was blazing so hard he couldn't go near it, waves of heat rolling out and stinging his eyes. The other man was standing, breathing rather less heavily than Saul, staring at the conflagration.

"What the devil happened?" he demanded aloud, in a decidedly upper-class tone.

Saul couldn't tell if the man was asking him or the empty air; he replied anyway. "I've no idea. I thought it was a mortar at first but—"

"We're not at bloody war any more."

"*At first*," Saul repeated. "That or lightning, but the sky's clear as you like. Did you see anything?"

"Such as what?"

Saul had no idea. "Someone with some kind of gasoline? That blaze is—"

"Unnatural," the man completed. He was regarding the tree with hard, sceptical eyes. Saul couldn't blame him. The tree had been a living thing; if you'd chopped it down the wood would have taken a good year to dry out for burning, but the fire was so fierce he felt it heating his cheeks, and so loud that they were almost shouting over the noise of branches crackling and snapping. How in God's name did a live tree burn like that?

"It must have been lightning," he said aloud. "I had a view of the whole park."

"And you saw a very small thunderstorm above?"

Saul had trained himself to endure contempt, but he didn't have to take sarcasm from a stranger. He turned away from the inferno and had his first good look at the other man.

He was of medium height, but thinnish and rangy, which made him appear taller: the sinew and whipcord build that Saul himself had, and liked. English from his features, with dark hair and much lighter hazel eyes under near-black, slanted brows. A saturnine, sardonic sort of face, clean-shaven; a mouth that seemed made to sneer. He looked like the kind of man Saul had met a great deal in the war in the officer ranks: a thoroughbred aristocrat, effortlessly superior, endlessly disdainful.

"See anything you like?" the man enquired, those finely shaped lips twisting, and Saul realised he'd been staring.

Well, sod you, fellow. "I can't say I do, no," he said affably, and wasn't sure if the flicker in the man's expression was amusement or affront.

By now there were others running up: a park keeper, passers-by, people demanding whether anyone had called the fire brigade. Saul found himself obliged to repeat his account a dozen times, in the face of blank incredulity to which he could scarcely take exception. There had been no mortar and no lightning strike, and the tree had ignited from the top, its branches burning before the trunk caught, which put paid to the gasoline theory unless an aeroplane had dropped the stuff from the sky. There was no explanation.

"Spontaneous combustion," said a matronly woman with a firm nod.

"Lot of nonsense," muttered a man dressed like a shopkeeper.

"It is not. It's in Dickens," the woman said triumphantly. "Spontaneous combustion, that's what this is."

"You mean, it caught fire?" Saul asked.

"That's right. Spontaneous combustion." She evidently relished the term. "That's what happened here."

Saul didn't agree that *It caught fire* answered the question *Why did it catch fire?* in any satisfactory way, but the nods around him suggested he was in the minority. He glanced to the saturnine man, feeling he might see something of his own disbelief on that lean, compelling face, and saw with a slight feeling of anticlimax that the fellow had gone. He must have slipped away some time ago, for though Saul looked around, he could see no sign of a departing form.

There was an elderly man standing some way apart. His arthritic hands were clenched on the stick on which he leaned, and he looked as though he was close to tears. Saul sidled up to him and asked, softly, "Sir? Are you all right?"

"The tree," the old fellow said. His mouth was working with palpable distress. "Her tree. Why?"

"It seems to have been some strange chance—"

"That was no chance," the old man said vehemently. "Not her tree."

"Whose tree?"

"The Woman Clothed by the Sun."

Saul could all but hear the capital letters, and the expression seemed vaguely familiar. "The...?"

"The Woman Clothed by the Sun. The Prophet. Mrs. Southcott."

"Mrs... *Joanna* Southcott?" Saul asked.

"This was her tree. Time and again she sat under it vouchsafing unto her followers the revelations of the Lord."

"Of course." As a normal sort of Englishman, Saul's reaction to religious enthusiasm was usually to remove himself from the conversation as quickly as possible. He couldn't. Major Peabody was going to be overjoyed by this. He smiled at the old man. "Tell me more."

The Major's reaction was all Saul could have desired. "Would that I had been there!" he kept repeating. "Would that I had seen it for myself! I must have observed some detail that would allow us to place this in its true context. You know Mrs. Southcott's work, of course, Lazenby?"

"You have mentioned her, sir. And my informant told me a great deal."

Major Peabody ignored that. Once he had decided he wanted to say something, a staff sergeant bellowing *Yes, I know!* in his ear would make no difference. "An ordinary servant girl who in the noonday of her life was touched by the gift of prophecy. She proclaimed herself to be the Woman of the Book of Revelation—"

"And visited East Barnet often, so her devotee told me," Saul put in. "He says the tree was widely known as Mrs. Southcott's tree. I confirmed that with the park keeper."

"Mrs. Southcott's tree," Major Peabody repeated. "A true case of spontaneous combustion to which you can bear eye witness!"

"Well, I saw a tree burst into flame, and could not find any reason for it." Saul would not put his name to any supernatural claim, but he had a sinking feeling that Major Peabody might do that for him.

"Yes, that is what I said. A remarkable phenomenon. I believe I begin to see. This confirms everything I have learned." He hurried to his map. Saul rubbed the bridge of his nose and wondered what he had started.

"I should like to examine the box," the Major muttered. "I must see the box."

Joanna Southcott, the prophetess—or the crazed old woman who spouted nonsense, according to point of view—had left behind a sealed box of secret prophecies, only to be opened at a time of national crisis and in the presence of twenty-four bishops of the Church of England. Despite strong representations from her band of followers, this had not been done during the war. Major Peabody said the bishops had been intimidated by the responsibility, which Saul translated as *declined to participate in such a farce.*

"You think the box should be opened? Is there a national crisis?"

"I shouldn't presume to decide when the box is to be opened," the Major said testily. "But if Mrs. Southcott's tree has spontaneously combusted, the box itself may display signs of supernatural activity."

"Does it really exist?" Saul asked thoughtlessly. The Major gave him a hurt look, and Saul altered that to, "Can it be seen? Who has it?"

"That, I do not know. Perhaps you might investigate. Yes, find out for me, Lazenby. I must think about the implications of today's event."

Saul had heard about this job a year ago, from a man whom he had once counted a friend, and who had put the notice his way out of pity. *A lunatic, harmless enough, but quite convinced by every piece of fantastical nonsense he hears. According to him, London is a hotbed of magical powers, haunted temples, and secret societies. He's a ridiculous crank, but he's rich, he's offering good money for an archaeologist to act out his games, he'd be delighted by a man of your educational accomplishments, and it's not as though you have anything to lose.*

His acquaintance had been quite right. Major Peabody had been ecstatic to employ Saul, with his doctorate from Oxford and his two years' work excavating alongside the great Leonard Woolley. He hadn't given a damn about Saul's war record or the conviction, and unlike the very few other people who'd been prepared to give him work since 1918, hadn't expected him to accept lower pay and worse treatment as a consequence. He was in every way a fair and reasonable employer, except that his theories were tripe, his credulity exasperating, and his obsessions laughable. He believed every bit of folklore that came his way, every medieval myth or Victorian fantasy of the past. If Saul had harboured any hope of returning to a career in archaeology, working for Major Peabody would have destroyed it. He had, repeatedly, to remind himself that he had and deserved no such hope.

The Major's great idea was that London was a mass of sacred sites laid out in mystical patterns. He'd covered a map in pins and connected them with threads, crowing with pride when he could connect five pins to form a pentacle or six for a Star of David. Worse, he'd concluded that if he had three likely sites that might be part of a pattern, the missing points in it could be logically inferred and a new, previously hidden sacred site discovered. This meant that he would stick a pin in a featureless bit of Metro-land, and then ask Saul to find evidence of a holy well, plague pit, or undiscovered Anglo-Saxon earthwork. Saul had wondered whether to warn him about the dangers of looking for data to fit one's theory, and decided that was akin to advising a deep-sea diver that it was a bit wet out.

It had been a year of astounding futility right up to the point the tree burst into flame.

Major Peabody regarded that admittedly bizarre event as a spectacular vindication of his theories. Saul considered that, since this was the first of some hundred and fifty "sacred sites" that had been anything more than a random rock or patch of grass, his strike rate was significantly lower than might be expected by chance. He didn't say so. Let the Major enjoy his triumph; it did no harm.

It proved surprisingly easy to track Mrs. Southcott's box down. Saul had harboured an idea that any such thing would be a closely guarded relic, but the prophetess's band of believers were only too happy to point him in the right direction, and two days later he and Major Peabody were at Paddington Station, taking a train to Newport. Saul had telegraphed ahead to the family who held the absurd thing, and had booked first-class seats for them both at his employer's generous insistence. He might be acting as the private secretary to a crank, but at least he would do it well.

His mild sense of satisfaction lasted until the train was about to move off. They sat in a six-person compartment, in the usual configuration of two facing benches. It was empty except for themselves, but as the whistle screeched and steam billowed, the door opened, and a man sprang in.

"Good day, gentlemen," he said, slamming the door and removing his hat. "I beg pardon for intruding."

"Not at all," cried Major Peabody as the train set off. "It is, after all, public transport; I trust my colleague and I won't disturb you with too much talk. Good day to you."

The man sat down opposite Saul, took up his newspaper, looked over it, and smiled. It was a sly, charming, insincere smile and it was worn by the man from the burning tree.

Saul was sure of it. He'd paid enough attention at the time, he'd had that sardonic, highly bred face and voice in his mind for hours after, and here he was, the man who'd been at the Southcott tree, as they set off to see the Southcott box.

It was the kind of coincidence that would delight the Major's heart, and Saul wasn't sure he could bear it. He could imagine the saturnine man's sneer as the Major spouted mystical nonsense, and for all his fussy employer exasperated him Saul didn't wish to see him mocked, any more than he wished to be known as a lunatic's jack-of-all-work.

The man was still looking over his newspaper at Saul, and as their eyes met, he tilted a brow in unmistakable question.

God. It couldn't be—

No, of course it wasn't an approach. Surely that was just Saul's own wishful thinking. Although there had been that *Like what you see?*...

No. And even if it was, Saul had no intention of entertaining it. The man was undeniably the kind he liked—those long, brown, strong fingers on the newspaper, the lean build, the winging brows—but Saul had been husbanding pennies and rationing himself to one meal a day before he secured this post; if he lost it he'd be ruined. He was not going to commit indecent acts in a railway station convenience with a total stranger on his employer's time, even if that was the stranger's intent, which, he told himself firmly, it probably wasn't.

The man was looking at him with amused puzzlement, as though Saul had spoken his determination out loud, and it dawned on him that if it *wasn't* an approach, he must seem deranged not to acknowledge the fellow.

"Pardon me, sir," he said. "I think we've met before?"

"I think we did," the man agreed, lowering his paper. "Randolph Glyde, at your service."

"Saul Lazenby."

"Charmed." Mr. Glyde glanced at Major Peabody, who hastened to introduce himself, and volunteered that he was an antiquarian researcher.

"How fascinating," Mr. Glyde said. "And are you an antiquarian as well, Mr. Lazenby?"

"Lazenby is an archaeologist," Major Peabody said over Saul. "An Oxford man, now devoting his time to my studies."

"And what do you do, Mr. Glyde?" Saul asked, before the Major could say any more. "Are you a man of leisure?" The suit he wore was sufficiently well-made to suggest wealth, whether earned or inherited.

"Ah, no, so few of us can afford leisure these days. Those iniquitous death duties, you know. I work for my bread. I'm a commercial traveller."

Death duties had hit the great landed estates very hard, and the newspapers were filled with stories of the newly labouring aristocracy. The heirs to earldoms were becoming radio announcers and photographers, while the daughters of dukes took up as mannequins or wrote pieces for magazines. Nevertheless, the disjunct between the man's appearance and the idea of a commercial traveller was such that Saul found his brows lifting sharply. "You're a salesman? Of what?"

"Wines and spirits," Mr. Glyde said promptly.

"For whom?"

Mr. Glyde's smile glinted. "Plummet and Rose."

"Where's your sample case?"

"I sent it on ahead." The smile was widening.

Major Peabody gave a harrumph. "There is no need to interrogate our fellow traveller, Lazenby. Wines and spirits are a most respectable business for a gentleman. Perhaps you could recommend me a port, Mr. Glyde? I have need to replenish my cellar."

They discussed port for a while. Saul stayed out of the conversation, watching Mr. Glyde's face. He knew nothing of the wines and spirits trade but he did feel sure that a commercial traveller of any competence would have a sales book with him, or make an effort to conclude a bargain, and Mr. Glyde was obviously competent. He had that air, the effortless confidence of a man who never questioned his own intelligence, fortitude, or judgement. Saul wouldn't have been able to put his finger on precisely what showed it, but you could tell it in a man, just as you could tell a man from whom it had gone.

But the clever Mr. Glyde wasn't making any effort to sell wines and spirits to a highly receptive audience, and Saul had an increasing sense that something didn't add up.

It had to be chance that Mr. Glyde was on this train, in his carriage. There was no other possibility, given they hadn't exchanged names. Or—had he still been there when Saul had given his name to the park keeper? Might he have tracked him down from that?

But why would he? Saul didn't believe for a moment that Mr. Randolph Glyde, with his well-cut suit and faint, lazy smile, would go to such trouble for a thin, sunburned man with defeated eyes. If he'd wanted a fuck, which was at least in principle not outwith the bounds of probability, Saul was of the opinion he'd have suggested one on the spot.

He had no reason to have tracked Saul down. But if his presence here was chance, why was he giving every impression of lying about his profession, and why hadn't he said anything about their previous meeting? *Jolly peculiar show with that tree bursting into flame for no reason, wasn't it?*

As he'd anticipated, his employer took the first opportunity to turn the conversation to his obsession. Mr. Glyde made some remark about a vintage port tasting better with a dusty old book by his side upon which Major Peabody leapt, launching into a description of his library. The self-described salesman made no effort to bring the conversation back to the topic of port, instead listening to the Major with a look that was just slightly sceptical as he described his great theory of the psychic patterns of London, giving Saul undeserved and unwanted credit as his collaborator. Saul could only sit, fuming, as Mr. Glyde's eyelids flickered occasionally in his direction.

After interminable miles, the train pulled in to a station where there would be a ten-minute stop for passengers' comfort. Major Peabody hurried out to use the facilities. Saul and Mr. Glyde sat and looked at one another.

"So," Glyde said. "Archaeologist. Have you dug up *very* many magical artefacts in North London?"

Saul set his teeth. "Major Peabody is my employer. I can't listen to any mockery of his enthusiasms."

"Then you must spend a great deal of time with your fingers stuffed in your ears. What drives an Oxford man to work on such tarradiddles? He must pay remarkably well to silence the objections of your academic training, if not your conscience."

"That is none of your damned business," Saul said furiously. "I might as well demand what makes a gentleman lie to total strangers about his profession."

Glyde's lips curved unpleasantly. "What a peculiar accusation."

"You're a highly peculiar salesman. I don't know what brings you to this train—"

"Do you not," Glyde said, and those light eyes snapped onto Saul's with almost physical force, drilling into him, a look so intense and commanding that Saul felt a momentary urge to curl up and agree to anything. "Do you not have an inkling of my purpose, Mr. Lazenby?"

Saul narrowed his eyes, a physical expression of defiance that seemed to help his inner resolve. "The only motive I can imagine is one entirely discreditable to a gentleman, and if that *is* the case, I suggest you don't try it. In fact, I suggest you find another carriage. I've no interest in your importunities and I shan't see my employer insulted."

Glyde's brows shot up, then he laughed. "Nicely deflected. I almost wonder if I believe you."

"I don't give a damn if you believe me or not. But I'll be happy to turf you out of this carriage if I must, and we shall see if that convinces you."

"How remarkably belligerent," Glyde said. "Do you have any idea what you're about?"

"I'm capable of removing your sort from decent company, if that's what you mean." Saul was less sure of that than he'd have liked to admit. He'd been underfed for some years, between a Mesopotamian gaol and unemployment in London, and Glyde looked to be in hard training. On the other hand, Saul was in a hell of a bad temper, and the prospect of shaking this sarcastic sod till his teeth rattled seemed worth the probable consequences.

Perhaps Glyde read that determination in his face. He shrugged one shoulder and, as Major Peabody opened the carriage door and bustled back in, he murmured a smooth word of farewell and disappeared, leaving Saul in a frustrated state of targetless anger, curiosity, and just a touch of disappointment, as though there had been an opportunity lost.

CHAPTER TWO

Randolph let himself into the house on Fetter Lane with a sense of deep relief and a cry of "Shop!"

"Here!" yelled Sam from the living room. Randolph dumped his wet hat and coat on the stand and came in to see his three fellows seated comfortably around the room, feet up, looking disgustingly warm and relaxed.

"I hope you idle swine know it's raining outside," he said, collapsing into a chair. "God, I'm tired. Someone pour me a drink."

"Pour it yourself," Sam said, but made a long arm for the whisky bottle and handed it over.

"Have a heart, I've been on my feet all day. Incident in Peckham. *Peckham,*" Randolph repeated with distaste.

"What's wrong with Peckham?" Isaacs demanded.

"It's not Belgravia or St. James's," Sam said. "You're an awful snob, Randolph."

"I try. Specifically what was wrong with Peckham was a corpse that had signally failed to lie down and be dead, and that's the second one this week. What a bloody day."

Sam groaned. "Did you find the cause?"

"Found it; dealt with it," Randolph said crisply. He had no urge to relive his messy afternoon in detail. "Are you swine really going to make me get up for a glass?"

Isaacs picked a tumbler off the shelf next to his chair and threw it. Randolph caught the heavy glass more by luck than judgement and gave him a glare in lieu of thanks, then poured himself a generous measure and knocked back half of it in a swallow.

The burn of the alcohol in his throat was sufficiently heartening that he found himself toying with a joke along the lines of *whines and spirits*. He didn't have the intellectual vigour to make it work; instead he struggled for a second to place the phrase, before remembering that absurd conversation a few days ago with the man Lazenby in the train.

If only more of his work involved sinewy, sunburned, sensitive men, rather than people who lacked the common decency to die properly. He downed the remaining whisky, topped up his glass, and said, "So how was everyone else's day?"

Barney pulled a face, making himself look more than usually boyish in that minor-public-school way of his. "Ugh. Well, Isaacs and I went to Smithfield, as you asked."

"So you did. What did you find?"

Barney waved a hand for the whisky bottle in lieu of answer; Isaacs got up to retrieve it. Randolph raised a brow. "Go on, tell us. Unless we're to understand from your unaccustomed indulgence that you have seen horrors the like of which no mortal man can bear."

"Nah," Isaacs said. "That was Wednesday."

Barney grinned. "Quite. No, today wasn't unwarrantedly ghastly at all. It's just..." He scratched the back of his hand, a light unconscious gesture that drew Isaacs's sharp gaze. "Well, it was uncomfortable. That rather nasty feeling in the air. So we had a look around, and asked a few questions, and, uh—"

"Turns out the problem was in Cock Lane." Isaacs completed Barney's sentence for him, as he so often did. Two minds with but a single thought, alternately expressed in the civilised English of Eton and Sandhurst, and a Cockney rasp. "Knocking and scratching. Which—"

"The fact is, we'd swear it was the Cock Lane Ghost," Barney concluded. "And I *know* you're going to say that's not possible."

"Well, yes, I am," Sam said. "The Cock Lane Ghost was a fraud. There was nothing to it."

"I must say, given the state of this ghost-raddled city, it takes a special gift to spend a day on one of the few manifestations that *doesn't* exist," Randolph added, applying as much acid as possible to his tone. He had had a trying week.

"Yes, we're aware it was a fake," Barney said. "Now it's real."

"Oh, God," Sam said. "Are you sure?"

Isaacs had dark eyes, heavily hooded at the best of times, narrowing to slits in moments of annoyance. "Not to say we're experts like you gentlemen, but we've been at this game more than five minutes."

"We're sure." Barney took a measured sip of whisky. "It's blasted uncomfortable. Malice, accusation, a mood of growing discomfort and distrust among neighbours—"

"Could it be a genius loci?" Randolph asked.

His three companions all looked blank. Barney remembered some Latin from his expensive education, but possessed only the slightest, scrabbled-together knowledge of the arcane; Sam knew more about the theory and practice of ghost-hunting than anyone Randolph had ever met, but had barely darkened a school's doors; Isaacs had neither formal nor occult learning. "Plebeians," Randolph told them all. "Genius loci, a spirit of place. One of those manifestations that arises from the atmosphere. A spiritual echo."

"Oh, yeah, I know what you mean," Isaacs said. "No."

"Definitely not," Barney added. "It's an entity."

Sam shut his eyes. "Fine. Did you get rid of it?"

The soldiers glanced at one another. "Well, it buggered off," Isaacs said. "I wouldn't feel quite comfortable in saying *got rid of.*"

"No, I agree. It felt a sticky sort of blighter and you know, this isn't our field."

"Ugh." Sam rubbed his forehead. "Randolph, do you have time to take a look tomorrow? I'll be tied up all day with Syrena Phan, and this doesn't sound right."

"If I must, dear fellow," Randolph said with dramatic gloom. Sam didn't bother with even a perfunctory smile, which was unusual. "Is there something bothering you, at all?"

"Oh, you know. Well. Another approach from Whitehall today."

"Arseholes," Isaacs muttered. "You told them to sling their hook, right?"

If there was one principle that united their little band, it was refusal to do Government work. The thoroughly decent Barney would unquestionably kill before he let bureaucrats get their soft, unaccountable hands on Isaacs again, while Sam, whose family had been destroyed by the War, regarded the British state with all the hatred of which his cheerful nature was capable. He looked fairly uncompromising now. "Of course. But they were very pressing. Threatening stiff penalties."

"I'll tell 'em where they can press their stiff penalties, whenever you like," Isaacs growled.

"Already did. They aren't listening. The Shadow Ministry would like us to know it's time for a united front."

"Nothing fills my heart with more optimism than the British ruling classes establishing a Front," Randolph said. "It was *such* fun last time."

Isaacs cackled; Barney got it a second later, and snorted. Sam didn't laugh. "Something seems to be going on over there, gents. Sir Ranjit's getting old; I've heard younger men are trying to force him out of the job. There'll be any amount of political coups and manoeuvring planned, and I have no doubt they'll be looking for pawns to play with. I wouldn't be worried by that alone, but I had a letter today. From Jo."

All three of the others sat up straight. Randolph had never met Jo, Sam's foster-sibling and the most talented soothsayer England had produced in a century, but he'd heard a fair bit, including that Jo, like many of the greatest seers, was neither man nor woman in the conventional sense, and should be referred to as "they". Jo had left Britain before the War, disappearing to an undisclosed location abroad rather than permit their prophetic powers to be used as a military weapon. They had never returned, for fear of detention; Sam couldn't visit them in case he was followed; even letters had to go through a complex poste restante system. If Jo had written, something was up.

"What did they say?" Randolph asked.

"How is they?" added Barney, who did his best. "Well, I hope?"

Sam made a face. "I think well, but troubled. They're having visions. Not terribly specific, but they wouldn't write if it wasn't important." He took a letter from his pocket. "They say, *It's hard to judge what is related. The veil is so thin and hangs in tatters in too many places. I must tell you this: no sign will guide you; no gun will save you; a fool and a knave may do what an emperor could not, and the unenlightened man brings light.*"

There was a respectful pause, which Isaacs broke with, "You what?"

"Not the faintest," Sam said. "It will make sense in the end one way or another but, as Uncle Robert used to say, the hard part is working out what it means while it's still useful. He was awfully good at it, but then he could do The Times crossword before breakfast. I don't suppose any of you—"

"I think I got a four across, once, in 1920. Let's have it again?" Barney repeated the words after Sam. "*No sign will guide you; no gun will save you; a fool and a knave may do what an emperor could not, and the unenlightened man brings light.* Umph. Any ideas?"

"An obvious one," Randolph said. "We know what an emperor, or at least the Kaiser, could not do as of 1918."

There was a nasty pause as the others considered that.

"Um," Barney said. "Sam, old fellow, would you say Jo might tackle quite such...large matters?"

"If you mean, did they just prophesy the fall of empire, I've no idea."

"Could we ask?"

"They won't know. They aren't obscure on purpose, believe me. If they could write, *Watch out for a fellow called Smith who's going to pick your pocket next week*, let alone, *The monarchy will fall*, they would." Sam was bristling slightly, as he always did at any imputed slight to his beloved foster-sibling.

"No doubt," Randolph said. "I have been dealing with the Southcott woman's gibberings recently; Jo is a marvel of clarity by comparison, and at least they don't insist on rhyming."

"You didn't say what happened there," Sam put in. "The Southcott business."

"With the tree, or the box?"

"Either."

"Nothing."

Sam exhaled audibly. "Could you do better, please?"

Randolph shrugged. "The Southcott tree burned. I don't know why. Mrs. Denton, who holds the Southcott box, reported that it grew very hot to the touch but that the clasp held. I don't know why. Does that help?"

"Randolph..."

"There's really no point asking me; it was Aunt Clothide's area. All I've ever known about the damned box is the importance of not opening it without at least two dozen holy people present in case it provokes a national calamity."

"I thought it was meant to save us all."

"God, you're optimistic," Randolph said. "On that note, and going back to our previous conversation, does the issue in Cock Lane suggest human activity, or might it be the state of the veil?"

"Let's have that again?" Barney asked a little hopelessly.

Randolph sighed. "From the beginning, then. Once upon a time, the divisions between this world and what lies outside were sufficiently substantial that one could use a scrying glass without having something tear one's eye out."

Barney was giving him a look. "We do know that much, thank you."

Randolph ought not to be impatient with Barney and Isaacs' ignorance, although he was. The soldiers been thrust unwillingly into this game, and had survived their abrupt introduction to the supernatural world without descending into terror and madness apparently by thinking about it as little as possible. He'd never known two people less inclined to introspection or study; they just got on with things. It worked as well as anything could in their situation, but meant they were mostly useless and somewhat trying when it came to theoretical discussion.

"Well, it's the crux of the matter," Sam said. "Before the War, it was *hard* to get through, in either direction. An entity turning up— well, before the War that wouldn't happen without a great deal of effort on someone's part to invite it in. And perhaps that's what's happened now. But the veil is in tatters and Cock Lane's a funny spot, and what Randolph and I are wondering is if something's arisen *without* being summoned. I can't say it's impossible. And that would be worrying," he concluded with admirable understatement.

Barney gave a vague shrug, mirrored by Isaacs. Sam sat back. "With any luck it's just someone buggering about, but I wish you'd take a look, Randolph. You'll have a better chance than me of telling if something's seriously wrong."

"I'm flattered you think so," Randolph said, almost meaning it. Sam had been brought up a practical ghost-hunter rather than an arcanist, but he was learning fast. "Sadly, the definition of *wrong* is changing so quickly these days I can barely keep up."

Sam grimaced. "Well. Nothing's how it used to be."

"Too true," Barney muttered.

It was seven years since the War, and the War Beneath, had ended. That was far too short a time for memories to lose their bite; quite long enough for the world to be turned on its head. Old families whose sons had died in Flanders sold their stately homes to war profiteers; the land was dotted with half-empty villages where the young men were dead and the young women gone; the cities and towns were full of hungry-eyed jobless men; the Empire that had covered a full quarter of the earth was beginning to look less like an immutable and unchanging truth and more like hubris, with nemesis attendant. And the veil between this world and the other, repeatedly slashed and burned by the Great Summonings of the War Beneath, was slowly, inexorably tearing apart.

Not everyone recognised that as truth. Some believed the damage mankind had inflicted would repair itself. But Randolph had lost almost every relation, professional colleague, and teacher he'd ever known in the War, just as Sam had lost his entire family, and Barney and Isaacs had near as dammit lost their souls. He was no longer prepared to believe that things would work out for the best.

"Right, well, one foot after another," he said briskly. "*No sign will guide you*, eh? How fortunate I already know the way to Cock Lane; I should be quite nervous to consult Bartholomew's Reference Atlas, under the circumstances."

He went the next day. Cock Lane was an alley of no account near the great Smithfield meat market, famous only for the notorious fraudulent haunting of a previous century. Randolph felt such a delightfully named thoroughfare was missing a trick; one should surely have been certain of picking up a telegraph boy or a guardsman there.

Not that he had the energy. He'd rather liked the way it had been in his war: casual encounters when one had the time and inclination, to which the authorities turned a blind eye because there weren't enough occultists to waste any over petty morality; no tiresome obligations afterwards, since there were more important matters afoot and anyway half the men one fucked would be going back to wives or sweethearts. He didn't have the strength for dodging around dark alleys any more, let alone the tedious palaver of winks and nods to ascertain shared inclinations. He'd nearly died for his country a great deal too often; if that country was as grateful as it claimed to be, it could demonstrate that by leaving him alone.

He'd been told things were changing. The new generation of gilded youth, nauseatingly referred to as Bright Young People, made a great parade of unconventional natures. "Darling, you can't *move* for homosexuals!" he'd been assured of some Piccadilly club by one of his fashionable acquaintance. Good for them, he supposed. It sounded like the sort of milieu in which a handsome, jaded, upper-class predator could have made absolute hay with fresh-faced innocents to the benefit of all concerned, if only his war had ended when everyone else's had. If he'd been like other men of his class, with nothing better to do than amuse himself; if he hadn't been so sodding busy with ghosts.

If he wasn't getting old. Randolph, who was thirty-five, chose not to pursue that thought.

He wasn't entirely sure why he was thinking of this at all, except, perhaps, for those encounters the previous week with the man

Lazenby. He let his mind roam over that as he headed up Farringdon Street, since idle thoughts were a useful way to free his less usual senses.

Saul Lazenby, who had looked like an ordinary bystander when that bloody tree had gone up and Randolph had been too damned late to see what happened. The diviner they used, an irritable pet-shop owner in Brixton, had sent a series of frantic but incoherent telegrams, and by the time Randolph had worked out there was some threat to the Southcott Oak, he'd had very little time to get there.

Randolph had immediately telephoned Mrs. Denton, whose family guarded the Southcott box, to be assured of its safety and ask for watchfulness. Two days later she'd telephoned back to say that a Major Peabody had requested permission to visit, and would Randolph please take a look. So he'd looked, and he'd seen: Saul Lazenby, the innocent bystander at the Southcott tree burning, innocently by-sitting in a railway carriage on his way to visit the Southcott box.

It could be innocent, was the damned thing of it. The Dentons had kept a very close eye on the visitors and reported no effort to open, steal, or damage the box. Peabody had been an obvious idiot, his head full of half-baked mystical notions and theories. If Lazenby had been in Oak Hill Park by chance, it was perfectly reasonable that his unicorn-chasing employer would follow up the Southcott connection.

If. Because Randolph still didn't know what had made the tree burn, and he had not quite liked the feeling he'd had from Lazenby. There was something out of true there, something off. It might be purely personal, of course: Lazenby was of the solid respectable middle classes and without doubt interested in men, and Randolph knew, if only by observation, the fear and shame that might have been heaped on him. If you told a fellow he was wrong long and convincingly enough, he often grew wrong. Perhaps Lazenby was simply a self-loathing queer working for an idiot and no more need be said. Perhaps Randolph should track him down and cheer him up. That sensitive, sun-browned face, that lean and hungry look, the banked fires in his dark, unhappy eyes—oh, he'd bet Mr. Lazenby would repay a man's efforts, given half a chance.

Randolph walked round the curve of Snow Hill in a pleasant reverie, imagining what it might have taken to persuade the intriguing Lazenby off the train and round the back of the station; came toward the right turn to Cock Lane; and felt the presence hit him like a hot, sodden towel in a bathhouse, so hard that he recoiled.

He set his teeth and his mind against it, instantly defensive. The presence wasn't attacking him, yet, but it squatted over the street like a toad and he wasn't the only one to sense it. People were crossing the road for no apparent reason, moving away. He could feel it scratching, a tiny irritant that would turn to torture sooner than one might think.

This wasn't a spirit of place. This was a malignant thing that felt spiteful and ancient, as though it had brooded over the street forever, and it hadn't been here at all six months ago. This was bad.

Cock Lane was almost deserted, with most of the few people on it hurrying to leave, just a couple of men standing and arguing. That was only to be expected; all the milk would doubtless have spoiled too. It was that sort of influence, a kind of mad-eyed mountainous pettiness that made everyone's soul a little shabbier.

He headed up Cock Lane, the air tainting his lips and nostrils, and as he approached the arguing pair, a tallish thin man and a short, fat, older man, he said aloud, "Oh God, *really?*"

Saul Lazenby turned with a look of unguarded dismay that would have been entertaining if Randolph hadn't been absolutely fucking furious. "What the— Are you following us?"

"I'm following trouble," Randolph said. "And here you are. What a coincidence. Did you do this?"

"Do what?" Lazenby demanded.

"Oh, it's the gentleman from the railway," Major Peabody said, with an air of revelation. "The traveller in port. I had meant to ask you—"

"Enough playing the buffoon," Randolph said. "What are you doing here?"

"That is none of your damned business, and I suggest you mind your manners," Lazenby said, as Major Peabody spluttered. "This is a public street and we didn't invite your company."

"But I'm inviting your absence." Randolph could feel the scratching on the inside of his skin now. Nasty remarks were rising to his tongue and he felt even less compunction than usual in voicing them.

Hell's bells. "Get away," he snapped. "Sling your hooks, *now.*"

"I have no idea—" Major Peabody began huffily.

Randolph had no time to debate. The force, the *thing* flowing into a Cock Lane Ghost-shaped hole in people's minds, had been swirling around since he'd stepped onto the street, and it was becoming aware of him. He'd felt it probing, nudging against his mind in the last few seconds, and now he felt the ear-popping suction as of a tide going out that told him something was gathering to strike.

If this pair of idiots were civilians, he had a responsibility to ensure their safety. If they were in the know, they could look after themselves or take the consequences. Randolph felt very strongly that he'd like to see them both die, and it was the strength of that feeling that gave him the warning of attack.

"Brace," he said, grabbing both men by the hand, and hissed out the First Line of the Saaamaaa Ritual as the thing descended.

It was malice, pure malignancy, without motive or object or reason. Randolph felt the wash of it despite the protection of the First Line, cramping his chest and tightening his throat with hatred. He saw it on Peabody's round face, distorted into a cruel parody of his amiably idiotic features, and on Lazenby, his lips drawing back, his eyes narrowing into an animal mask, and he knew he would look much the same.

This thing was hellish strong. He repeated the First Line, putting more of himself behind it and, since he couldn't use his hands without letting go of the damned fools he was protecting, he scraped a sigil on the pavement with his toe. Once, twice, a third time, and the protection sprang to life, flaring around him like blue fire.

Not to either Lazenby or Peabody's dull sight, of course. Peabody looked baffled, Lazenby frankly alarmed, and even as Randolph registered the change from hate to concern on his face, he tried to wrench his hand away. It was all Randolph could do to keep a grip.

"Let go!" Lazenby yelped.

"Love to," Randolph rasped. "I let go, you run. Understand? You run to the end of this street and you don't stop till you're out of the line of fire, and whatever you're doing, you bloody well pack it in. Cross my path again and I'll make you sorry. Go now and nobody has to get hurt. Clear?"

Lazenby's brows drew together. He hesitated, a thought obviously dawning, and then spoke much more calmly. "Yes, very clear. I tell you what, old chap, though, why don't I stay with you for now? Major Peabody will pop off just as you asked, won't you, sir?"

"What?" said the Major.

"I think this gentleman's having some bad memories," Lazenby said, and turned his face away from Randolph to mouth something. "So I'll stay with him while you find someone who might be able to help, do you see?"

"Oh!" The Major nodded, enlightened. "Of course. You just stay here with Lazenby, you poor fellow, and I'll fetch a policeman."

"Will you both sod off," Randolph said, holding onto what was never very impressive patience by his fingernails.

"I know how it is," Lazenby said, gentle and reassuring. "But we all need a pal sometimes, even when we don't feel like it. I'll stick with you. Don't worry, old man. You're safe now."

Christ alive, Lazenby thought he was a shell-shock case. Of all the times to be kind and considerate instead of taking umbrage and marching off. Randolph could have screamed, or laughed. He did neither, because in the second his attention was occupied, Major Peabody pulled his hand free, walked obliviously through the protective circle with a cry of, "Just a minute, now!", and set off down the street at a trot. Fast enough to get away unscathed, Randolph hoped.

"For the love of God. How long do we have before that imbecile brings back a policeman?"

"What?"

"Never mind. Oh, what the hell." Randolph jerked Lazenby closer, a small but ever-curious part of his brain noting how the man's eyes widened, slapped his free hand against the wall behind him, and let the impressions crowd in. Malice, lust, fear, envy, the usual slurry of human insignificance, but something more behind it. A sense of empty idiocy, as great and vacant as the sky.

"Right," he said aloud. "Right. I need a—" The *oculus fatui* turned on him at that moment, and Randolph felt its attention gathering to a point. "Fuck."

"I beg your pardon?" Lazenby said, with outrage.

"Shut up and let me get on."

"Certainly not!" Lazenby snapped, but Randolph wasn't listening. His mind was focused on the thing he had to fight, feeling its nature. It filled a ghost-shaped hole in the street's belief, that was worryingly clear, but it wasn't anchored by summoning or purpose or history. For all its power, for all its sneaking, the damn thing didn't *belong* here, and that gave him the edge.

"Not in this land, not in this city," he said aloud, and spoke six of Wayland's words.

They jarred through his body, clanging in his bones, scorching his eyeballs, hung deafeningly in the air for a fraction of a second that lasted an eternity, and then everything stank of molten metal and the presence was gone. Randolph took a very long breath.

"What the." Lazenby evidently hadn't spent enough time in the Army, since he got no further. "What the— *What?*"

"Lovely meeting you," Randolph rasped through dry lips, disengaging his hand. He'd left red finger marks on Lazenby's wrist. "Pleasure. Goodbye."

"Just a blasted minute!" Under the brim of his hat the ends of Lazenby's fair-brown hair looked wild and flyaway, as if with electrostatic charge. "What did you just say? That—that— What *was* it?"

"What do you think I said?" Randolph enquired unkindly. He'd undergone nine excruciating days of ritual to keep Wayland's words. The human mind was not equipped by nature to contain them; they slipped from the ears as soon as spoken. It was a rather unpleasant experience, although not nearly as unpleasant as actually remembering the things.

"I... But..." Lazenby's mouth opened and shut in bafflement at his inexplicably failed memory.

Randolph patted him on the cheek. "There, there. Thank you greatly for your consideration, and enjoy your policeman, he's just coming. And if I can remind you...don't cross my path again. There's a good chap."

CHAPTER THREE

Several days later, Saul still couldn't stop thinking about that bizarre incident. Too much about it was puzzling. Glyde turning up for the third time could no longer be blamed on coincidence, let alone interest; that he believed Saul to be following him made no sense at all.

Saul had been on Cock Lane because the Major speculated it might be one point of a mystical pattern beginning at Temple Church. Temple Church was his new Key to All the Mythologies, which Saul ascribed to the book he'd recently received through the post: a cheapjack private printing bound in brown card. The Major claimed it was a great rarity and had been sent to him on strict conditions of secrecy by a mysterious and anonymous correspondent. Saul took that with an extremely large pinch of salt, but the Major was caught up in his fantasy, and had insisted they explore the various lines of connection on foot.

It had been a reasonably pleasant stroll through busy streets on a nice day. Major Peabody had spoken of currents of spiritual energy and the harmonies of the spheres, repeatedly adding, "As above, so below," while gesturing to the sky with his umbrella and nearly taking Saul's eye out. It was the usual nonsense that he humoured as he always did, and then they'd found themselves on Cock Lane, and...

He'd lost his temper, that was all. Suddenly, abruptly, after a year with Major Peabody and six years before that of hard-learned self-control, he'd found himself raging bitterly at his employer as the man retaliated with equal savagery. He couldn't even remember what either of them had said, or why: it had been a red-mist fury, a wave of anger so great it had blotted out everything else. Major Peabody, once they'd managed to get rid of the confused and annoyed policeman, had decreed that they had walked into an area of great psychic darkness and forgiven Saul's insubordination on the spot.

Saul didn't believe in psychic darkness, whatever that might mean—though if it meant not losing his job, he'd take it. They had had a meaningless quarrel, that was all.

Only, Glyde had turned up again, and he'd said...something.

Saul couldn't remember, and his attempts to do so gave him a nauseous sensation of something missing, like probing the cavity of a just-pulled tooth. Glyde had—he'd said— There had been a noise, Saul was sure, not exactly loud but with a loud *feeling* to it, like the ringing after a great hammer blow. A noise, and words that had slid away from his ears like water off an oiled surface, leaving the barest trace of their passing.

But that was nonsense. He'd stopped paying attention for a moment; gone off into his head, as his mother had used to call it. He'd been distracted and missed what Glyde had said, and it had been disconcerting to be jerked back to awareness of the world around him.

That raised the question of what had preoccupied him to such a great extent, and he was afraid he knew the answer. The press of Glyde's fingers, which he'd felt on his wrist for days afterwards, and that powerful tug, jerking Saul towards him. Nature had given Saul a taste for lean strength, hard brains, harder will. It had let him down quite spectacularly to date, and the evidently disturbed Randolph Glyde would be no different.

Glyde, grabbing his wrist, spouting jabber that suggested he'd come out of the trenches with a persecution complex or a tendency to hallucination, voicing obscene invitations for all the world as though he'd been thinking about something else. He must be a madman. The only emotion anyone should feel towards the poor fellow was pity; one should certainly not dwell on the touch of his fingers or the shape of his mouth. Randolph Glyde was unbalanced and aggressive, perhaps dangerous, even if, during his periods of lucidity, he was also the most unnervingly attractive man Saul had met in years.

God damn it. He *was* going to stop thinking about this.

He'd been letting Glyde occupy his mind in self-defence. The Major was riding high on his recent successes with the burning tree and the 'psychic darkness', and he'd barely stopped talking since Saul had arrived that morning.

"It is all thanks to the book," he announced, waving it indicatively. "This fellow has produced research of astounding proportions; I count myself fortunate that I was able to procure a copy. Combining this new information with my own studies leads to so many new avenues of discovery. The Great Hexagram is revealing its secrets at long last!"

The Great Hexagram, which Saul was positive the Major had thought up no more than a few days ago, was a huge six-pointed pattern with its base at Temple Church, extending well north of London. Bits of thread dangled from many pins on the map as Major Peabody attempted to realise his vision, while Saul went through books in search of the required supporting evidence.

The Major's library was extensive and eclectic, combining rare old maps and local histories with implausible medievalist folklore and books about magic, which the Major insisted on calling grimoires. Most of those were simply gibberish; others made an effort at scholarship. Saul had read a few to acquaint himself with the subject, including a *History of Witchcraft* by one Julian Karswell which had been genuinely disturbing, leaving him in no doubt that the author believed every sinister word he wrote. Saul had gone so far as to look Mr. Karswell up, wondering what sort of man could have been behind such an unpleasant piece of work, but discovered only that he had died in France well before the war. He couldn't regret the fellow's passing. The *History of Witchcraft* left some rather ugly phrases fixed in his memory, and after a couple of days with it sitting on his desk, unaccountably noticeable at the corner of his eye and giving the irritating impression that it moved a tiny bit every time he looked away, he'd put it firmly back on the shelf. Much longer in this job and he'd probably find himself a believer.

"I have it! Enfield Chase," Major Peabody announced. "*That* is where the apogee of the hexagram surely lies. A crucial site."

"I don't know of it."

"The ancient name of what was once a royal hunting ground. In what we now call Cockfosters." Major Peabody swept his hand over north-west London on the map. "The land was once in the possession of Geoffrey de Mandeville; that is what gave me the clue. Do you know of de Mandeville?"

"The turncoat earl of Essex during the Anarchy," Saul offered. "He changed sides several times between King Stephen and Empress Matilda." That was all he remembered about the civil wars of the twelfth century, and he was surprised to have retained even that much from long-ago history lessons, but he felt quite sure that Major Peabody would enlighten him. Or, at least, tell him things.

"Quite right. Once neither claimant to the throne was prepared to trust him again, de Mandeville launched a rebellion and lived as an outlaw. He died excommunicate, and nobody would accept his body for burial except the mystical order of the Knights Templar. The Templars, Lazenby! The ancient founders of Temple Church! It all makes sense!"

"So what has he to do with Cockfosters?" Saul asked, in lieu of agreeing.

"De Mandeville once had a manor house there, on a site called Camlet Moat." He tapped the map, indicating an area some two or three miles north-west of Oak Hill Park. "Does the name Camlet Moat suggest anything to you?"

"Not really, sir."

"Camlet," Major Peabody repeated with relish. "Or, as it was called in the fourteenth century, Camelot."

Saul contemplated him. He appeared serious.

"Camelot. Isn't that meant to be in Glastonbury?"

"A common misapprehension. Nobody knows where the true Camelot was located. Perhaps it was the name of the court and not the castle; perhaps it moved with the king. I do not assert as a fact that the legendary seat of King Arthur is in Cockfosters," Major Peabody said, with scrupulous fairness, "not yet. But the name alone merits further investigation. And, let me add, there is a well remaining on Camlet Moat to which all kinds of legends are attached. Supposedly it contains his treasure chest, which sinks whenever drawn up by seekers after his fortune."

Saul was moved to make a noise of protest. Major Peabody gave him a reproachful look. "I'm not a treasure hunter. The point is that legends cluster around important sites, such as holy wells. You must make a preliminary visit to Camlet Moat; this is where your training will come into its own. It is possible we may need to apply for permission to excavate there one day, but all in good time. Regrettably, Temple Church is closed for rebuilding work, but I shall trace the patterns around the area and see if I can learn more of de Mandeville's connection to the Templars. What a revelation this may prove to be! I am delighted to have you with me in this, Lazenby. It was a lucky day for me when I took you on."

He was beaming at Saul with such pleasure that Saul couldn't help but smile back. "Yes, sir. For me, too."

This latest freak meant another trip on the railway. Saul found a seat and settled back. He had a copy of the *Archaeology Review* in his coat pocket, but he didn't feel quite like reading it, somehow. It contained a long piece about Leonard Woolley's excavations at Ur. The great Sumerian city had not caught the popular imagination, unlike Howard Carter's work in the Valley of the Kings, but it tugged at Saul as though he had a fishhook in his mouth.

He could have been there. He could have been under the Mesopotamian sun—they called it the State of Iraq now—working with Woolley, who had told him that a place would be kept for him after the War. He'd felt so lucky back in 1914. Billeted in the desert he loved rather than the mud and blood of Flanders, where one in three of his Oxford contemporaries would die before the slaughter ended; a plum role waiting for him that would, by now, have established him for life. All he'd had to do was get through the War without death or disgrace.

People said one out of two wasn't bad. They were wrong.

He hadn't presumed to approach Woolley after his release, but a curt note had arrived anyway, withdrawing the offer. He didn't blame the man, just as he didn't blame his family for disowning him. It was only what he'd deserved. Still, he stared out of the window rather than reading.

Trent Park was closest to Cockfosters station, no more than a mile's walk through the red-brick suburban streets creeping outward from London. Extraordinary to think that this had all been a royal chase once, where kings and noblemen rode to hounds over what Major Peabody would doubtless call greensward. Saul wasn't quite sure how the vision of a mystical, magical, medieval England fit with de Mandeville's life of sordid betrayal and savagery, but inconvenient reality obviously didn't worry the Major.

Trent Park was private land, the surrounds of a great house now thrown open to the public. Many landowners were offering their fellows that courtesy in these changed times, attempting to learn from the example made of the Russian aristocracy. Saul appreciated it. He had shinned over plenty of walls but it was easier to stroll through a gate.

He followed a path along a very long drive through a spread of oak trees, none of which caught fire; skirted the impressive Georgian house to cross the bridge over an ornamental lake; and walked along a path up the incline of what a wooden signpost told him was Camlet Hill. At the top of the hill, visible from some distance and standing on a patch of rough, bare grass, was a stone obelisk. It seemed to be a couple of centuries old: a Georgian faux-ancient folly. From its vantage point he had a magnificent view of the house, and the spread of London beyond the park. He couldn't see anything that looked like it might be Camlet Moat through the foliage, though he did note that there seemed to be a peculiarly lush area, its greens brighter and thicker, in the direction he needed to go. Different planting or soil, perhaps.

He headed down the hill, enjoying the birdsong and the dappled sunlight, and trying to remember anything of the poem that went, *Oh, to be in England, Now that April's here*, such as the title, author, or any of its other lines. The trees closed in quickly around the path, and the planting here was gnarled, twiggy hawthorn and mountain ash: lower and less elegant trees than the slender birches and mighty oaks elsewhere. It gave a sense of enclosure.

There were no signposts to Camlet Moat. Saul followed the path as it led him, and was forced to remind himself that the area was actually rather small. It didn't *feel* small. It had the atmosphere of a much larger forest, with nothing at all visible through the trees and the green-brown haze of shrubs, ferns and brush. Once it had stretched over mile upon mile, and deer would have stepped through the thickets, unafraid.

Something even greener than the rest a little way away caught his eye, a lurid shade almost too bright to be natural. Saul left the path, pushing through ferns to approach it, and saw a body of still water, some twenty feet wide, densely covered in vivid green algae that looked thick enough to walk on. He'd come to the water as its banks bent sharply in a corner, and it stretched away from him to left and right in near-straight lines.

This was Camlet Moat, a squarish islet surrounded by water, and if he walked around the moat, presumably he'd find a bridge.

Saul would have liked to keep to the water edge, but he didn't want to cause irreparable damage to his shoes or trousers; he couldn't afford to be wasteful. He went back to the path and followed it. It appeared to head only away from the moat, and he had to double back on himself twice and walk what seemed a very long and circuitous route before he finally spotted the dark, rough wooden planks sitting low in the algae-coated water that apparently constituted a bridge. Saul had a momentary qualm, wondering how deep the moat was and picturing himself sodden and covered in green slime, before he set a tentative foot on it.

It shifted slightly under his weight, but didn't tip him into the slimy sea. Saul crossed as quickly as was compatible with care, and found himself on solid ground inside Camlet Moat, Major Peabody's highly dubious Camelot.

He took a deep breath, and felt the air expand in his lungs. It was fresh and clean here, and it made his heart lift in a way he hadn't experienced in too long. He came from a small country town, and this woodland spring reminded him of his boyhood, before he'd left for the stink of cities or the unforgiving glare of Mesopotamian sun. He could feel the old remembered hope and exuberance as though it were welling up inside him with every breath, so that he almost laughed aloud, filled with the green joy that pulsed from the ground through his feet, just as it rose through roots out into a flourish of foliage and life. He walked without thinking, ferns brushing against his legs, not looking for anything, enjoying the solitude and the movement and the stillness—

There was no birdsong.

The thought stopped him in his tracks. He stood, listening, but heard nothing. Not a chirrup or a warble, not a rustle of wings, barely a rustle of leaves, because the breeze seemed to have dropped and the air was cool but very still. Still, and absolutely silent except for his own pulse, which seemed somehow to be very loud indeed in his ears. He stood, and the wood stood around him, and quite suddenly he was afraid.

That was absurd. There was no living creature but himself on this tiny island, and nothing to do him harm. He wasn't lost in a vast and pathless ancient forest; he was in a Cockfosters park, with work to do, and if the birds weren't singing, well, that was merely...something ornithological, not his field. He made himself walk forward, and *not* turn and look, because it was ridiculous to feel as though there was a presence around him, watching.

After a few steps, the feeling receded and he could breathe easily once more. He walked with purpose, not because he knew where he was going but simply so as not to stand still again, and after a moment—because this really was a very small overgrown bit of land, and it *didn't* stretch out just a little further than a man could walk before his legs failed him—he found himself approaching one corner of the isle, where a flash of colour caught his eye.

There were bright rags hanging off the branches of a tree. A lot of rags, and not all bright any more. Some were new, others fading, and now he could see that what he'd at first taken for swags of lichen or rotting leaves were yet more bits of cloth, mouldering away to nothing. He wondered for a second how the wind had brought so many rags to a single tree, and then saw that each was knotted on.

He walked closer to examine the peculiar decorations, staring at what seemed to be a baby's lacy cap tied to one branch, and his forward foot came down half on hard stone and half on nothing at all. He reeled backwards, flailing to keep his balance, and realised he'd nearly stepped into a well.

It had no raised edge, no fencing. It was merely a hole in the ground, lined with moss in a way that suggested stonework as far down as he could clearly see. It smelled of old, cold water but he couldn't see any water, just dark empty dampness. This was presumably the well of de Mandeville's manor house, but in impossibly good condition for its age. He could see a few suspiciously regular mossy stones scattered around, which were probably the remains of walls, but no other sign of human habitation. The centuries had smoothed away all evidence of a house; a well would have collapsed into itself, or filled up with leaf-mulch that turned to earth.

Evidently people had kept it in some sort of repair at some point, though it didn't look as though it had been tended to for decades. Perhaps it had been at the behest of the treasure hunters who believed it might contain a chest of gold? They'd had a similar legend in Saul's village, of a treasure trove buried in a field. The story went that it had to be dug for, but always sank away when it was almost in the hunters' grasp. He'd dug himself, aged six, feeling all the thrill of seeking hidden secrets even when he'd found nothing but worms.

It was a commonplace enough myth for a well. But why the rags tied to a tree?

He was reaching for one to examine it when he heard a rustle. It wasn't particularly loud, but it was the first noise he'd heard in this weirdly silent place, and it made him jump. He swung around, and saw another man coming through the trees. The man registered him at the same time, and they both said, in unison, "For God's sake!"

Saul put his hands on his hips. Randolph Glyde spread his own hands out in a frustrated gesture. They glared at one another.

"At this point," Saul said, "I think it's fairly obvious that you're following me. Would you care to explain?"

"At this point," Glyde mimicked, "I think it's fairly obvious that you're getting to places before me. I should like to know how and why."

"Getting to what places? This is a wood!"

"Disingenuous, Mr. Lazenby. It's an unmarked part of private grounds reached by a bridge, and yet here you are. You didn't come here by accident. What the devil are you up to?"

Saul opened his mouth to respond with equal brusqueness and stopped himself, remembering abruptly that the man was unbalanced.

He didn't *look* unbalanced. Actually, he looked quite extraordinarily good. He was hatless, and the dappled light touched his sleek, dark hair giving it a tinted sheen, as though he were wearing a coronet of green. He was lean and long and glowing with health, and his casual brown tweed suit, well cut and modern in style as it was, somehow gave him the look of a forester.

Glyde was scrutinising Saul too, a frown between his eyes. "You look...well."

"Uh, thank you?" It had sounded nothing like a civility; more as if looking well were an odd thing for him to do. "Speaking of health, you left last time before we could summon assistance. I must ask—"

"I am not a shell-shock case," Glyde said. "Let's dispose of that red herring right now. I am as sane as any man in England, if that's anything to boast of. I did spend my war in Flanders, but shells were the least of my troubles. And you, Mr. Lazenby, spent yours in Mesopotamia."

Saul felt the blood surge in his face. It was a sickening shock every time he was identified, even if it was something he constantly expected and dreaded. He had to struggle to control his voice. "I see you have been looking me up."

"I have, yes. It isn't the most edifying history I've ever read."

"Major Peabody knows," Saul said abruptly. "In case you were planning to inform him. I have not hidden my past from him or anyone."

"A bold decision, considering that you seem very lucky to have escaped the firing squad. Most people would not care to admit to a war record like yours."

"I may be a damned fool and worse, but I'm not a coward, and I'm not a bloody liar," Saul said through his teeth. "And you may go to hell. I have done nothing except obey my employer's orders; you're the one following me around and looking me up. If you don't like me, leave me alone!"

Glyde was watching him intently. Saul gave him the nastiest look he could. "Well?"

"Would you care for a drink?"

"*What?*"

"A drink. You're probably thirsty." Glyde walked forward, taking something from a battered leather satchel incongruously slung over his elegantly clad shoulder. Saul realised it was a tin cup on a piece of string. He stared, speechless, as the man came up to the well, opened his mouth to point out that if the well had any water at all it was far too low to reach, and was prevented by an almost immediate splash. He must have been mistaken.

"What the— Do you intend to drink that?" he demanded.

"Any reason why not?"

"Liver fluke? Dead newts? It's not a working well; heaven knows what the water's like."

"Indeed. I think you'll find it clean." Glyde pulled up the cup, brim-full. From the length of the string, it appeared the water was no more than four feet down; Saul was baffled he hadn't seen it. "Here. Have a drink."

The water in the cup looked clear, and contained no obvious amphibians, but this was still ridiculous, and enraging when Saul had been gearing up for a fight. "I don't think so."

"Drink it," Glyde said, the words close to an order.

"Why the devil should I?"

"Because either you'll find it refreshing or I'll find it informative."

"All right, that's enough. I've had my fill of nonsensical remarks."

"Well, you chose to work for Peabody." Glyde's eyes were the colour of woodland: light brown, green-dappled, gold-flecked, fascinating. Compelling. "You want to drink. You *need* to drink. The water is good and pure, Mr. Lazenby. The question is, are you?"

Saul had a vague feeling he should object to that but he was still looking at Glyde's eyes, he couldn't look away, and he could feel the tin cup being pressed into his fingers even as the hat was twitched from his head. He could smell the water, cool and fresh, could feel how deliciously it would sluice a throat parched by heat and sun and the red dust of ancient pottery.

He raised the cup to his lips and drank.

The water slid down his throat, into his chest, and spread through him, cool and soothing, leaving a trail of tingles behind it. There were only a few swallows in the tin mug, but he relished each as he had never relished water before, and when he took the cup from his lips he felt replete, refreshed, and as though he'd been drinking for a very long time.

He blinked.

"Good?" Glyde enquired, plucking the mug from his fingers.

"Excellent." Saul's mouth felt rather odd. That must be the cold.

"No violent cramps, urge to vomit black bile, or bleeding from eyes, ears, or nose?"

"Not more than usual, thank you. It's delicious. Are you not going to drink?" Somehow his anger with Glyde seemed to have been washed away with the water.

"Not my time." Glyde shook out the moisture from the mug and stowed it in his satchel. "Well. Well, well. You puzzle me, Mr. Lazenby, you really do. What were you doing with the cloutie tree?"

"The—?"

Glyde indicated the rag-strewn tree. Saul shrugged. "Looking at it and wondering about the rags. What did you say it was called?"

"A cloutie tree. Cloutie, meaning cloths in some dialects. It's for healing."

"The Major said something about a superstition of a holy well."

"Did he indeed. Yes. Where a tree grows by a holy well, one may dip a rag in the water and use it to wash the afflicted part. Tie the rag to the tree and the affliction rots away with the cloth." Glyde gave him a glinting smile. "If you believe in that sort of twaddle, of course."

"It's a tempting idea. I can see why people come here." Saul glanced over the tree, estimating perhaps forty visible rags. How many people had tried to wash away their pain and desperation on this peaceful islet? The thought stung his eyes, and he found himself blurting, "Does it work for everything?"

"You mean, can it minister to a mind diseased?"

"Broken minds, broken hearts." Saul tried to say it lightly, but he felt his throat tighten.

Glyde met his eyes again, but not with the intense, compelling look of before. Saul might almost have called his expression sympathetic. "Yes, they need healing as much as legs and arms, don't they, even if the injuries are less visible. Ah... I think one might simply wash one's face, you know. The water knows its business. Have you a handkerchief?"

Saul pulled it from his pocket. Glyde knelt by the well on the mossy stone, careless of his beautiful suit, and leaned in, stretching downward. His long arms were not remotely long enough to reach water four feet down, but when he straightened, the handkerchief was soaked and dripping.

Saul stood, helpless. Glyde stepped close, eyes intent and full of something Saul couldn't understand. He reached out and carefully, tenderly, wiped the wet cloth over Saul's cheek.

It was so cold. Far colder than when he'd drunk, searingly cold, so cold that it felt hot. It burned his skin, and he gasped and shuddered under the touch, but he didn't pull away. Glyde ran the handkerchief along his cheekbone, down to his jaw, then up, over his eyebrows and his forehead, until every part of Saul's face was quivering under cold water that blazed like flame. He shut his eyes as the cloth skimmed his eyelids and thought he heard Glyde whisper something, then the cloth was lifted away.

Glyde held out the handkerchief. Saul took it and, because there was nothing else he could or should do, he tied it to the tree that grew by the well and thought, *Please take it away, please take the pain away.*

And there they stood, he and Glyde, looking at one another.

"Clean," Glyde said, with a flicker of a smile. He reached out to run a finger down Saul's damp jawline, and his touch wasn't priestly any more. Saul sucked in a sharp breath and saw the response in the fractional widening of Glyde's eyes.

"I..." he began, and had nothing to say.

"Yes." Glyde's fingertip brushed, very lightly, over Saul's lips. "I wish to heaven I understood the role you're playing."

"I'm not playing a role," Saul managed. Glyde's fingers were sliding up the other side of his face now, into his hair, sending shivers over his scalp. The blood was pounding through him. He wanted to fall to his knees, or simply to stand here with Glyde's fingers on his face for ever.

"We're all playing roles." Glyde had that little frown of concentration again as he stroked the hair that sprang from Saul's temples. It didn't take much of an angle to turn his winging eyebrows into something positively Satanic. "The only question is, are you an actor or a puppet?"

"Oh, a puppet." Saul wanted to lift his hand to Glyde's face in return, and didn't dare. He didn't think it would be unwelcome, but he couldn't find the courage. It had been too long since the last time; it had hurt too much. "That's quite clear."

"Mmm. I wish you'd find another job."

Saul jerked away. "What?"

"I don't like this." Glyde lowered his hand, and the strange moment of intimacy shivered into nothing, leaving Saul feeling bare and absurd. "I don't like the way I keep meeting you, and I don't think puppethood suits you."

"I don't know what you're talking about."

"No, that's rather the point." Glyde looked, for a second, extraordinarily weary. "You're getting mixed up in something ill-judged at best, and I very much wish you would take my advice and stop."

"Leave my position?"

"Let Peabody play his game out, whatever it may be. He seems to me a man liable to end up with ancient masonry falling on his head, and I don't think you ought to be at his side when it happens. Find a different post."

"You saw my record," Saul said "How many employers do you think would jump at the chance to have me? I can't get a place as a third-rate clerk; I've tried. This is the first position I've found since I came back to England, and if I leave it I'll starve. What on earth do you have against Major Peabody? He's a harmless old coot obsessed with fairy tales, and the worst he's doing is wasting his time and mine on half-baked ideas. Isn't it?"

"I know nothing against him, except that he and you keep turning up in the wrong places." Glyde grimaced. "Or the right ones. What brought you here today?"

Saul opened his hands. "This is the site of a manor house that was owned by Geoffrey de Mandeville in the twelfth century. Major Peabody thinks it's a sacred site." He felt awkward, somehow, using the word as he stood here.

"What has a medieval nobleman to do with the price of fish?"

"He's buried in Temple Church, which is another sacred site. Don't ask me to explain; all I do is follow the bees in the Major's bonnet. And given that, how is it that I keep running into you? What are *you* doing here?"

"That, unfortunately, would be telling." Glyde reached for Saul's hat, which was hanging on a tree branch, and handed it to him. "I understand your predicament, and I am inclined to believe in your innocence, or at least your ignorance. But if you were able to point your employer to a different hobby—macramé, say, or stamp collecting—I think it would be to everyone's advantage, including his. Otherwise who knows where this may lead, and I shouldn't like anything unpleasant to happen to you."

His voice was so smoothly meaningful that Saul couldn't tell if the words were an expression of goodwill or an open threat. He met Glyde's eyes, startled, and found himself held once more by their compelling gaze.

"Goodbye, Mr. Lazenby," Glyde said softly. "It's time to leave the island."

Saul didn't quite think about anything as he crossed the bridge back to the park, where the birdsong sounded deafening, or walked back to Cockfosters station. He didn't begin to think, in fact, until he was safely on the train, at which point the utterly bizarre nature of the encounter dawned on him, like the belated realisation while shaving that a troubling memory was nothing but a dream. Except that, in this case, it had happened.

"What the *devil*," he said under his breath.

Glyde wasn't mad, even if his behaviour was inexplicable. Saul was increasingly sure of that. He was beginning to harbour a theory that the man worked for the Government in some hush-hush aspect, and to feel very afraid that perhaps Major Peabody had stumbled on some, some...

That was the problem. Saul couldn't imagine the Major's researches pointing to anything important at all. Had the tree in Oak Hill Park been ignited by a new weapon, perhaps, the kind of which one read in pulp novels? Was there some strange chemical compound in that well-water? Saul could still feel a lingering tingle on his skin and a coolness in his chest, and there had been something else, an effect on his mind. He was sure of that, the more he thought about it. The entire experience had felt like a hallucination from the point he crossed onto Camlet Moat.

Which was, of course, *before* he'd drunk the water.

God rot it. Saul had an urge to get off the train, take the next northbound one back to Cockfosters, find Glyde up to whatever he was doing, and blasted well demand what was going on. That or to push him against a tree and tell him to finish what he'd started, because the memory of Glyde's fingers caressing his face, combing through his hair, was making it hard for him to breathe.

He'd wanted so much in that moment. Not just the touch, not just the promise those stroking fingers made to his skin, but the care with which they moved. The understanding in Glyde's eyes. The kindness. Saul was a man of science; he would never, even alone, have given in to the urge to make a superstitious gesture. Glyde had dirtied a fine pair of trousers to soak that handkerchief, and done it in such a serious, priestly way that Saul had been left with a feeling of something almost like absolution. It was a comfort, even if an illusory one, to imagine his sin and shame rotting away with the cloth, and Glyde had given him that when other men had spat.

He'd given comfort and made a lot of cryptic remarks, and he'd also managed to make Saul do as he was told, twice. Drinking the water, walking away on command like a child, as though he'd had no control of his own will. The word *mesmerism* pricked at his mind. He didn't like it.

One thing was for certain: Saul didn't intend to dissuade Major Peabody from his researches. He wanted to meet Randolph Glyde again. He had questions.

The answer to one of those questions came to him that afternoon. Glyde had described the Major as *a man liable to end up with ancient masonry falling on his head*, a peculiar remark that had rung a vague bell at the time. Saul thought of it again in the Major's library, and this time the bell was loud and clear. He hurried to find the obituary of Mr. Julian Karswell, author of that deeply unpleasant *History of Witchcraft*, and read over the text with decided uneasiness.

While examining the front of St. Wulfram's Church at Abbeville, then under extensive repair, Mr. Karswell was struck on the head and instantly killed by a stone falling from the scaffold erected round the north-western tower, there being, as was clearly proved, no workman on the scaffold at that moment.

"Well," Saul said aloud and stood in the library, wondering what the devil it all meant.

CHAPTER FOUR

With the usual infinite variety of an English spring, the next day was a downpour. Randolph resented that. If it had rained like this yesterday he probably wouldn't have found Lazenby prowling around the undergrowth of Camlet Moat and thereby given himself a headache.

You could never tell with Camlet Moat, that was the problem. The well would go dry for months at a time; sometimes Randolph couldn't find the bridge for hours. Nevertheless, if the water had been foul to Lazenby's mouth, that would have been conclusive. The Moat had its own ways, and he was terrifyingly aware how little he knew of them, but it had let Lazenby in and offered him healing.

Or, at least, he thought it had. He'd had a strong impulse to come to the Moat in the first place, and an equally strong one to give Lazenby the water, but he lacked any understanding of why. He couldn't even swear, now, that he'd wanted to test the man entirely on the Moat's behalf, given the relief he'd felt when Lazenby had found the water good. Randolph would have been...disappointed, one might say, to learn that Lazenby was a villain.

Of course he could still be a puppet, or a blunderer: Randolph had four years, several nasty scars, and a lot of dead friends to remind him of the damage good intentions could do. Come to that, Lazenby could easily be a villain who suited the Moat's obscure purposes. Randolph, the last and by far the worst-informed Walker of Camlet Moat, didn't know enough to guess. But he was not happy that he had found the man there, and he needed to look into this.

He clapped on a hat, turned up his collar, bade a reluctant farewell to his warm, dry bachelor rooms in the Albany, and went to 166 Fetter Lane.

It was a tall, thin house with a profoundly odd atmosphere, thanks to two centuries' occupation by occultists. In recent times the appalling runecaster Karswell had lived here, then his daughter Miss Kay, a diviner, along with the ghost-hunter Simon Feximal, his companion Robert Caldwell, and the homeless youngsters they'd acquired, Jo and Sam. Now only Sam Caldwell was left. He'd opened the house to the rest of their group because, Randolph suspected, he found its emptiness unbearable.

Barney and Isaacs each had a room on the top floor, for which Sam had provided reinforced locks and bolts on the outside of the doors, as if that would do any good. Randolph had no intention of leaving his luxurious and solitary rooms in the Albany, but had joined the Fetter Lane household to the extent of carrying a key.

He let himself in now, and shouted a greeting that echoed in disappointing silence, which made him realise he hoped Sam was in. That was absurd; he was here to work, not chat. He headed up to the first floor, and shouted, "Shop!"

"Hello!" Sam yelled from the book room, so Randolph went in.

Sam was glaring at a pile of papers, but looked up long enough to give Randolph a nod. "Morning. How are you?"

"Tolerable. Yourself?"

"Mustn't grumble."

"I don't know why not," Randolph said. "There's nothing I'd rather do. I don't suppose you know anything about Geoffrey de Mandeville?"

"Is that a research topic, a ghost, or someone who owes you money?"

"You're a lot of use." Randolph looked around the shelves. It wasn't a huge room; occult libraries rarely were. There were only so many books of any value, though the supply of rubbish was endless. "Ugh. I'm not sure where to start with this."

"What are you after?"

"I don't know."

"Ah," Sam said. "One of those. Was that why you hared off yesterday?"

Randolph made a face. "I had a very strong feeling that I needed to go to Camlet Moat, and when I arrived, that Lazenby character was there. The one who was at Cock Lane and the Southcott tree."

Sam put his pen down. "Again? Who *is* this chap? He couldn't be Shadow Ministry, could he?"

Randolph hadn't thought of that possibility. "Surely not. My God, if they're interfering at Camlet Moat— No, I can't think it. And he drank the water."

Sam's eyebrows went up. "He drew it himself?"

"I gave it to him."

"Did you. And if there had been a repeat of the incident with Dennis Whetstone—"

"Nasty piece of work, Dennis. I always thought so."

"I couldn't agree more, but he lost half his tongue."

"If someone buggers around at Camlet Moat, they can take the consequences," Randolph said. "It is my duty to prevent buggering around at Camlet Moat. That was how I did it."

"If you say so. How was the water?"

"Good and plentiful."

Sam made a face. "Could be worse, then."

"It probably is worse." Randolph leaned back against a bookshelf, shutting his eyes. "I don't know what's going on. I met Lazenby's employer, Peabody, and I would swear the man's as hopeless as he looks. But the Southcott Oak burns and Lazenby pops up to see it, on, he claims, this man Peabody's instructions. An entity takes advantage of a rent in the veil at Cock Lane, and Peabody and Lazenby are there again. I used Wayland's words, did I tell you?" Sam whistled. "Indeed. Then yesterday I feel compelled to go to Camlet Moat and there Lazenby is *again*, this time with de Mandeville's connection to Temple Church as the paper-thin reason du jour. It can't be coincidence. But I gave him the water and I—" He didn't want to tell Sam about the washing. That felt intensely private. "I don't quite know why. It makes me uncomfortable."

"Uncomfortable," Sam said. "That's not the word, is it? What do you fear?"

"I don't know."

"Randolph—"

"I don't know what I fear," Randolph said, "because I don't know a fucking thing about Camlet Moat. As you are well aware."

"I am. And you know what I think about that."

They'd had this argument all too often. "I can't let someone else do it. I have to be the Walker. It's my family responsibility."

"Your family are dead." Sam was a cheerful, likeable, undistinguished sort of chap in appearance, and the more Randolph got to know him, the less he'd have liked to square off against him. "You can't carry all their responsibilities yourself, even if you knew how. You *have* to give this one to someone else."

"I don't have anything to give. Theresa was trained to be the Walker of Camlet Moat, not me. She knew the secrets. All I have to justify investing myself Walker in her place is that I'm a Glyde with twenty-three generations of service behind me; someone else wouldn't even have that."

"Then someone else needs to start again from scratch," Sam said. "It's no good telling me about hereditary responsibilities when you're all out of heredity. The Glydes are done with, Randolph. You know it as well as I."

"I know I'll be the last, thank you. I'm well aware I've already failed. It's just a matter of discovering how badly."

Sam exhaled. "If your upper lip got any stiffer you wouldn't be able to speak. It isn't your fault your family is dead, their duties undone. You didn't create this problem any more than the rest of us did. But we need to fix it. Not the last lone Glyde. *We.*"

"Do you know how long—"

"Twenty-three generations," Sam said over him. "You've mentioned it. Do you know how little I want to share Jo's prophecies with you when it should be my family talking about them, or how it feels to live here without Uncle Simon and Uncle Robert? I assume you've noticed how much Barney and Max hate what they've become? None of us wanted the world this way, but we're stuck with it, and you don't have the luxury of being the great and noble Heir of Glyde any more. The Shadow Ministry's right about that, I'm sorry to say."

"I shan't be handing over my family's responsibilities to Whitehall," Randolph snapped. "You may be sure of that."

The thought of submitting his duty to a civil servant or even an arcanist in bureaucratic service was profoundly wrong, and all too possible. With most of Britain's senior occultists dead in the War Beneath the War, Whitehall had taken control of much, and wanted all. Randolph had been informed on several occasions that he was obliged by family responsibility, national obligation, and patriotic duty to report to the Department of Special Affairs, known as the Shadow Ministry, and take orders therefrom.

Be damned to that. The Glyde family held royal warrants, the first signed by Queen Elizabeth on the advice of Dr. John Dee, and reported to the monarch alone, not that anyone had asked them to do so since Charles II. Randolph might be the last Glyde, but he would keep the secrets with which he had been entrusted and take them to his grave rather than hand them over to the people who had run that fucking, fucking war.

Which sounded very grand, but he knew what standing heroically alone and clinging to your principles in the face of overwhelming force looked like. It looked like his father's last stand at Ypres, attempting to hold back hell, dead within three minutes.

"You're right," he said. "Someone ought to take it on. I *know*. But Camlet Moat matters too much, and we've already been criminally careless, and I've nothing to give. I wondered about passing it to Syrena Phan, actually, as the most practical academic I've ever met, but we need her work on the veil."

"Lord, please don't try," Sam said. "She's burning the candle at both ends as it is, and has hauled her mother out of retirement too. If you offer her any more work, your hand will come back a stump."

"As I suspected. I don't suppose you'd care to do it?"

"Ha, no. I'm a ghost-hunter. Don't come to me for ancient sacred ritual, you might as well give it to Barney. Um... I admit that nobody's leaping out at me. You need to think about this a bit more."

"How ineffably useful. Thank you so much."

"And meanwhile, what about the immediate problem?" Sam asked. "Jack-in-the-box man?"

"Lazenby. I don't know, except that he keeps turning up, supposedly on his eccentric employer's whims."

"An undiagnosed prophet? Instincts he doesn't understand?"

"Possibly. Or it might be simple coincidence."

"Uncle Simon had very strong views on coincidence," Sam said. "Mind you, Uncle Robert said it was the driving force of literature and indeed humanity, so there you are."

Uncle Simon and Uncle Robert. Randolph had never met the writer Robert Caldwell who had lived and died with Feximal, giving

Sam his surname on the way. He'd heard muttered imputations about the pair; he'd also heard Sam coupling their names for three years. He'd never asked—it was no more his business than Glyde secrets were Sam's—but something propelled him to remark, "This must have been an unusual home in which to grow up. With Mr. Feximal, I mean. He was the most intimidating man I've ever met in my life."

"Uncle Simon was deeply chivalrous and deeply kind," Sam said, instantly defensive. "He could be alarming when he wanted, but Aunt Theodosia was the one to fear."

"God, wasn't she." Randolph turned to the bookshelves, since he ought to be working if they were going to indulge in chit-chat. "Did I ever tell you how I first met them both? I had just turned twenty-one and my father took me to the Remnant to introduce me as the Keeper of the Words, heir to England's occult aristocracy, all that. It was something of a procession, impressing the greatness of my inheritance and my duty on me, and the greatness of the Glyde name on everyone else. Well, we came across Miss Kay and Mr. Feximal in the display hall, and my father presented me as if he rather thought they might wish to kiss my hand, and I have never seen such withering contempt on human faces. Mr. Feximal just *looked* at me, and Miss Kay pointed at me with those dreadful nails of hers, and said, 'You should beware of arrogance, young man.' My father asked if that was a divination, and she said, 'No, just his face.'"

Sam threw back his head and laughed. "That sounds like Auntie Theo."

"I was crushed," Randolph assured him, smiling, although it was entirely true. "It was salutary. My father was very much of the old guard, the equivalent of those military men who thought bright red was a jolly good colour for war and regarded wearing khakis as a form of cheating. He considered Mr. Feximal as little more than a tradesman, and the German war machine as an insult to the occult craft."

"I thought they were rather good," Sam said drily.

"Oh, but *mechanised*, dear boy," Randolph drawled. "The occult ought to be the preserve of gentlemen, you see. Hand-crafted, with all incantations said in the right accent, and only the most elevated spirits to be dealt with."

Sam gave him a sideways look. "That doesn't sound entirely unlike you."

"Father and I were always in full agreement that a rapier is a more gentlemanly weapon than a Sten gun. The difference is, when our opponents started using Sten guns, I was happy to sacrifice centuries of Glyde tradition on the altar of survival. He was not." He flicked through the book, replaced it, and took down another. "Mr. Feximal made it through almost to the end, didn't he? I never crossed his path out there."

"Mmm. They were listed as missing in action after Passchendaele."

They. Randolph allowed his curiosity to get the better of him. "He and Mr. Caldwell were inseparable, I believe."

"Entirely, for twenty-three years. I miss them both appallingly but I'm glad they're together."

Randolph contemplated the book he held, not really looking at the pages. He'd never seen that kind of thing, or perhaps he'd seen it and hadn't noticed it. He'd certainly never considered the kind of relationship that Sam was talking about for himself.

Before the War, his future had been mapped out. He would marry his cousin Theresa, who was a superb dancer, ornament of the most fashionable boites de nuit, and a brilliant arcanist, and they would carry on the Glyde family line. That was a cold-blooded way to look at things, perhaps, and it wouldn't have been a love match in the normal sense, but they'd both been happy with a practical arrangement, pleasure to be taken elsewhere. Randolph's childhood had been ruled by his parents' mutual hatred; he and Theresa would have been married friends. Not Darby and Joan, not a lifetime romance, but he'd never have had that anyway, and really, who did?

He'd have grown old with his best friend and considered himself blessed, but the War had taken her, and everyone else, and since then he'd had only empty encounters, nothing and nobody worth remembering, because what was the point in wanting more? Theresa was gone, and there was no lifelong companionship to be had with another man.

Except, on Sam's word, there was. Twenty-three years.

"Did you mind?" he asked abruptly. "I mean, about your uncles. The two of them."

That was a damned intrusive question, but Sam didn't seem moved. "It wasn't up to me to mind. Uncle Simon and Uncle Robert belonged together, and it was nobody else's business. And Jo isn't quite usual either, come to that. I can't see why it should have mattered a damn to me or anyone. They plucked me and Jo off the streets, you know. Everything they gave us, everything they did—they *deserved* to be together, and instead it was used against them."

"How?"

"Oh, the Shadow Ministry blackmailed them into service in the War," Sam said, in the kind of calm tone one laid like planks to bridge a pit of rage. "Uncle Simon was a conscientious objector, and over age too, but there were letters, indiscretions. You know the sort of thing. The Ministry said it was because the war effort needed every man, but Uncle Robert always thought it was spite. He and Uncle Simon had made sure Jo wasn't installed as HQ's private crystal ball, you see, so Whitehall took its revenge by sending them to the trenches instead."

"Dear God." Randolph had known Sam's loathing for the Shadow Ministry; he hadn't known this. "Sam, I am appalled. Disgusted. I had no idea."

"I can't tell you how much I hate those pen-pushing bastards. I truly can't. My uncles— Oh, the devil. I miss them hellishly."

"I'm sorry."

Sam shut his eyes, exhaling hard. "Well. You lost your father."

"We weren't close," Randolph said, with some understatement.

Sam tapped the desk with his pen. "Look, not to insult you by suggesting that you have human feelings, but—"

"I should bloody well hope not."

"*But*," Sam repeated, "if you wanted—"

The bell rang in the hall, a long urgent clanging that meant *Come down right now*. Randolph turned and ran, taking the stairs two at a time. It was a tall, thin house so the stairs turned on each floor; he cantered down, vaulted the handrail at the bottom, and skidded into the parlour, Sam thundering after him.

There were four men in there. Randolph didn't bother to look at the other two, because Barney was scarlet in the face, his jaw set, and Isaacs, by his side, had his hands clasped tight behind his back.

"Report," Randolph snapped. Military discipline had saved them before.

"Gentlemen from the Shadow Ministry, sir," Barney said through his teeth.

"I'll handle this. Dismiss."

The soldiers turned on their heels as one and stalked out, making Randolph's skin prickle unpleasantly as they passed. Sam would manage them far better than Randolph could, so he swung back to the two remaining men. One of them wore a scornful expression; the other was sweating. If Randolph hadn't already known which of them had occult senses, that fact would have told him.

"Bracknell, you bloody fool," he said, without preamble. "What do you think you're playing at?"

Bracknell set his quivering jaw. He was in his late fifties, as were many of the arcanists who worked for the Shadow Ministry. That was inevitable: the younger generations were mostly dead, and those still upright tended not to think fondly of Whitehall. "I might ask you the same thing, Glyde. Those two—"

"Are war heroes, honourably discharged, with more medals than they can carry."

"Are not safe." Bracknell pulled out a handkerchief to mop at his face. "Good Lord, man, do you think they ought to be running around London without supervision?"

"They've been running around London for three years," Randolph said. "You seem to have driven them to incoherent fury in three minutes. As an argument for you assuming control, it fails to convince. Who's your friend?"

"Mr. Delingpole is the new Under-Secretary at the Department of Special Affairs. Mr. Delingpole, this is Randolph Glyde, of the great family."

"A family that has served the British government long and well." Mr. Delingpole extended his hand.

Randolph looked at it, unmoving, until the man took it away again. "My hands are dirty, Mr. Delingpole. That happens when one works. And, to be clear, my family serves England. Not Britain, since the Welsh and Scots and Irish are their own lands, and *not* the Government, because the forces we handle are not temporal, bureaucratic, or at man's disposal."

Mr. Delingpole smiled tightly. "That is very quaint, but I fear it is hardly an attitude for the modern world. Parochial individualism belongs to a gentler, kinder era. We are facing new challenges, and we must face them together."

"Under your authority?"

"Under the authority of the Chief Secretary, who serves the Crown."

"I already serve the Crown. My duty is mine, Mr. Delingpole. I have been bred to my knowledge. You are not in a position to tell me how to do it."

Delingpole's eyelids drooped. "My department seeks to coordinate those who can serve the country in time of need. Is there any reason you cannot discharge your duties within a wider structure of administration and support that will allow us to work together? Your responsibilities may be hereditary, but your family suffered appalling losses in the War, and you are unmarried. Ought there not to be arrangements in place?"

"I will make those."

"And if you step in front of an omnibus tomorrow?" Mr. Delingpole asked swiftly. "We no longer have the luxury of the old ways."

"Captain Barnaby and Mr. Isaacs are walking proof of that," Bracknell put in. "They don't have your generations of knowledge and tradition, and just look at them. And if it comes to that, I'm sorry to observe that you no longer have those generations. We all need to pull together now, Glyde, just as we did in the War."

"Ah, the War," Randolph said. "Jolly good. Remind me what regiment you served in."

"You well know that I was over age."

"So was Simon Feximal, by more than a decade," Sam said from behind him. "That didn't stop Whitehall forcing him to France, to *pull together* while people like you stayed at home."

"My father was sixty, and volunteered," Randolph added. "We're acquainted with sacrifice for the common good in this house. You may spare us your lectures."

"I don't agree, I'm afraid." Mr. Delingpole was thin-lipped. "It is very appealing to dismiss the importance of organisation and planning in favour of the individual hero, but it is also, if I may say so, fantastical, and rather childish. The country has limited resources to face serious threats. We as a nation need to understand those threats and use our resources wisely. How much work is duplicated? How much potentially vital information goes unshared? How much more efficiently could you do your duty with proper support? Mr. Caldwell, you submitted to Navy discipline in the war; do you believe your battle cruiser could have done its duty with no captain and every man making his own judgement of what was best to do?"

"Do you know how many men on my ship died?" Sam demanded. "Are you using the War as an argument *for* government organisation? Have you any shame?"

"Let's not get bogged down in the trenches of the argument," Randolph said. "The point isn't whether you would organise well or badly, is it, Mr. Delingpole? The point is that you are offering support and structure and simplicity and all these wonderful ways of taking work and responsibility off our shoulders in exchange for us accepting your authority. That's what's going on here, isn't it? Bringing us under central command. You don't want arcanists and occultists carrying on in our several ways. You want us reporting to you, and believing we *ought* to report to you, because it's more efficient, more practical, more *modern*."

"And it is all those things."

"It may be," Randolph said. "Amazingly, I don't consider efficiency the sole and only good."

"And we can spot a power grab when one is being attempted under our eyes," Sam added. "Whitehall's tried to bring occultists into line before. Last time, someone ended up being eaten by eels."

"Is that true? I always thought it was a pleasant fantasy. How satisfying," Randolph said. "Let's be clear, Mr. Delingpole. I'm sure you'd be terribly efficient, and organise things to dedicate our resources to the benefit of the nation. And I know that's very tempting for people like Bracknell here, who want nothing more than to believe in a strong man at the top and a steady hand at the tiller, and to have someone else be responsible for it all. But I don't believe in your strong men, I don't trust your hands, I take my own responsibility, and I *will not* obey orders that run counter to my judgement. I have done that in the past. I won't do it again."

"We have not given you any orders that would clash with your judgement," Mr. Delingpole said.

Randolph smiled at him, unpleasantly. "You will, Oscar. You will."

"What? My name is Horatio."

"It would be. Is there anything else we can help you with before you leave?"

"This won't do." Bracknell was red in the face. "You are being obstinate and obstructive and irresponsible. We need people like you on side. Why, we need you on the secretarial committee. You talk of taking orders: we want you *giving* them. You're a Glyde: every occultist in the country will accept your authority. You have a chance to direct this department and shape its policy. Isn't that right, Mr. Delingpole?"

"Quite right," Mr. Delingpole said without enthusiasm.

"God help the department," Sam said. "And what unique and singular blessing is it that I could bring to Whitehall, as if I didn't know?"

"Indeed," Randolph agreed. "Let's not play the fool. You want my name, and Jo Caldwell's gifts, and Captain Barnaby and Mr. Isaacs as weapons. You may not have any of them. And don't try to bribe me with your penny-ante offices again or I will take it *poorly*."

Bracknell pointed a finger at Randolph. It shook slightly. "Are you aware of the consequences of your defiance?"

"Is that intended to intimidate me?"

"I'm warning you," Bracknell said. "We can all see what's going on. We all see who's doing his bit, and who isn't, and we'll all know who to blame when things go wrong, as they will if you aren't prepared to work in harness like a sensible man. Your arrogance will be your downfall, Glyde. You were told that."

"No, he was told to beware of arrogance," Sam said. "And I'm looking at a dollop of it right here if you think you know more or better than Randolph. I've had enough of this conversation. Get out of my house."

"Thank you for the show of faith," Randolph said, once they had shut the door on the Shadow Ministry men. "I wish I shared it."

"Don't we all," Sam said. "What a shambles. I feel like a weaver or some such, watching the masters bring in the Spinning Jennies and move everyone to the factories. Seeing everything industrialised. Ugh."

"I feel more like the ancient relic of an outmoded regime watching his world crumble, but at least I'm used to that," Randolph said. "The trick will doubtless be to avoid the guillotine."

"I'm afraid it's firing squads these days, that's progress for you. You need to watch yourself with those bastards, Randolph. I'm just a jobbing ghost-hunter with a useful sibling, but you're a problem."

Randolph knew all too well that was true. He had no desire to lead anyone, least of all the motley selection of arcanists and occultists who had lived past 1918, but he was the last Glyde, and people followed him. If he bowed the knee to Whitehall, others would conclude it was the right thing to do. While he didn't, his refusal was noticeable, and imitated, and irritating.

And there was very little to be done about that. He shrugged; Sam sighed. "I know, I know. I'd better go and check Barney and Max have simmered down."

"You left them angry?"

"Let me handle them," Sam said firmly. "And you'd better do something about this Lazenby character. The last thing we need is the Ministry finding out about our problem with Camlet Moat the hard way."

"Indeed. If only I knew what to do about him."

"Not to tell you your business," Sam said, "and I realise this may seem an extreme measure, and very much outside your area of expertise..."

"What are you suggesting?"

Sam grinned. "Have you considered talking to him?"

CHAPTER FIVE

Saul gathered up his coat and hat, bade goodbye to Major Peabody, and stepped out of the door. The Major lived comfortably on Berners Street; Saul's tiny rented room was a good half-hour's walk north, in the much less salubrious area towards Camden Town. At least it was cheap, and the landlady uninterested.

He walked up Berners Street, only vaguely registering a man who lounged against a shop-front at the corner with Goodge Street. The tall, lean figure straightened as he passed with a tip of his hat and said, "Good evening."

"Surely you're joking," Saul said. Somewhat irritatingly, he had to work to repress a smile. The fact that he kept meeting Glyde did not make the man a friend.

"Not at all," Glyde returned, falling into step. "It's undeniably evening, the weather is undeniably good—"

"You were waiting for me, Mr. Glyde. And there's no point pretending otherwise, since I'm not heading anywhere more complicated than my own home."

"How disappointing. I thought you might care for a drink."

Saul stopped and turned. "Sorry?"

"Drink. They're sold in public houses, I believe."

"I've heard that too. Why would I have a drink with you?"

"You already did."

"Yes," Saul said. "I have some questions about that."

"You could ask them over a drink."

Jesus wept. "Do you intend to answer them? Over a drink or otherwise?"

Glyde's smile glinted. "Come and find out."

What exactly would I be signing up to? Saul wanted to ask. He didn't. Glyde was peculiar, and worrying, and supercilious, but he was also the first person who'd suggested going for a drink to Saul since July 1916. He went into pubs alone when the need for fellowship became intolerably strong, but never chatted; he hadn't become a regular anywhere, even a silent one, because it seemed unjust to impose himself under false pretences.

Glyde knew who he was and still wanted a drink. If that was all he wanted. Saul could feel those fingers on his face, over his scalp, and the longing stabbed at him.

Blast it. "All right, then. Where?"

Glyde shrugged, pointed, and led the way across the street to a little old place with wooden beams. It was busy enough that nobody looked twice at them—not that there was anything at which to look twice. Glyde bought a gin and tonic for himself and a pint for Saul, and they sat opposite one another at a small, round, sticky table, as one did. As Saul did, anyway. Glyde's expression as he touched the tabletop with experimental distaste suggested otherwise.

"Do you not go to pubs much?" Saul asked.

"Frequently. *A* pub, at least. I go to *a* pub frequently, or perhaps it would be more accurate to say sometimes, but they wipe up the spilled beer there."

"Ah. A classy place."

Glyde snorted with what seemed real amusement. Saul leaned back, weighing him up.

He was upper class to a fault. Saul's father was a country solicitor, and his upbringing had been by no means humble, but Glyde reeked of the right schools, the right connections. Saul had met plenty of his sort at Oxford, cool, confident, older than their years, and had found them attractive and repellent in equal measure.

"All right," he said. "You wanted me here. What's this about?"

"My insatiable curiosity." Glyde sipped his gin with a grimace. "You are, as noted, a highly educated man—"

"And a disgraced one. Which is why I work for the Major, because nobody else will have me. Next question."

"At ease. If I may continue? A highly educated man, and one who has worked in strange and ancient places. Do you think there's anything in Major Peabody's theories?"

"I beg your pardon?"

"It's a serious question." Glyde's voice remained light, a slight smile on those thin lips. "Do you think there's more to the world than meets the eye?"

"I think there's plenty I don't understand," Saul said, feeling his way. "And that the human mind has remarkable and insufficiently explored capacities. For example, mesmerism. What did you do to me?"

"I?"

Saul gave him a look. "You did something I don't understand on Camlet Moat, and something on Cock Lane, too. I'd like to know what you're playing at."

Glyde's brows rose. "I dare say, but you haven't answered my question. No, no, Mr. Lazenby: you go first."

"Whether there's more to the world than meets the eye? Of course there is, one way or another. People create poetry and mustard gas. We invent gods and monsters and gods that might as well be monsters. We act with extraordinary grace and unfathomable cruelty. We're so terribly intelligent, and dreadfully easy to fool. I'm ready to believe you mesmerised me on Camlet Moat; I've seen odder things done. I don't need to believe in mystical hexagrams to explain a tree bursting into flame—"

"How do you explain it?"

"I don't," Saul said. "It may have been a natural phenomenon, a new undetectable secret weapon, or divine intervention. I couldn't say which."

"You aren't curious?"

"Do you have an answer? Because if so, then yes, I am damned curious, but I've heard enough meaningless speculation for a lifetime."

"You don't think there is method in Major Peabody's madness?"

"Not to speak of, or any meaning either."

"Mmm. And yet you keep turning up."

"What do you mean, I keep turning up?" Saul demanded with justifiable outrage. "*You* keep turning up. I've been there before you every time, on Cock Lane, and Camlet Moat, and even at the tree. You came to find me on that train, and you were waiting for me today. And I'm acting at the dictates of a luna—uh, an eccentric, so what is it that brings you to the same destinations as me? What mystical patterns are *you* following, Mr. Glyde?"

"That's an extremely good question," Glyde said. "Which I don't intend to answer."

Saul sighed. "You astonish me."

Glyde's lips curved. One couldn't call it a grin, but it was certainly a smile, and a real one at that, crinkling his eyes and parting his lips for the first time that Saul could recall. He didn't have much to smile about himself; it struck him now that Glyde seemed not to find much joy in the world either.

He looked better smiling. It cut through the cool superiority of his manner, turning his bony aristocratic features into something warmer, more human. It made him touchable, or it made Saul want to touch him.

"I think you owe me some sort of answer, though," he said, more or less at random. Anything to keep this going, not to have Glyde walk off and to be alone again. "Don't tell me: you're searching for Geoffrey de Mandeville's lost treasure. Following clues through London from Temple Church to Camlet Moat."

"Damnation," Glyde said. "I should have thought of that, shouldn't I? Yes, this is a case of rival treasure hunters across London. Peabody will sweep you off to the Pyramids next, for inscrutable reasons, and I shall step out from behind the Sphinx—"

"Looking much like its shorter cousin."

Glyde gave a crack of laughter. "Ha! Yes, indeed. I shall make gnomic utterances swathed in a headscarf and vanish into a sandstorm."

Saul was smiling too now. "It's clearly your metier. Wines, spirits, and cryptic disappearances."

"Wines and spirits take up much of my life," Glyde assured him. "Is Major Peabody looking for treasure?"

"Not to my knowledge. He seems to me nothing more than a harmless crank with a mind open to every passing wind of belief. You would—you would tell me if he was not? If you knew any ill of him?"

"What ill do you fear?"

"Oh, you know." Saul strove for his previous tone. "If you're actually a spy for some top secret government department. If Major Peabody is using the cover of a harmless eccentric to work for the Germans, and I'm unwittingly helping him—" He broke off, raising his pint to his lips, but his hand shook, the beer splashing his face. He put the glass down too hard, and felt beer run down its sides, over his fingers.

Glyde's eyes were on him, intent. "I can't tell you Major Peabody is harmless, or if he intends ill, or if he is doing ill without intending it.

I don't know *what* he's doing, or if it's for anyone but himself. I will not lie to you: I am concerned. On the other hand, I do not work for the Government." He said that with extreme distaste, as though denying being a common prostitute. "I have no reason to believe Major Peabody is a traitor to his country, in the way you fear. Honestly, I don't know what's going on."

"But something is going on."

Glyde picked up his drink. He looked suddenly very tired. "Plenty of things, one way and another. It never stops, does it? 'It isn't the fighting that fucks you up—'"

"'It's the fucking fucking around,'" Saul completed automatically. Their eyes met again. Saul knew the expression Glyde wore; he wore it himself, as so many men did. "Where were you?"

"Flanders."

"Doing what?" He could imagine this lean, superior man mud-covered and yelling. Glyde would, he thought, have been a good commander. A commander to whom a man could come in trouble; one who might well head trouble off for you.

"Special battalion."

That knocked the wind out of Saul's sails. It sounded hush-hush, and if it was—

Glyde evidently saw something on Saul's face, because he shook his head. "I'm not a spy. I repeat, I don't work for the Government. Let me put it this way: if I had any reason to think you're playing a part in something you shouldn't, I would say so. If I learn any such thing in the future, I will say so. I believe that you do not want to do harm, to England or to others; I shan't let you be tricked into it if I can avoid it."

Saul stared at him, speechless. Glyde looked, for once, quite serious, no trace of the habitual faintly mocking half-smile, and what he'd said...

I believe that you do not want to do harm; I shan't let you be tricked into it.

Saul wanted to clutch the words to him, to curl round them, to write them down and keep them pressed between the pages of a book. He wanted to believe them, and he hated the small scarred part of his mind that pointed out, *He knows your story. He knows what will bring you to your knees. If he wanted to manipulate you, how better?*

"I think you're a decent man," Glyde went on. "I think, if I warned you off, you would take the warning, rather than risk another mistake."

"Another villainy," Saul said, stifled, because Glyde might as well have kicked his chair from under him. He was habituated to contempt or abuse; he couldn't take this.

"Mistake. You aren't the only one who made a hash of things in the War; many of us have the wrong sort of blood on our hands. If I find reason to be concerned, I will tell you. And—if you have concerns, will you tell me?"

"But what concerns?" Saul asked hopelessly. "I don't understand why any of this should be more than Major Peabody's demented rambling."

"I hope it isn't. If it begins to seem meaningful, or if you should find yourself out of your depth, come to me." Glyde extracted a silver case from his pocket and handed Saul a card. Engraved, expensive. *Randolph Glyde*, it read, with the address of a flat in the Albany and a telephone number. "I don't promise I'll be able to help, but I can try."

"Why would you? Why do you think—?" His voice cracked, and he clamped his lips shut before he betrayed himself utterly.

Glyde looked at him for just a second with an expression appallingly close to sympathy, then his face smoothed into the habitually mocking look and he tilted a brow. "I'd like to say, because I'm an impeccable judge of character," he drawled. "It's not true, naturally, but feel free to give me that credit anyway: I do like a bit of unearned credit. I should have been a general, really. I'm quite cut out for the role."

"This cryptic posture of yours could become trying," Saul returned in his best stab at the same light tone, profoundly grateful for the respite. "Do you always speak in double talk?"

"Habitually. It's terribly vulgar to say what one means." Glyde's eyes met Saul's for a second. "Despite which, I meant what I said. Call on me. Any time."

The edges of the card were hard against Saul's fingers. He wanted this to be an invitation, an approach; he hoped or feared it was something far less familiar, for which he longed even more. He wanted it to be kindness.

And maybe also an approach. Could he imagine himself going to an expensive address, ringing a doorbell, giving his name to a porter? Walking through marble halls and taking a brass-fitted lift to Glyde's door and saying...

He couldn't imagine what he would say to this sophisticated, superior man. He'd have had the confidence once, and the desire, but he wanted something else now, something far harder to find than a quick suck in a back alley. He wanted his belief back. He wanted to know the things he'd thought he had—love, liking, companionship, and trust— could be real. He wasn't going to get any of that from a man he didn't know who seemed constitutionally incapable of giving a direct answer, but he wanted them so much the longing clawed at his insides.

Glyde was watching him, face unreadable. He didn't speak for a moment, as if he knew Saul had been struck dumb, and then he said, gravely, "You've had a hell of a time, haven't you?"

"Others worse," Saul managed.

"That is the most specious form of consolation possible. One can always find someone who has it worse. If I'm having my fingernails torn out with pincers, it is unhelpful to observe that my neighbour has been hanged, drawn, and quartered."

"Well, yes. But if one has brought one's trouble on oneself—"

"You had your nature turned against you," Glyde said. "That is not a condition to be envied."

"I don't want anyone feeling sorry for me."

"I shouldn't worry, dear chap, I am notoriously unsympathetic. But I do strive to be fair. I say again, if you're worried, come to me." Glyde drained his glass. "Or, indeed, if you need a listening ear. I don't claim to be good at that, but I'm probably better than nothing."

"Why would you?" Saul demanded.

"The War took too many decent people. I find myself disinclined to let it take any more."

The visiting card gave suddenly in Saul's hand, folding almost in half. It was thick stock, expensive. He realised he must have been crushing it even as he noticed the sharp line of pain along his finger ends.

Glyde's eyebrow twitched. "Tut. Allow me."

He extracted another card and held it out. Saul dropped his in the ashtray and reached for the new, unspoiled one. He took hold of it just as Glyde moved it forward, so the ends of his finger and thumb bumped into Glyde's. Saul held on; Glyde didn't let go.

They stared at each other over the card. The touch of skin to skin was so tiny, so trivial, and it tingled through Saul's hand like a caress.

Glyde's hazel-dappled eyes were intent, but the only compulsion going on was the one in Saul's blood, throbbing through fingers and heart and groin. He licked his lips, and saw Glyde's gaze track the movement, still didn't dare speak.

"Yes," Glyde said at last. "Do call on me, should you wish to. I must go. I'd say goodbye but it feels almost inevitable that it will be au revoir. One way or another."

He picked up hat and coat on that shot and departed, leaving Saul to stare after his lean form. He finished his pint slowly, not really paying attention, and set off home.

That was the strangest conversation he'd had since—well, since any of the other conversations with Glyde. It was the longest he'd had in years with anyone who wasn't Major Peabody, and those barely counted since they were punctuated monologues. It was also the most painful since his father had informed him he was no longer considered a son.

Glyde had offered help, and even perhaps friendship, and Saul knew that could be a trick or a trap. He'd been caught by his longings before; wanting made you vulnerable, and he was afraid to be vulnerable again. And God knew what the man was playing at with his cloak-and-dagger business. It was eccentricity, or a game—or it was meaningful, which made it doubly dangerous. Saul had been unwillingly caught up in the secret side of the War; he had no desire to find himself dragged back into anything. All he wanted—

All I want is to be left alone. That was what he'd have said yesterday, and meant it. To do no more harm, to risk no more hurt.

But in that conversation he'd wanted something else. He'd wanted—well, he'd wanted Glyde, without question; he'd have come to heel like a dog if Glyde had suggested a back alley, but there was more. He wanted the touch of fingers, and a sympathetic voice, and someone with whom to laugh, or talk, or be silent. He wanted to know that someone thought well of him again; to feel for someone in return. And for the first time in years, he found himself believing that one day he might.

It didn't make him happy. It hurt like hell, like the agony of blood returning to a long-numbed limb, but, Saul realised, the painful prospect of hoping again was better than the dull knowledge he never would.

They said time healed all wounds. Maybe by the time his handkerchief had rotted away on the cloutie tree, his own gaping wound would have scarred over.

Over the next few days Saul took a closer look than he'd have liked to admit at his employer and his work. He couldn't, when thinking clearly, imagine Major Peabody being of any use to foreign governments. The man was a fool and a fanatic, but surely nothing worse, and he clearly didn't know anything of value. Nevertheless, Saul looked, so that he could not in future rebuke himself for failing to do so, and perhaps a little because if he had found anything, he could have taken it to Glyde.

He was not going to indulge those thoughts. It was, he'd discovered, very easy to imagine walking into a palatial flat, taking hold of Glyde's face, kissing him fiercely and wordlessly, sliding to his knees. He could picture any number of acts of pleasure and need carried out in panting, hungry silence, and he did imagine them on his own in his bare room. What he couldn't imagine was an actual conversation that would lead them there.

The fact was, Saul had lost his nerve. He didn't trust himself or his judgement, and Glyde had left the pub first. If Saul had imagined the attraction between them—or, because he wasn't a fool, if Glyde had felt it but chosen not to act—Saul didn't want to take the risk of being refused. It didn't matter anyway. If his imagination and his heart were coming back to life, he'd be grateful, and not ask for more. He told himself that very firmly, several times.

Today he was compiling the dossier Major Peabody had requested, into which he defied anyone to read sinister meaning. It was a summary of the various accounts of Geoffrey de Mandeville's twelfth-century death and burial, on which no two chroniclers seemed able to agree. His corpse had been gibbetted in Temple Church orchard, or he'd hidden in a tree that had broken and dropped him into a sacred well, or he'd simply been killed in battle up near Ramsey Abbey in Cambridgeshire. The litany of possible dooms ran through Saul's head, adapting itself to the tune of 'What Shall We Do With the Drunken Sailor'. *Hanging off a tree in a leaden coffin; drowned in a well with a tree grown over it; arrow to the eye and lost in fenland; ear-lie in the morning.* He didn't realise he was whistling until Major Peabody walked in.

"You're in a cheery mood today, Lazenby. God's in his heaven, all's well with the world, eh? In the merry, merry month of May."

"You seem quite cheerful yourself, sir. Good news?" It wasn't much of a guess; the Major had punctuated his remarks by waving a letter in the air.

"Yes indeed. How do you feel about a jaunt to the country? Fresh air, exercise, and perhaps the answer to some questions?"

"It sounds delightful. Where do you have in mind?"

"Cambridgeshire. The Fens."

"Geoffrey de Mandeville?" Saul suggested, this not requiring a great intuitive leap, and was rewarded with a beaming smile.

"Indeed! My correspondent is a Mr. Abchurch who lives outside Burwell, where as you know Geoffrey met his end. He is something of an antiquarian with an interest in de Mandeville and has most generously invited us to stay at his home and look over his collection. Perhaps you will arrange the railway tickets for us both?"

They left for the Fens two days later. Saul had hastily purchased new shoes and some decent clothes in which to dine—probably an unnecessary expense, but he felt awkward enough imposing himself on a stranger who didn't know his history without appearing shabby too.

The train took them to Cambridge, where Mr. Abchurch's motor-car awaited them. Saul didn't know this part of the country, and looked around with a certain dismay as they drove through an endless expanse of flatland. This had all been marsh once, long drained for agriculture; it looked like the paintings he had seen of Holland. Endless fields, spiked by the occasional tree, separated by long straight dykes and channels. The wind whipped over them directly from the North Sea, and behind them the great towers and spires of the university were visible for far too long. You could see for miles, because there was damn all to see. The skies were huge.

Their destination, Roestock House, stood outside the village of Burwell. It was a little sort of place, houses and cottages huddled low against the scything wind, held down by a huge grey stone church, fifteenth century or so, with an octagonal tower. They reached the house, a big red-brick Georgian construction a couple of miles outside the village, as twilight was setting in, streaking the great grey sky with yellow-gold.

Mr. Abchurch himself opened the door as Saul and the Major emerged from the motor-car, and greeted them both warmly. "Major Peabody? And Mr. Lazenby? I am delighted to meet you both, and thrilled that my little hobby of Geoffrey de Mandeville has attracted so much attention. That old villain, eh? It's a great pleasure to meet fellow enthusiasts. Do please come in, and Hetty will show you your rooms. My wife. Henrietta, my dear, Major Peabody and Mr. Lazenby."

Mrs. Abchurch was as short and round as her husband was tall and thin, and every bit as friendly. She and the maid bustled round to relieve the visitors of coats and hats, then she led the way upstairs. "We don't have much company so far out of the way of things, so you must take us as we are, I fear. I hope you aren't too tired by your journey? We will be quite alone this evening so James can talk old Geoffrey with you to his heart's content, but I've invited a few neighbours to join us for dinner tomorrow. We like to make the most of company when we have it."

Saul made polite noises, grateful he'd thought to equip himself with dining clothes. The room made ready for him was warm, with a coal fire blazing and a thick quilt on a comfortable bed. Mrs. Abchurch seemed charming; her husband was evidently something of a monomaniac but a pleasant one, and would doubtless enjoy Major Peabody's avid interest. This felt like a holiday, and he determined to enjoy it.

Dinner began with chitchat. The Abchurches were older and childless and this was farmland, so the War hadn't loomed as large here as it might have, and nobody brought the subject up. Instead they discussed local history, and folklore, and how the two intertwined in the topic Saul and the Major had come here to study.

"They called him the Devil in Human Form," Mr. Abchurch said. He sipped a glass of wine, wiped a stray drop of red from his lips. "The story as I have heard it becomes a mix of truth and legend, de Mandeville a monster of the Fens, a Grendel. If you would like to hear it—"

Major Peabody indicated he would, very much. Saul added his voice. The wind had risen outside, and it was a fine night for a story.

"The Anarchy, then, when King Stephen and Empress Matilda battled for supremacy. The old men who tell the tale place it in 'days gone by', or 'the Dark Ages'. They will all tell you that this was 'when God and his angels slept'; that phrase has become as much part of the language of this tale as *Once upon a time*. But it might be the first century, or the fifth, or the fifteenth for all they know. They speak only of a King and a Queen fighting over England's crown; and some say that the battle was between King Arthur and his sorceress sister Morgan le Fay."

"Do they? Do they indeed? I must tell you—but please, go on." If Major Peabody failed to shanghai a conversation, he was rapt indeed. Saul couldn't help a smile.

"Now." Mr. Abchurch leaned forward. "During the wars of the King and Queen, when God and his angels slept, there lived a baron named Geoffrey Man-Devil, for he was the devil in human form. He turned his coat from King to Queen and Queen to King again as the fortunes of war ebbed and flowed between them, and at each turning, the treacherous baron was rewarded. Geoffrey became lord of three counties, and even Master of London.

"But the people loathed him for his cruelty and arrogance, and at last his pride became too much for the King. He was arrested and given a choice: execution, or giving up his lands and his castles— which meant breaking his word. For Geoffrey had sworn as he hoped for salvation to serve as Master of London and Custodian of its Tower, and to renounce that oath put his soul at hazard.

"Devil in man's form as he was, Geoffrey chose disgrace over death. He gave up his castles and his honour with them, and fled to the Fens, raising an army of cut-throats and murderers as he went. Since he could no longer live as a lord, he chose to live as a monster. He seized the city of Ely, and from there took Ramsey Abbey itself, murdering the monks and driving out the Abbot, who rained down curses as he fled. Geoffrey's killers used the Abbey as their lair, plundering and ransacking the lands around, dragging innocents back to the sacred ground for ransom, rapine, and torture. The very statues in the church covered their faces from what they saw, and as Geoffrey passed along the cloisters, the stone walls wept blood."

His voice had taken on the cadences of the storyteller, with extraordinary effectiveness. Saul felt all too conscious of the house's lonely position in this bleak land. The fire and candles seemed less comforting now, more of a fragile bubble of warmth and light in the midst of a very great darkness. He could hear the wind, a mindless howling that whipped and tugged at the walls.

"As Geoffrey was more devil than man, so his hordes became monstrous in their cruelty and appearance. They were beasts of the Fens, poised between man and animal, land and water. They ravaged the land so that not an ox could plough, a man dig, or a woman spin her wool in safety for thirty miles around. The people cried out for help, but no army could make its way through the watery Fens to defeat Geoffrey's evil.

"At last the King decreed that a great castle should be raised at Burwell, and garrisoned against Geoffrey's monstrous horde. Geoffrey in his pride attacked the castle, holding that he and only he was master of the Fenland. The dispossessed Abbot of Ramsey blessed the arrows that were handed out to the archers of the King as they defended Burwell, and as Geoffrey's howling horde descended on the castle, a single bowstring was pulled. The arrow flew true, and struck Geoffrey in the head. Yet he did not die, but crawled away into the marshlands, begging for the rites that would save his soul as his beast-men fled. But no man would help him, monster as he was; no priest would pray for him, excommunicate as he was."

Candlelight danced on Mr. Abchurch's spectacles, making his eyes a sheet of flame.

"As Geoffrey lay dying, a party of holy knights came by, wearing the red crosses of their order. They were knights of London, and some say they had been set to kill the oathbreaker. They laid a surplice on Geoffrey, claiming him for their order, and took his body back in solemn procession to London. There they encased him in a shroud of lead and suspended him from a tree in the orchard of London's ancient Temple, for they dared not bury a body whose soul the Church had refused. And there we leave him, whether buried or not buried, damned or saved, I do not know; I cannot tell."

He sat back. Saul couldn't speak. His mind was full of pictures, of medieval knights and fur-draggled man-beasts dripping with slime, statues that hid their faces and walls that bled, and the bleak endlessness of the untamed fens.

Major Peabody licked his lips. He opened his mouth to speak, and the lights went out.

Every light. The candles on the dining table; the fire in the hearth. The electric light in the corridor that had limned the door with its brightness. It was dark, and it was as cold as though the fire had never burned, and damp too, with the cold, wet, stinking breath of the fen.

Mr. Abchurch, or possibly the Major, made a strangled noise. Saul jerked out, "What the—" and managed to stop himself. Mrs. Abchurch shrieked, a high shrill sound.

Something outside chuckled.

It was deep, slow, and huge, a laugh without joy or pleasure, and it came from all around at once. *Outside*, Saul told himself. *It's outside.*

"What was that?" Mrs. Abchurch asked. "What *was* that?"

"A b-bird," her husband said. "A bittern?"

"That wasn't a bittern!"

"The lights," Major Peabody said. "Something must have—have fallen down the chimney."

"Yes. Yes, it must."

"If you get the matches, dear," Mrs. Abchurch said, in a voice that was very nearly calm. "We could relight the candles if you get the matches."

"They're on the mantelpiece," Mr. Abchurch whispered, in quiet horror.

Saul felt it too. He didn't want to get up from the table, because to move would be to draw the attention of whatever was outside, whatever was wrapping its breath and cold fingers around the house, pressing in. The smell of wet rot was unbearable.

If he lit a candle, he might see something in the room.

The thought gripped him with a terror so cold and all-encompassing that he had to speak, just to know he was still there. "I'll get them."

"No!" Major Peabody said sharply. "Don't get up!"

Christ, Saul thought. *He feels it too.*

"We'll just wait," Mr. Abchurch said. "I'm sure if—if we wait a moment, the electricity will come on."

"What if it doesn't?" Mrs. Abchurch's voice was thin. "What if it doesn't come on? What if it doesn't *ever*—"

The laughter came again, sweeping around them, filling the air, and at the end of it a last little noise. It was almost a giggle, and it came from right behind Saul's ear.

"It's behind me," Major Peabody rasped, and Mrs. Abchurch gave a low wail. Mr. Abchurch was muttering what sounded like fragments of prayer, brokenly. None of them moved.

Saul would have liked to pray. He couldn't even remember how it was done, but he knew, urgently, that there must be a way, and the thought brought a sudden vivid image to him: Randolph Glyde on Camlet Moat, wiping the handkerchief over his face like a sacred rite. The vibrant life of the great forest around him, the well water cool in his throat, the green and gold light through the leaves, as dappled as Glyde's hazel eyes. He shut his own eyes in the darkness, willing the image into his mind, and told himself the wet cold on his face was the clear burn of the well water.

"I'm getting the matches," he said, and stood.

The howl of wind outside rose to a shriek. Major Peabody gasped, a shrill sound. The giggling turned to a snarl, and Saul's hands were shaking, his muscles stiff with fear, because his senses were screaming: *it's right behind you*. He felt with his hands, shuffling forward until his fingers bumped something, waved them up and down till they hit the mantelpiece.

"Lazenby?" Major Peabody demanded. "Lazenby!"

Saul felt along the mantelpiece, every moment expecting he would touch something wet and draggle-haired from the marsh. His fingers rasped against a dry rough surface and he sucked in a breath to avoid screaming, then realised what he had. He gripped the matchbox, easing it open to be sure it was the right way up, fumbled one out, struck it.

Light flared, blinding in the absolute dark. There was nothing but the flame for a second, and then Saul could see. He leaned over Major Peabody's shoulder and held the flame to a candle, which spluttered and resisted for too long but finally burst into life.

The match was burning down. Saul took out another with shaking fingers and lit the other candles. His companions at the table were rigid for a few seconds more, then as light filled the room, Mr. Abchurch took a deep breath.

"Thank you, Mr. Lazenby. Good heavens, that was startling."

"Yes, wasn't it?" Major Peabody said, and Saul was astonished to see the smile return to the man's face. "Goodness me. It certainly added a frisson to your storytelling!"

"Didn't it just," Mr. Abchurch agreed with a chuckle. "Look, there's some sort of weed on the fire. It must have been picked up by the wind and fallen down the chimney."

"Is that likely?" Saul felt compelled to ask. He could see it too, a clump of matted, rotted black-green stuff smothering the coals.

"Oh, well, the winds here," Mrs. Abchurch said. "I suppose that's what made the birds sound so extraordinary."

Saul looked between his companions. He was absolutely sure they had felt the terror too, and he was all too familiar with the stiff upper lip as required response to bowel-loosening fear, but this wasn't people putting a brave face on things. Mrs. Abchurch was rising now, plucking the matchbox from Saul's hand. "I must go and check on the kitchen. I dare say Joan will have had a nasty shock too, poor thing. Oh, look, the electricity is back on." She pulled open the dining room door, admitting the yellow artificial light from the hall. "Jolly good. It's such a nuisance when we lose it altogether."

She went out, not a care in the world. Mr. Abchurch beamed at his guests. "Well, since we've lost the fire in here and while Hetty takes charge, may I suggest we retire to the drawing room and take a glass of port there?"

"That would be delightful," Major Peabody agreed, and they trooped out to settle down in front of a still-blazing fire and discuss the Prime Minister's likely replacement in the event of his resignation.

Nobody mentioned Geoffrey de Mandeville again that night.

CHAPTER SIX

Randolph sat in the pew, stretched his legs in front of him, crossed his arms, and leaned back to look.

Stone pillars rose around him to a high clerestory, a dark-timbered roof, and elaborate curling carvings framing a rose window in the chancel arch. The clerestory windows were green, as was the huge chancel window, tinting the sunlight that streamed in to turn the church interior to a petrified forest.

It wasn't, despite that, a beautiful place on the inside. The stone didn't soar, or sing; the carving was regimented. It wasn't an *inspired* church, because inspiration was a luxury. St. Mary's Burwell was rock solid and nailed to the floor.

Not that most of its builders, let alone those who had paid for it, would have seen it that way. To the lay observer it was simply a fine church in the Perpendicular style, absurdly large for the surrounding village, with a few unusual features.

Randolph wasn't a lay observer, and nor was the Vicar of St. Mary's.

"A shocking attack," that worthy said. "Worse than since the War, far worse. I don't understand it."

"Where was it?"

"Outside the village, is all I can say. And it didn't last long. I was asleep, you see, after dinner." The Vicar's face was lined with age and care, his voice tremulous. "By the time I was fully awake it had stopped. It was old, as everything here is old. Old and deep, and it came out roaring. From *nothing*. I should not have expected it to come from nothing."

"I had a similar experience recently," Randolph said. "Perhaps we should expect more."

"The veil is hanging in tatters, I know, but that has been the case since the War. It surely ought to be getting better, not worse. Why now?"

"Damned—I beg your pardon—*bothered* if I know. I'll take a look around."

"I wish you would. I don't like it, Mr. Glyde. I—frankly I find myself struggling. I have told you I would like to be relieved of this responsibility."

"Wouldn't we all," Randolph said with perfunctory sympathy. "A shame it's not possible."

"I am, I regret to say, too old," the Vicar persisted. "Surely a younger man—"

"Of course, of course. If only they weren't all dead."

The Vicar recoiled slightly. Randolph supposed he should be kinder, but he had limited patience for shirkers at the best of times and he'd got up at five in the morning to come here, sustained only by railway coffee. "Since you're here, let me try something on you, Mr. Herbert. *No sign will guide you; no gun will save you; a fool and a knave may do what an emperor could not, and the unenlightened man brings light.* Ring any bells?"

The Vicar gave that due consideration and said, "Not a one. The light-bearer—could that be a reference to Lucifer?"

"We can only hope not. Never mind, it was a long shot. May I make free of your church?"

"Of course. Er, you may wish to..." He tailed off, indicating a corner of the chancel arch. "The locals call it the silent watcher. I try not to look at it."

Mr. Herbert retreated. Randolph stood, stretched, and began to prowl.

He wasn't a religious man in any normal sense, although he bore the words of a god, but churches were a vital part of the land's fabric, and lasting ones too. St. Mary's had stood for at least six centuries in something like this form, with worship on this site for far longer. It was a place of sanctuary and protection, a candle against the dark. Randolph would take any of those he could get.

The corner to which he'd been directed was dark, pierced by beams of glowing green from the corner of a window, and one of those made it just possible to discern a crude carving in one of the oak supports. The light, Randolph calculated, would never fall directly on it. It was a rough shape in which at first one could only see deep bores for eyes, and a gaping square-edged pillarbox mouth from which tendrils curled.

Ivy. Randolph could taste it in his own mouth, feel the push of roots and branches, the spring of leaves. The face in the forest, the watcher in the woods. The Green Man.

What have you beheld? he asked the silent watcher in his mind, and let the impressions flood in.

He was sitting in a pew in the green glass light some time later, nursing a persistent headache, when a creak and footsteps indicated visitors to the church. Someone coming to pray, he hoped; he could use a bit of honest faith.

The footsteps came forward, paused, approached again, and an all too familiar voice said, "Do you know, I'm not even surprised."

"Do you know, nor am I. Have a pew." He slid along the wood polished by years of reverent bottoms.

"That's the first time I've heard that offered literally." Lazenby came and sat by him. Randolph glanced round and thought: *yes, still beautiful*.

He really was. Dark, intent passionate eyes; that constant little frown; the curved perfection of his top lip. The aching need and want and vulnerability that Randolph recognised too well, as though whatever strings he plucked in Lazenby resonated in his own chest.

Beautiful, wanting, and in the wrong bloody place *again*.

"Well," he said.

"Yes, well. Are you— No." Lazenby had his hands locked together, knuckles showing white. "I suppose you're here for your usual mysterious reasons."

"For my own reasons, yes. And you are—?"

"With Major Peabody. You said I could come to you if I found myself out of my depth." Lazenby was looking straight ahead, chin up, but his hands were working. "Did you mean it?"

"I did. Have you?"

"In the sense that either I'm going mad or the world is."

"Sadly," Randolph said, "it's probably not you. Would you care to come for a walk?"

They left the church together. Randolph paused in the porch, taking a quick look up at the ancient stonework.

"What are you looking at?"

"Wodewoses." Randolph indicated the shaggy semi-human figures carved on the arch above them, lines blunted by the centuries. "Wild men of the woods, although that's in areas with more trees. They call them fen-grendels here."

"Yes, I expect they'd be more...fenny, wouldn't they. Bedraggled fur. Wet and reedy and stinking."

Lazenby wasn't panicking, but only because he wasn't letting himself panic. Randolph knew that note in a man's voice. "I expect so," he said, keeping his tone light and unemotional. "Off you go, Mr. Lazenby, talk to me. Whatever you have to say, I assure you I'll have heard stranger."

They set off on the road out of the village together as the clock chimed eleven. Randolph rarely walked with anyone who kept a satisfactory pace, but Lazenby strolled at just the right speed, a leisurely stride that would eat up the ground without tiring. The fenland stretched around them in shades of green, grey, and brown under the May sun.

Lazenby took a deep breath. "Something odd happened last night. I don't know what it was, but it was damned odd, and since damned oddness seems to be associated with you—"

"If it's odd, I'm interested."

"Yes but— It's absurd in the light of day. I don't know how it will sound."

"Find out by telling me."

Lazenby narrowed his eyes but launched into the tale, which chimed all too well with what Randolph knew from the Rector and the silent watcher. He told it clearly and well, neither attempting to minimise his own fear, nor adding the usual details that people seemed to think gave verisimilitude.

"And we went to bed," he finished. "I lay awake half the night, but nothing else happened. It sounds ridiculous."

"It doesn't. What did you skip?"

"What do you mean?"

"You sat in the dark, afraid to move, with something gibbering in the room and the hand of terror on you. Believe me, I know how that feels. And then you rose and found the matches, against every instinct. What helped you there? What determination, or prayer? It may be important."

"How could it—" Lazenby stopped himself and then said, "Camlet Moat."

Randolph had been hoping for almost anything else. "Camlet Moat," he repeated.

"There was something about the atmosphere— I don't know. It was completely different in every possible way, but I thought of that place—the well water—what you did—"

He broke off again. Randolph couldn't blame him.

"You thought of Camlet Moat, and you could act."

"If you must know, I pretended I was there. I shut my eyes and imagined it. Have you ever been in a bad situation and you needed to be in a better place, in your head?"

"Often and often."

"It's a habit I have, I've always done it. Especially in—well, in bad times. I imagined I was at Camlet Moat and it helped, that's all. But I can't see any way in which that could be relevant."

He said that too defiantly. Randolph cast him a sideways look. "You can't think of any connection at all?"

"Nothing. Unless one considers that the lights went out when our host told the story of Geoffrey de Mandeville, and Camlet Moat was Geoffrey de Mandeville's house, and you baptised me from his *well*—"

"And we're a brief stroll from the ruins of the castle where he received his mortal wound. Aside from that, no connection at all."

"What's going on?" Lazenby halted, grabbing his arm and pulling him round to glare into his eyes. "What in hell's name is this?"

He looked afraid, and angry too, the kind of anger bred by fear. "Specifically, I don't know," Randolph said. "I'm trying to find out. More generally— My advice, in all honesty, is that you get as far from Peabody as possible. Leave the silly sod to it."

"No."

"Yes." If he did Randolph would never see him again, and that would be...call it a missed opportunity, or even a connection lost, but probably Lazenby's life saved. "Vanish, man. Change your name, start again, and leave the Major to his idiocy before he drags you down with him. I said I'd tell you if I was concerned; well, I am. Get on a train to London and then a train to somewhere else, and don't come back. I shall miss our meetings, naturally," he added. It didn't come out as ironically as he'd meant it to.

"No," Lazenby said again. "I can't do that. For one thing, I like my name."

Saul. An odd name, with a sound to it that suited him. Raw, sullied soul. "I like it too."

They looked at each other, there on the road under the great flat open sky, and then Lazenby went on with determination. "For another, the Major has been decent to me. If he's in trouble by accident, I owe him something. Tell me this: were we in danger last night? Of—of any kind?"

Spiritual, was what he meant. He didn't know the half of it.

"Yes," Randolph said. "You were. If you want the truth, I suspect you saved four lives, or at least four minds, by lighting that candle. No, I am quite serious. If you had not resisted, if you hadn't brought back the light—" He stopped dead.

"What is it?"

"You brought the light. You...brought... Fuck."

"Excuse me?"

"Saul, the character in the Bible. Wasn't he unenlightened?"

"Well, he was a pagan," Saul said. "His name was changed to Paul when he turned to Christ. Better known as the Apostle Paul, if that rings any bells? You did *have* an education?"

"You don't want to know about my education. *The unenlightened man brings light.* Hell's teeth."

"What, if anything, are you talking about?"

"Saul."

"Yes, Randolph?" Lazenby enquired, in tones of extreme courtesy, and even in the middle of this, Randolph felt himself smile.

"Damn it. Right. I have an unpleasant feeling that you may not have a choice in this matter, but I'm giving you one anyway. I will get you to a railway station, to a port, out of the country even, if you will go *now*. That means leaving Peabody to his own devices, but I will endeavour to stop him doing whatever he started. Or, God help me, I will tell you what's going on, fully and truthfully to the extent of my ability to do so, and then you'll be sorry. Your choice, but make it now."

"You'll tell me what's going on. Really?"

"Yes. You doubtless won't believe me, and if you do, you won't like it."

They were still standing on the road, looking at one another, the flatlands stretching around them. Randolph felt intensely visible, as though he could be seen for miles. As though Saul could see everything of him.

"Suppose you start to tell me," Saul said, "and I don't like it. What's to stop me leaving the Major or the country then?"

"No act of mine. I'd ask for your word to keep silent, that's all. But, fair warning, once one gets tangled in these matters it can prove difficult to escape again." *It may already be too late*, Randolph wanted to add, and wasn't sure if that would be fair or the opposite. "Come on, let's walk."

Saul fell into step with him. "Where are we going?"

"Nowhere in particular. Swaffham Prior, apparently," he added, since there was a low waystone indicating that such a place lay at a distance of two miles. "Prior to what, I couldn't say. I find it easier to think when I walk."

"So do I. Tell me, then."

"Are you sure?" Randolph asked. "This is not a terribly pleasant business."

"It's been a long time since things were terribly pleasant. I want to know what's going on."

Randolph took a deep breath. "Probably exactly what you think, or fear. What you don't want to believe."

Silence.

"You're saying it was supernatural."

"You saw a tree burst into flame," Randolph said. "You were in Cock Lane when an entity struck, and you felt it strike, and you heard me speak words you were not able to apprehend then or after. You *know*. You knew last night."

Nothing but the scrunch of feet on dry ground, the faint hiss of the wind.

"Who are you?" Saul asked at last. "What are you?"

Randolph stuck his hands in his pockets. "The easy answer: I'm Randolph Glyde, and I keep an eye on a number of things on behalf of the country."

"You said you didn't work for the Government."

"I don't. My duty is to England. I am answerable to the King and my conscience."

Saul nodded slowly. "And what's the difficult answer?"

"That there is more in heaven and earth than is dreamed of in your philosophy. Intelligences other than human, and places other than this. I'm not trying to be cryptic: these things are complicated and best not spoken of, as you discovered last night."

"Last night, a man told us a story," Saul said. "A legend, a folktale. Geoffrey de Mandeville was a twelfth-century thug, not a devil in human form. Walls did not bleed as he passed, because walls don't bleed."

"Wrong. I don't know what de Mandeville was originally, and damned if I know what he is now, but belief works in strange ways. You told me Abchurch used ritual phrasing."

"No, he— Well, I suppose you could call it ritual."

"He recited a set form of words and summoned something. What would you call it?"

"But it's a story!" Saul yelped. "That's why it's *become* a set form of words! If something terrifying turned up right behind you giggling in your ear every time you told the bloody thing, people wouldn't tell it!"

"Five shillings says otherwise. But in general, you are quite right. I expect people have been telling the story harmlessly, or almost harmlessly, for centuries. Letting the repository of belief build up, creating the shape of a tale, bleeding it into other forces, growing like ivy round oak. That's how it works, how it's always worked. Only, you see, things have changed recently. There's no point making strangulated noises, I'm trying to explain a very large matter here."

"Let me help," Saul said. "You are telling me that the supernatural—which is to say, superstition, folklore, myth—is real?"

"Some of it. People, like your Major Peabody, talk a lot of rubbish, and are frequently wrong. Let me see. Did you ever read the Casebooks of Simon Feximal?"

"The ghost stories? About fifteen times over. The *Strand Magazine* changed hands for vast sums at school."

"That's a start. Very well: you should know that Simon Feximal was a real man, and Robert Caldwell wrote those stories as accurately as he could within the limits of what's safe to tell."

"Balls," Saul said explosively. "*Balls.*"

"My word on it. I know Caldwell's adoptive son very well; he's a ghost-hunter himself. He still lives in Feximal's house on Fetter Lane. The Casebooks are exactly what they purport to be. Not fiction."

"But—"

"If you read an account of what happened to you last night in the *Strand*, under Robert Caldwell's name, would it seem a departure from his usual content?"

Saul made a choking noise. They walked on.

"Right," Saul said at last. "It is difficult to believe that this isn't some huge, immensely cruel practical joke."

"I dare say. I was brought up to it."

"What are you?" Saul asked again. "A proper answer, please."

"I am an occultist. I am a protector of the realm under the King's seal. I am the twenty-third Glyde to carry out an extremely ancient duty, and I am also, faute de mieux, carrying out someone else's extremely ancient duty because there's nobody else to do it. Before the War, I was a wealthy and privileged scion of one of the great and ancient families. Now I'm half a ghost-hunter and half I don't know what, with my world hanging in shreds around me, staring into a pit most people don't even see, but it's there. It's bloody there."

He clamped his mouth shut, not sure how that had come tumbling out, except that he couldn't bear to be the Heir of Glyde now. Not with this vulnerable, frightened man in this inhumanly empty place. Saul's eyes were on him, wide, watching.

"That sounds bad," Saul said after a while. "Are you all right?"

"Of course I am. Ah, God. Do you want the truth?"

"Yes."

"There are other worlds, other places, beyond or behind, outside or under our own, a breath away. Sometimes people summon the denizens of those places to ours. Sometimes they try to get in all by themselves."

"Last night, the thing that was laughing," Saul said. "It was outside and it was in the room, both at once. I heard it right behind me and so did Major Peabody, at the same time."

"Yes. Don't expect them to play by the rules, including geometry. There are no rules."

"You said Abchurch's story called it because things have changed. What do you mean?"

Randolph didn't want to tell this part. He glanced at a waystone, its grey top poking out of the rank grass. *Swaffham Prior, 2 miles.* "The other worlds have always been with us, and so have people like myself. Occultists like my family maintained the health of the land, and the monarch—latterly the government—let us get on with it. Towards the end of the last century, though, things began to change. Warfare was becoming more mechanised, more industrial in scope and nature. A big war was coming, as any fool could see, and governments were casting round for new and larger weapons. Machine-guns. Dreadnoughts. Mustard gas. Us."

"Wait a moment," Saul said. "You don't mean—"

"Of course they used it. All that power, that potential for destruction? They all did, as though they'd just been waiting for a chance. The Germans, the Belgians, the French, the British. There was a war going on beneath yours—that's what we call it, the War Beneath—and you probably even heard about it. You read about the event at Mons, I suppose?"

"You mean the Angel of Mons?"

"Those weren't angels," Randolph said. "Oh, my friend, those weren't angels. That was the first Great Summoning. We started it there, the British. We—arcanists who ought to have known better, under direction of generals who ought to have been shot—we summoned things that should never have been, in unimaginable quantities . And we ripped the veil to shreds."

"The veil. As in, 'beyond the veil'?"

Randolph wasn't sure how he'd gone from the lofty keeper of knowledge to a blubbering penitent pouring out his shame, but if he had to do this, it was a relief to have an intelligent confessor. "It's an imperfect metaphor for an intangible thing. A veil or a curtain, a barrier of sorts between our world and what's outside. The act of summoning tears a hole in the veil and invites the outside in. It's an act of supreme stupidity, and we summoned, and summoned, and summoned. Before the War Beneath, perhaps Abchurch's story was just a folktale. Now it's a calling. He called, something came."

"What came? I mean—what was it?"

"Something eight hundred years dead in the fens," Randolph said. "Something that wanted to put out the lights."

Scrunch, scrunch, went their feet on the road. The sun was warm on Randolph's neck, casting a short shadow in front of his feet.

"If you're trying to alarm me, you've succeeded," Saul said at last.

"Good. I want you to run away."

"What happened on Cock Lane?"

"Something came through. It's a place of belief, and that seems to have weakened the veil."

"And you sent whatever it was away." Saul had a kind of baffled acceptance in his voice now. "You said—what did you say?"

"Certain words, a protection. Old and deep. It's my duty to keep the words, and speak them when needed."

"I couldn't remember them. I tried to tell myself I wasn't paying attention."

"There's no attention in the world that would let you remember them," Randolph said. "If I wrote down the sounds for you, you couldn't speak them. I paid a significant price to be their keeper."

"Who else knows them?"

"Nobody. I'll pass them on to someone else before I shuffle off this mortal coil. That's how it works."

Saul turned to look at him, frowning. "And at Camlet Moat? What did you do there?"

"God knows."

"What?"

"I don't know," Randolph said. "Sorry. The Glyde family has provided the Keeper of the Words and the Walker of the Moat for twenty-three generations. I'm the Keeper; my cousin Theresa was the Walker. She studied it for years, taking over from our Uncle

Archibald. She'd have known what medieval noblemen have to do with it all, and what Camlet Moat wanted with you. I don't."

"Wanted with *me*?"

"Camlet Moat is one of London's cornerstones, a vital protection. If you had intended harm to the city, or the Moat, drinking the water would not have been an enjoyable experience. That's why I gave it to you; I wanted to find out if you were a threat. Whether that might have attracted the hostility you experienced last night, I couldn't say."

"Why don't you ask the, uh, Walker?"

"Because he's me."

"Sorry?"

"Theresa was the Walker of Camlet Moat," Randolph said. "The role was passed down through my family by word of mouth alone. Before the War three people knew those deep secrets: Uncle Archibald, who was retired, Theresa as the Walker, and our young nephew Gerry, in training. But Theresa died at Ypres, and when I got back to England it was to find Archibald and Gerry dead and buried. Spanish flu, apparently, and the amusing thing is, Archibald hadn't written down a fucking word. I spent six months ripping the house apart in the hope of finding anything I could use, and then I called myself the Walker of Camlet Moat because nobody else could do better. Since when I've been trying to maintain one of London's most important arcane protections without a single solitary clue what I'm doing. I probably shouldn't have given you the water but it seemed like a good idea at the time, and that's all I've had to go on for years. I'm sorry."

"That all sounds extremely bad," Saul said after a moment. "And it must have been damned hard for you. To lose three family members so quickly—"

"Oh, I lost the lot. There were seven of us at the Second Great Summoning, and I was the only one who walked away. My cousin

Valentine had already been lost in action at Mons, Vernon burned to death in a French chateau to nobody's regret, and Gerry was the sole child any of my generation had yet produced. I'm the last Glyde."

Saul stopped and swung round to face him, touching him lightly on the arm. "My God, Randolph. I am so very sorry." His dark eyes were intense with feeling, brows pulling together, thoughts only for Randolph's loss in the middle of his own hellish mess. It was, Randolph realised, precisely what he'd have expected.

"Thank you. It was a long time ago." He began to walk again rather than receive sympathy he didn't deserve, let alone do anything damned stupid such as falling into Saul's arms on a public road just because he had a childish need for comfort.

Saul caught up after a few paces. Randolph spoke before he could say anything else. "So that's your story. The truth after which idiots like your Peabrain are groping."

"Peabody. You don't think— Does he know about this?"

"He seems to have scrabbled some sort of information together. I'll see what I can get out of him tonight."

"What happens tonight?"

"The Vicar of St. Mary's and I will be coming to dinner with the Abchurches. If any sinister manifestations appear, you may leave them to me. I'd enjoy the exercise."

"How on earth—"

"The Vicar is a colleague of mine."

"The Vicar," Saul repeated. "Of course he is."

"There are a number of us. Arcanists and academics and ghost-hunters, religious men, highly irreligious women. All of us with an urgent interest in making sure the veil tears no further than it has."

"A secret society?"

"An informal association."

"Hang on a moment. You say that the—the thing that happened in the War was mandated, that the Government knows about this veil business. Why isn't there a formal association?"

"There is. There's a Whitehall department entirely dedicated to occult affairs."

"Great Scott. Well, good."

"Not at all, no," Randolph said. "It's a power grab. Most of the country's leading arcanists died in the War; those who remain are young, old, or cowards. Whitehall saw an extraordinary opportunity to seize control of an area that has hitherto eluded government grasp. That is beneficial to them, and appealing to people who are frightened of hard truths. The Shadow Ministry offers us all a structure on which to rely and an authority in whom to place one's faith. Unfortunately, doing so rather depends on not acknowledging that these are the blundering fools who caused the current situation."

"Well, I see that. But if someone is trying to take action—"

"If only. The Shadow Ministry's first priority is to establish its authority. To discuss the current crisis is to question Whitehall's competence. The Department will listen to me when I join it; until then my protests are alarmist, unpatriotic, and damaging to morale."

"Shouldn't you join it, then?"

"Oh, I could demand a seat at the highest table and use it to make a great fuss about what needs doing," Randolph said. "But people wouldn't see that. They'd only see the Heir of Glyde joining the Shadow Ministry, lending it my name, my approval. It would encourage people to take orders from Whitehall, and I know the sorts of orders they'll give, you see."

"Christ," Saul said. "How is it possible that everything you say makes things worse?"

"Someone else observed much the same to me recently. Would that I could take the credit, but it's just the way things are."

"Yes, well, that's— Sorry, have we missed a turning?"

"Metaphorically?"

"No, literally. I could have sworn it was two miles to Swaffham Prior when we started."

Randolph looked at the waystone. It read, *Swaffham Prior, 2 miles*.

"The sodding countryside. The last one said that as well."

"Country miles," Saul said. "We must have missed a side road, I can't say I was paying attention. Should we go back? Major Peabody is at Roestock House looking at Mr. Abchurch's collection, and I told him I was just popping out."

"We can retrace our steps." They turned in unison and began to walk back along the long straight road. A few minutes passed in silence. Randolph was grateful for that. He wasn't in the habit of speaking frankly; he hadn't meant to spill out nearly so much, still less to speak of his many failures. He preferred to lock those within rather than face sympathy or acknowledge weakness. He wasn't sure why he had told Saul more than a fraction of this, except that the man was afraid and alone and had needed to know, and it seemed a brutal cruelty to leave him bewildered, even if the price was to make him terrified.

That, and Randolph was alone too.

Which couldn't be helped, and wasn't a matter for self-pity or self-indulgence. He'd just wanted to talk, that was all, and Saul was remarkably easy to talk to. Also to look at, but now was not the time for such thoughts, having pulled the rug of reality from under the poor sod's feet.

"What did you mean about my name?" Saul asked eventually. "Unenlightened whatever it was?"

"How do you feel about soothsayers?"

"You mean, like Joanna Southcott?"

"Yes, except that her prophecies are drivel. In fact I meant Jo Caldwell, Sam's sibling, a diviner of remarkable gifts and only relative incomprehensibility. Jo wrote to us recently with a warning."

"Of what?"

"No idea. That's prophecies for you. It goes, *No sign will guide you; no gun will save you; a fool and a knave may do what an emperor could not, and the unenlightened man brings light.* What it means I could not say, but gifts like Jo's are seen once in a century. And you were unenlightened—in name, in fact, and in metaphor—when you went to find those matches. You brought the light back and believe me, the dark was closing in on you."

"But..." Saul looked as though he was groping for words. "Why would a soothsayer have anything to say about me?"

"God knows. Maybe it isn't about you at all; I might be wrong. But it doesn't do to ignore Jo Caldwell." The sun was warm on the back of his neck. Randolph tilted his hat back at an angle to cast a little more shadow.

"No, really, though," Saul said. "It doesn't make sense. Well, none of what you've said makes sense, but it particularly doesn't make sense that this should be about me. I'm not doing anything! And Major Peabody is— What on earth is wrong with these people?"

"Sorry?"

Saul gestured at the waystone in front of them. "For pity's sake. I'd say it was a practical joke except I can't imagine going to so much pointless effort."

Randolph looked at it. The waystone read, *Swaffham Prior, 2 miles.*

"We turned around," he said.

"What a bizarre thing."

"We turned around," Randolph repeated. "We turned around on a straight road and retraced our steps. Didn't we?"

"Of course we did."

"So how is it that the sun was behind us just before we turned, and is behind us now?"

Saul's hand moved to the back of his neck. "Have we been walking that long?" He pulled out a cheap fob watch, and clicked his tongue. "Blast. It's stopped."

Randolph took out his own watch and saw, with a disheartening lack of surprise, that it had also stopped. "Let me take a wild stab in the dark. Yours says twenty-one minutes past eleven?"

"How the devil do you know that?"

Randolph looked down at the shadow that pooled in front of his feet, feeling warmth on the back of his neck, then turned deliberately. The shadow and the heat moved with him. He looked up and, not greatly to his surprise, noted that the sky had a hazy cast that made the sun impossible to see.

Saul hadn't noticed that yet, though he was turning in a circle too. "I can't see any town. I can't see any buildings at all. How the devil— Right, look, it can't be more than a mile to either Burwell or Swaffham. If we just keep walking we'll reach one of them."

Randolph wasn't nearly so sure of that, but it was worth a try. "Indeed. Which way?"

"Back to Burwell. Oh, for heaven's sake." Saul turned again, looking around, and gave a frustrated laugh. "I can't tell which way we were going. I've been less disoriented than this in a desert. Well, if we find ourselves in Swaffham we can hire a car, perhaps, or even telephone the Abchurches so Major Peabody doesn't think I've fallen in a ditch."

"I'd be delighted to find ourselves in Swaffham," Randolph said. "Let's go." He set off, counting steps, whispering the numbers aloud. Saul gave him a look but didn't ask him what he was doing, simply paced in silence as they walked, the only figures in this great flat landscape.

They reached the next waystone at four hundred and thirty-three steps, and Randolph wasn't surprised at all at what he read.

"Swaffham Prior, two miles," Saul said. "Swaffham— What the *devil*?"

"What indeed. It was twenty-one minutes past eleven and two miles to Swaffham Prior when we were walking along this road without a care in the world," Randolph said. "It is twenty-one minutes past eleven and two miles to Swaffham Prior now, and I very much fear it's going to be twenty-one minutes past eleven and two miles to Swaffham Prior for some time to come. I'm sorry, Saul. We've been caught."

CHAPTER SEVEN

They tried walking more, in the same direction. This time they both counted, Randolph aloud, Saul under his breath. There was another waystone reading *Swaffham Prior, 2 miles* at just under seven hundred steps, and yet another about six hundred paces after that.

"Well," Randolph said. "That's that theory confirmed. *No sign will guide you*, indeed."

"What is going on?" Saul asked. He could feel the panic rising. It wasn't unnatural fear, like the terror from that night—*last* night, he reminded himself. It was very normal, natural panic at being hopelessly lost on a straight road in the middle of England. If you could call it England. This grey-green endless flatness didn't feel like a place that had a name. "Randolph—"

"I know. I'm not happy about this either. And I wish I could tell you what's going on, other than that we're stuck. I have a feeling that if we walked off in different directions, we'd meet one another coming the other way."

"I don't want to try," Saul said. The thought of being alone in this place was appalling. "Are we—is this— It's not natural. Is it?"

"Of course it bloody isn't." Randolph looked at the landscape with narrowed eyes.

"How do we get out?"

"Your conviction that I have the answers is flattering."

"Randolph." Saul grabbed his arm, pulling him around. "I appreciate your love of avoiding a question, but I am very worried now, and thinking all sorts of dreadful things, so a bit of help—"

"What are you thinking?" Randolph asked.

"Honestly?"

"Believe me, I shan't laugh."

Saul licked his lips and glanced up again, to the huge hazy sunless sky. "We spoke of ritual phrasing in folktales. The phrase currently in my mind is *east of the sun and west of the moon.*" That had been the title of a book of fairy tales his mother had used to read to him. He remembered one of the illustrations now: a small figure in an empty land, under a bleak and indeterminate sky.

"Yes," Randolph said. "That's rather what I'm thinking too."

Saul stared at him. He was still gripping Randolph's arm, but now more hanging on than holding. Its sinewy strength was a comfort. "Don't joke," he whispered.

"I'm not. I wish I were."

"But—"

The skies were so large here, so featureless, without sun or cloud or colour. The fens stretched out, neither land nor water, endless and empty and eternal, and they were such tiny specks on the land, flies crawling on a huge carcass...

He knew this feeling. It was desert sickness, terror of a landscape that paid not the slightest regard to people. Europeans notoriously suffered it, coming from more malleable lands adapted to serve them over centuries. *The locals don't bloody panic,* he remembered Woolley saying to a sobbing first-timer. *Open your mind.*

He shut his eyes, refusing to fold to his knees, and felt Randolph's other arm around his shoulders, a warm body pressing close. "Hold up, now. Hold up."

"Just a moment. I'll do very well if you give me a moment."

"I know you will. You're a damned brave man. People talk about courage, but sometimes I think it's just a matter of how long one can grit one's teeth and hold on. You know how to do that, don't you?"

Saul had somehow got his head resting against Randolph's neck and shoulder. He could smell warm male body, a hint of some eau de toilette, a stronger whiff of something green and growing, like ivy. "There's rarely much choice."

"There's always a choice. But here you are, still on your feet." Saul could feel Randolph's hand at the back of his head, stroking his hair, sending shivers down his skin.

Saul looked up, didn't step back. Randolph's face was close to his, his dappled eyes intent, and he didn't step away either. They were body to body, so close, looking at one another.

"I suppose you know you're beautiful," Randolph said, very softly.

Saul had no idea how to respond. All he could do was stare, hopelessly lost and wanting, hopelessly trapped.

Randolph's lips curved. "Would you have any violent objection to being kissed?"

They were in the open road, visible for miles. They were in an empty land, where no birds sang and the road never ended. He was with Randolph, who'd looked at him and seen beauty. It was all unreal.

He leaned forward and met Randolph's mouth with his own.

It was a careful touch, each feeling his way through need and loneliness and too many years of refusing to feel. Saul didn't have illusions there. Randolph might be self-possessed to a fault, his lips controlled, but his fingers were digging into Saul's shoulder, clutching as hard as Saul's own fingers, and he thought for the same reason: to prevent them shaking.

Saul moved his other hand, and found a hard hip. Randolph stilled for just a second, then jerked him close with a muffled grunt.

Then they were kissing wildly, mouths open. Saul felt his hat tossed aside, a hand in his hair, the other sliding down his back. He managed to release his death grip on Randolph's arm in order to get a hand to his face, cupping his smooth-shaved jaw. Mouth to mouth and tongue to tongue under the sunless sky, kissing for dear life in a dead land.

Randolph pulled his mouth away with a gasp. Saul, instinctively alarmed, attempted to step away, and felt Randolph's hands tighten, stopping him. "Don't go anywhere."

"Are we safe?"

"No, but there's nobody around."

Saul let himself lean into Randolph's strength. He hadn't leaned on anyone in a very long time. "If you meant to raise my morale just now, it worked."

"That wasn't what I intended to raise."

Saul laughed aloud, and felt Randolph's shoulders shake. "I have to tell you, that worked too."

"So I notice." As well he might, with their hips pressed close. Saul could feel Randolph's arousal as easily. He pushed forward almost without intending it, rubbing himself up against Randolph, and heard the low groan.

"Hell's teeth. Saul."

"Is there really nobody here? Because—"

"I don't know what there is," Randolph said. "I'm not sure where we are. I feel the urge to lay you down and make love to you till the sun sets, if it ever does, but I can't help thinking we should get out of here first."

"Yes. Of course."

Randolph did not let go. "I'm exerting common sense and self-control, you understand. Were we not rather up a gum tree..." His hands slid down Saul's flanks. "You have been occupying my thoughts for some time."

"I'm sure you're aware it's mutual. To be clear, when you gave me your card—"

"I hoped you might turn up on your own account, yes. And you will be very welcome to do so once we're out of this—whatever it is. But, and I hope I won't sound too eccentric, I'm not sure how good an idea it would be to fuck on this road. I have a feeling that once we start, we might not stop. Which doesn't sound like the worst fate in the world, but..."

Saul could feel it. Randolph's hands on bare skin, his mouth, bodies moving and twisting with pleasure. He wanted to kneel, to let himself be taken, to lose himself in panting and sweat. To give his body up to Randolph and be endlessly, helplessly, timelessly fucked till they were nothing but wanting and spending, wanting and spending, an expense of spirit in a waste of fens.

"I think I see what you mean," he said. "Is it—well, a trap? In the same way that one shouldn't eat or drink in this sort of place?"

Randolph leaned back to get a look at him, brows tilting. Saul shifted. "Well?"

"Just impressed at your capacity for acceptance. I abominate whining in the face of facts. People who stand there moaning, *Oh, this is impossible, it can't be happening,* ignoring whatever horror is hurtling toward them because they'd rather not know. So tiresome."

"You told me you were unsympathetic. I didn't know the half of it. Good Lord, man."

"What? I'm delighted at your mental flexibility."

Saul wasn't sure he deserved that. The realisation of Randolph's nightmarish, impossible truth had been creeping up on him for a long time and he hadn't wanted to believe it. If anything, he was accepting it more easily now because he'd been here before. He knew what it was to feel dreadful awareness dawn like the pitiless desert sun, illuminating everything he thought he knew and scorching it to ashes.

Last time one man had betrayed him. This time his entire known world was a lie but he had one man standing by him. Saul was almost afraid to realise how much better that felt.

"You're being a brick," he said inadequately. "Thanks."

"Nonsense. I can't think of anyone with whom I'd rather be stuck in an endlessly recurring loop of bloody bogland. That said, shall we get out of here?"

"Let's. How?"

"Absolutely no idea." Randolph released him, and they both stooped to retrieve discarded hats. "Hmph. Well, the road just goes on. Shall we see what happens if we leave it?"

"What might happen?"

"We might break out of the loop. We might find ourselves in another loop. We might emerge somewhere, or somewhen, else. It might be exactly what they want us to do. I tell you what." He hung his hat on the waystone. "Let's walk on and see what happens to that."

"All right." Saul wasn't at all tired. Or hungry, thirsty, or in need of relieving himself. That, he felt fairly sure, wasn't good.

Randolph shot him a sideways look. "I did mean it, you know. Your upper lip is an example to us all."

"Oh, well. When one expects terrible things to happen for long enough, it's almost a relief when they do."

"If you were expecting this, you could have bloody warned me."

Saul grinned. "Hardly. No, it's just that things were all going too well. Major Peabody, a safe berth. This feels more how it should be."

"Balls. Do you want to talk about what happened to you?"

Silence except for footsteps and the whisper of the wind.

"Oh, I don't know," Saul said at last. "If you've read the trial report, or any summary, it's entirely fair."

"Forgive me if I don't believe you."

"It is. Don't imagine there's a better telling that excuses me. I was stationed in Mesopotamia, in a garrison town. I had a lover, a local man. It never even occurred to me that he might be an Ottoman agent—or, rather, that his priority was his own land, and not mine. Or me. I didn't think. I didn't think I was telling him anything, either. But of course I had to slip out to meet him, we had to arrange assignations—I might as well have handed him the layout of the fort and the rotas, in the end, with everything I told him." He looked up at the sky, not wanting to see Randolph's face. "I loved him, you see. It wasn't just casual for me, and I thought he cared for me too. I believed it." That was then, when his life had been charmed, the world ripe for the taking.

"He sent me an urgent letter, that last night, summoning me to an assignation. It meant I wasn't there when the Ottomans attacked, so I lived, unlike very many others. I was court martialled with all the attendant humiliation, spent two years in gaol, and came back to my family disowning me and the end of everything I'd worked for. I still don't know if he sent me that letter because he cared for me or the opposite. Certainly, if he'd hated every second we spent together and everything we did, sending that letter would have been a fitting revenge. I can't tell you how often I have wished I'd died that night."

"That, I understand," Randolph said. "It does seem such an easy way out, to those of us left behind. Take the heroic end, and let someone else clear up the mess. Have you ever wondered what your lover felt?"

"I beg your pardon?"

"Well, perhaps he hated you and your touch." Randolph spoke with clinical calm. "Or perhaps he had to make a choice between love and country. Perhaps he set out to entrap you, but perhaps someone said to him, *Get us this information or we'll expose your man, we'll kill him. We'll kill you.* There were no easy choices in that bloody war, and no single decisions. And if you were considered as culpable as all that, they'd have shot you."

"They wanted me to shoot myself," Saul said. "When they let me out, I was put in a room with a bottle of whisky, a revolver, and a single bullet."

Randolph paused for slightly too long. "That's a hell of a hint."

"It was, rather." He'd sat there for an hour or more, turning the bullet between his fingers. "I didn't take it, obviously. I, uh, had some idea that, since I'd served my sentence, I might find a more positive way to atone than blowing my brains out."

"It would have been a waste of brains," Randolph said. "God knows we don't have any to spare. You do realise that you were far from the only man spilling secrets in bed? There was a British general in France whose desire to impress Parisian whores was such that his staff eventually used him to leak doctored information. The only rooms they put him in had comfortable beds, but that's rank for you."

"Are you serious?"

"Entirely."

"That...doesn't make me feel better, in fact."

"I'm not trying to make you feel better. You made a bloody great balls-up with appalling consequences. With a slightly different set of circumstances it would have been a minor mistake and no harm done."

"But it was done. People died. We, they, only just held the fort against the Ottoman attack. If it had fallen—"

"If. What if your lover had felt Britain would be a better ally for his country than the Ottoman Empire, or Russia? What if our glorious nation had given a damn for Mesopotamia's wants?"

"What if, knowing the hostility of the locals, I hadn't started an affair with one?"

"What if we didn't have damn fool laws about who to fuck?" Randolph suggested. "Really, dear chap, if we were permitted to conduct our business without fear or shame or gaol, would you have been sneaking secretly out, or would you have been in your bunk with a charming sergeant, or writing letters to the boy you left behind?"

"But—"

"But me no buts. You were a pawn in a damned complex game, and you were played and sacrificed as such. I'm glad you weren't taken off the board altogether."

There was no pity in his voice, no awkward searching for excuses. It was profoundly refreshing. "But pawns have to obey orders. I didn't. The simple, clear rules—"

"Oh no, no, no," Randolph said. "Don't give me *simple*. Do not give me the done thing or the rules of behaviour. We both know better than that."

"Why not? Those rules are there for a reason."

Randolph put his hands in his pockets, tipping his head back to squint at the hazy sky. "Flanders, the War Beneath. My family was there from the start. The Glydes are the oldest family of arcanists in England, with letters patent from half a dozen monarchs. If there is occult aristocracy, it's us. And we marched out to war: my father, Uncle Jessamy, Aunt Clothide, my cousin Theresa, her brother Gerald and his wife, my cousins Vernon and Valentine, me. Doing our duty under the orders of a pack of power-hungry generals who believed they could wield our knowledge as weapons.

"And we let them use us, Saul. We obeyed orders. *I* did. I— Christ, I am ashamed to say this, but I was part of the circle at Mons, and in three smaller summonings after. I did it, Saul. I played as big a part in ripping the veil to pieces as anyone alive. I *saw* the damage that was being done, I knew it was wrong even as I did it, but we were at war, we had orders, and I followed them."

He was looking straight ahead, his profile set in an emotionless cast. Saul knew what that hid, and felt his chest contract in sympathy with the old familiar pain.

"I didn't start to speak against those orders until, what, September 1915, and then only to my family, quietly. It was already too late. The generals understood the scale of the weapon they had; they weren't going to let it go unused. Some arcanists were drunk on power, and many more were too caught up to stop, and an awful lot of us knew it was catastrophic, but we believed in those simple rules. It's so much easier to obey orders. It's not much fun to think."

Saul watched him. The bones of his face stood clear under the skin.

"I had row after row with my father. By the end we were screaming in one another's faces. I said he could pull every British occultist off the job, use his standing to end the madness. The Germans were having exactly the same rows on their side, and we were related to a dozen senior people at Heidelberg. We could have stood together across the battle lines and said no, this weapon is too great, the damage will be incalculable.

"But we didn't. My father wouldn't hear me and in the end nor would anyone else. Because the Germans were beginning the second Great Summoning, you see. We'd started it with the Great Summoning at Mons; the Germans intended to finish it at Ypres. We knew it was coming—how could we not; the air was full of grease and tin. We hadn't stopped our summonings so they didn't stop theirs, and that just proved one couldn't trust the bloody Krauts. Or the bloody Brits, depending on point of view. So there we were at Ypres, the German summoning under way, and we were ordered to throw everything we had at them. And I said no."

"You were a conscientious objector?"

"Hardly that. I killed, before and after. I was quite happy to fight, but not to lead an obviously catastrophic charge to certain death. Whereas my father was old, and old-fashioned, and he couldn't or wouldn't see what was going on. I called him a bloody fool; he called me a coward, and said he was ashamed to name me his son. He marched the Glydes, my whole family but me, out to fight for our country, and within three minutes they were all dead, their lungs turned to glass."

"Glass," Saul repeated.

"They did their duty, and died coughing up shards in the mud. I broke the rules and lived, and I'm the one who has to sort out the mess we all left. Tell me more about *what if*, Saul, tell me more about playing your part in catastrophe. The veil is hanging in tatters because we obeyed orders, three-quarters of England's occultists are dead, and now two of London's most vital protections depend on a stupid sod who's let himself get trapped into being eternally two miles from Swaffham fucking Prior. Oh look, more good news."

Saul had been staring at the hard, savage lines of his companion's face. He turned now at Randolph's finger, and saw the waystone. It said *Swaffham Prior, 2 miles*, and on top of it lay a limp, faded rag that might, a century ago, have been a fashionable Homburg hat.

"How long have we been here?" he asked, thinking of Rip van Winkle, of tales of ancient sleepers falling to dust. "How long—"

"Don't panic," Randolph said. "They don't play by the rules. Nevertheless, I'm not feeling particularly inclined to stay on this road."

"Can't you do something? Use these words of yours?"

"I am even less inclined to do that." Randolph picked up the felt remnants with two fingers. "I don't know what impact they might have here. I suspect it would be large and destructive, and the veil is too damned torn to risk more damage. The words might send us back to where we should be; they might equally rend a hole between here and there which would let more through to our side than just us."

"There isn't anything else here."

"Would you care to bet on that?"

Skin prickled all the way down Saul's neck. "What do you mean?"

"I don't feel alone." Randolph dropped the rag and glanced around. "Have you observed the shadows?"

Saul looked down. His shadow stretched out in front of him, a foot or so of black on the dusty road. He grabbed for his watch. "It's working! No, wait—what?"

Randolph consulted his own watch. "Stopped at twenty-five to three? Marvellous. Sodding marvellous. Because if time is passing in some manner, you may imagine what that means."

Saul thought about it. "Are you saying that night will come?"

"And who knows what with it. I don't want to be here at night."

"What do we do?" Saul could feel the terror rising, like an echo of that long-ago evening with the Abchurches—*no, last night, it was just last night*. "Randolph?"

Randolph was looking around, eyes narrowed. "I should like to find Burwell Castle. I would guess it will be here, and potentially useful, but the question is how to reach it. It was right behind the church, but damned if I know which way to Burwell."

"The road isn't going there anyway."

"We're leaving the road. It's terribly dull."

Saul thought about that, then licked a finger and held it up. "All right. The road to Swaffham Prior runs southwest from Burwell. The prevailing winds in Cambridgeshire are southwesterly, coming off the sea. Therefore, if we walk into the wind, we'll give ourselves a good chance of heading for Burwell. So, that way. Yes?"

"How in blazes do you know about Cambridgeshire's prevailing winds?" Randolph demanded, sounding somewhat affronted.

"They're always worth noting. They shape landscape and human behaviour. The world changes when the wind does."

"How handy to have an archaeologist around. Of course, the question is whether we can trust the winds here to be as they should, but that keeps life exciting. Very well, over the fields and far away?"

Saul stepped up onto the verge, and looked out at the land. It should have been fields, with neat lines and rows of crops; instead it was all grey-green, reeds and rank grasses.

"When you said you think Burwell Castle will be here," he began, carefully.

Randolph stepped over the verge and into the fen. He was wearing what looked like handmade leather shoes and an extremely elegant grey tweed suit, neither of which seemed appropriate for a marshy walk. Saul followed. The ground underfoot was springy, if not precisely wet or boggy.

"Let's cut a little away from the road. I very much doubt we can follow it," Randolph said. "To answer your question: I don't know when we are, if that even applies. I don't know what's ruling this. I do, however, know that we have a common factor in everything that's going on. That blasted medieval thug is a key part of the picture, so the place of his doom should be relevant. I'm banking on that."

"I'll take your word. But if he's a malevolent force then how is Camlet Moat not malevolent?"

"Protections are not necessarily kindly. In the story you heard, the dear old chap swore an oath to be Master of London, yes? To protect it with all his might. And the holy knights came to make him keep that oath, like it or not. Took him back to the Temple, where they hung him on a tree."

There was something precise and rather nasty in Randolph's voice. It made Saul look round. "Something wrong?"

"Can you see the road from here?"

Saul turned. He couldn't see anything except reeds and low scrub. "No."

"Let's head into the wind, then. Tell me something: did Peabody give you any instructions when he sent you to the Southcott Oak?"

"He didn't send me to the oak. He sent me to Oak Hill Park because he thought there would be a point of his pattern there. It was sheer chance that the oak burned then."

"Was it?"

Saul blinked. "Wasn't it?"

"That's the question. What set Peabrain off on this path, any idea?"

"It could have been anything. No, wait, it was a book. Someone sent him a book, privately printed. I don't recall if he had it when he sent me to Oak Hill Park, but it was definitely what set him on to Camlet Moat. And brought us up here, actually, because of Abchurch's collection."

Randolph tapped his fingers together. "Because of this book. Who's it by? Who sent it?"

"I haven't read it. Blank cover. Major Peabody said it was sent to him anonymously by a mysterious contact." He held up a hand as Randolph whipped round. "He always says that kind of thing, even when he got it in a bookshop. It's part of his fantasy. He claims that he's had a brilliant inspiration, or that his patterns have revealed some wonderful secret, and then I find the precise words in whatever he's been reading. He's desperate to make a wonderful discovery. It seems grossly unjust that all this is happening to me rather than him."

"Speak for yourself. I prefer it this way." Randolph tilted his head. "So when you say that it was chance you happened on the Southcott Oak—in fact he might have read it in this book? Sent you to 'discover' something he knew very well you'd find, thus proving his theory to you?"

"He certainly sent me to the west side of Oak Hill Park," Saul said. "And there wasn't much else there."

"No. If you'd asked anyone for an interesting local landmark— the park keeper, even—they'd have pointed you to the tree. Which caught fire. Blast and damn."

Randolph strode on, faster. Saul hurried to keep up, trampling on thick rank grasses that grew in clumps. "What's the significance of the oak?"

"Don't know. That was Aunt Clothilde's job. One can assume it catching fire wasn't a good sign, though."

"So little is," Saul said. "What are you afraid of?"

"Everything. Most specifically, of being trapped here failing to carry out the last remnants of my duty to my lineage, city, and nation. Christ, I'm useless. I should have listened to the Shadow Ministry."

"Are they really called that?"

"Department for Special Affairs. I don't actually think I should have listened to them, needless to say. That was just an outpouring of dismay. Anything else about this book?"

"It mentioned Temple Church too," Saul said reluctantly. "It does seem to have focused on Geoffrey de Mandeville."

The noise came from under them, and around them. It was deep and throbbing; it might have been a laugh, or a cry, or a call; it was not so much loud as everywhere. Saul could feel the vibrations in his feet.

It rose around them and fell, and the wind whipped salty-cold in Saul's face.

"Hell," Randolph said.

"What was that?"

"I don't know, but it came when you mentioned a name, so don't do that again. Hurry."

Saul hurried, striding forward, not running because Randolph wasn't, but walking as fast as he could without tripping on the coarse grass. His feet splashed a little. "It's getting boggy."

"Mmm."

"It shouldn't really." Saul tried to keep his tone academic. "We're very much on the edge of the fens."

"Mmm."

"Where's the bloody castle?"

"Good question."

The wind came again, harder, pushing against them, with a whine in it like the edge of a razor. Saul, used to flying sand, put one arm over his face and turned his head. Randolph's dark hair was whipping in the wind, his coat flapping; they were both leaning forward.

"Keep going," Randolph shouted. "Where it doesn't want."

Saul set his teeth. The wind was bitterly cold now, with the unnatural heat of an absent sun gone from his back. The noise rose again: sobbing, whooping, he couldn't tell.

His ankle turned on a tuft of grass. He stumbled, and Randolph caught his arm and tugged him to his side. Saul leaned in, feeling his warmth, and something more. Randolph's face was set, he was muttering, and the smell of ivy around him was very strong.

Ivy, green growing things. Trees. That was what this blasted landscape needed, Saul thought. He wanted solid earth under his feet, great oaks wrapped with ivy, graceful birches, the protective hawthorns and rowans of Camlet Moat. He brought the memory to mind again, making himself see the dappled sunlight, gold and green; feel the water on his face and in his throat. That was his England: not the brown peat-water and rank grass of a landscape that at best tolerated humankind, and had been broken because it would not be tamed. He made himself think of woodland that might stretch for miles, and birdsong, and thick foliage through which bright eyes glanced and darted away again.

"I don't know what you're doing but keep at it," Randolph said. "It's helping."

It didn't look like it was helping. Saul had been so lost in his self-created reverie that he hadn't looked around. Now he did, and saw that evening was drawing in. The sky was dark grey, shot with red and purple lights that looked more like blood poisoning than sunset, and the plants and scrubby shrubs were no more than dim black shapes.

"Christ."

"Focus," Randolph snapped. "Harder. Now."

Camlet Moat, Saul told himself. He'd got good at this over two years in a military gaol in Mesopotamia. There he'd put himself into the sunny chalk uplands of his boyhood, and remembered-created-learned that imaginary landscape in such detail that he could slip back into it during the worst times. He made himself do the same with Camlet Moat now, stumbling into the shrieking wind with Randolph's arm hard against his, imagining the endless forest, the sunlight, the cool water splashing over his skin. Faces in the leaves and sweet-smelling mulch of years under his feet; bright rags tied to the cloutie tree and a woman's laughter, here and gone. He didn't let himself feel the icy bog-water that soaked through his shoes or the whip of the wind; he let the throbbing sound that was more a roar drift through his mind and away.

Randolph's arm pulled at his. "There."

There was—oh Christ—a stand of trees. Actual trees. He and Randolph ran then, stumbling forward, holding one another up as in some parody of a child's three-legged race, heading for the trees while they could still see them against the darkening wind-whipped sky. Saul hurled himself forward, one long stride, another, then his foot came down on nothing and he was stumbling and splashing forward, face down, arm torn from Randolph's grasp.

The impact on uneven earth and knife-edged grasses, and the shock of the sudden soaking, knocked the air from him. He struggled to push himself up, arms elbow-deep in freezing water, and something gripped his foot.

It's a hand! was his first wild thought, and then, *It's weeds, just weeds, calm down.* He tugged hard, shoving himself to his knees, but couldn't dislodge whatever held him. He twisted, and turned his head, and saw it.

"*Randolph!*" he shrieked, and kicked frantically at the bedraggled thing, humanoid, weed-drowned and waterlogged, that rose from the fens like a growth, its too-long arms ending in a ragged, jagged tangle of branchlike fingers that held his foot. The stench of something rotten on the bottom of a pond was all around him, and the joyless laughter was all around him too as the thing dragged him sliding on his back, inexorably down into the marsh.

Something caught his collar and pulled back with startling force against the creature's grip. The fen-monster shrieked with rage, its open mouth revealing an eel's chaos of needle teeth, white in the dimness. It lunged forward and Randolph, behind Saul and gripping his jacket, came down on one knee with his free hand out and shouted, "*Forthlaede!*"

Ivy exploded from the thing's mouth, eyes, and ears, tendrils looping and throttling, its green stink drowning the bog-rot. The creature let go Saul's foot to scrabble frantically at the shoots that burst from its every orifice, and Saul felt himself hauled up.

"Run," Randolph said with force, and grabbed his hand.

They ran, stumbling and choking. Randolph was shouting something in an odd language which Saul only knew wasn't English or Latin, and the earth felt more solid, less splashy under his feet, and then they were on grass, and the dark stand of trees was ahead. Saul's legs, encased in sodden trousers, felt as though he wore armour; it was like running in a nightmare, every step too hard, too slow. But Randolph was dragging him, so that even if Saul was more falling than running he stayed upright, and they hurtled up the side of a grassy incline, tumbled over the top, and collapsed, gasping for breath.

"What the," Saul managed. "What."

"Fen-grendel," Randolph said. "Watery wodewose. A monster of the marshes. Did it cut your skin?"

Saul struggled to pull up his sopping trouser leg and felt the cold, wet skin. "I don't think so."

"Good. Christ above." Randolph sat up and leaned forward, elbows on knees. "That was all very inconvenient."

"Are we at the castle?"

"Such as it is. It feels safer here, for what that's worth."

Saul looked around, but couldn't see much except dark shapes, certainly no buildings. If they were at the castle site, either it hadn't been built yet, or it had long fallen down. There was nowhere to shelter against the cold. He shuddered violently.

"You must be freezing," Randolph said. "Blast and bugger. All right, take those off. You can have my jacket. Come on, damn it. I don't like you being covered in that water."

Saul peeled off his coat, his waistcoat, his shirt, which was sodden half way up his torso, and his undershirt, dropping the unwieldy, water-soaked clothing to the ground. By him, Randolph was doing the same thing. "Er—"

"We need to get you dry. Come on."

Saul shed shoes, socks, trousers, finally his drawers. Randolph pushed something into his hand. "Use that as a towel."

It seemed to be his undershirt, warm from Randolph's body. Saul scrubbed at himself, legs and arms and hair. Randolph was a barely visible shape by him as the last light faded horribly fast.

"Here." Randolph handed him the warm, dry coat. Saul slipped it on, shuddering with cold and gratitude, as Randolph picked up his discarded clothing and started wringing it out. "Huddle up there, by the, what, earthwork? Out of the wind anyway. I'll see if I can do anything here."

Saul stumbled to where the bank rose and sat against it, grass rough and cool under his bare arse and legs. He wrapped his arms round his knees, hearing the sounds of Randolph's movements. There were no stars above, no moon, no fires or windows in the distance, no sign that any thinking thing existed or ever had in this bleak waterland plain, and in a moment he couldn't see at all, no matter how he strained. It was as dark as an underground cell.

He dug his fingernails into his palms. This was bad enough for them both without him making a fuss, but he was sickeningly afraid in too many ways, memory and reality and the dreadful unknown all at once. He wanted comfort, or connection, or another human being in this abyss.

And, he realised, he could ask. He licked his lips. "Randolph?"

"Here." He sounded so matter-of-fact. Saul had always loathed upper-class unflappability, as though inhumanity was anything to be proud of, but the calm in Randolph's voice was a lifeline to which he clung. "All right?"

"I, uh. I can't see you," Saul said. The words sounded horribly thin and childlike in his own ears.

"Well, I can see you, very clearly. Don't worry. I'm here."

"What?" Saul seized the distraction. "How can you possibly see anything? It's black as the armpit of hell!"

"Imagine my shrug. I can see in the dark, I promise you."

Of course he could. That was typical Randolph, and reminded Saul of something that, under saner circumstances, would have been his first question. "What on earth did you do to that thing, before? With the plants?"

"It's a knack."

"I could hear what you said. It wasn't like the other words, before. What language was that?"

"An old one. How are you doing?"

"You're not going to answer, are you? Better than with a fengrendel dragging me under the water. I think you saved my life."

"My pleasure," Randolph said absently. "You were doing us both proud before that. Is that what you did back at the Abchurches, when the dark came?"

"More or less. I'm not sure quite *what* I did, though. I just imagined being at Camlet Moat."

"Imagination is a marvellous thing, particularly off the beaten track as we are."

"Right. Yes." Saul swallowed. "What do we do now?"

There was a whisper of movement and Randolph lowered himself to sit beside him, warm and ivy-smelling. He put an arm around Saul's shoulders, pulling him close. "We live through the night, old fellow, whatever it may bring, and in the morning, we go back home."

"As simple as that?"

"It's perhaps not the most elaborate plan, but it's what I have. If you don't like it...?"

"I like it."

"That's all right." Randolph's arm tightened. Saul let out a deep breath, and allowed himself to lean sideways, against him, and be held. "And until then, we'll just have to pass the time."

CHAPTER EIGHT

Of all the ways one might recline against a grassy bank with a beautiful half-naked man in one's arms, Randolph reflected, this was perhaps the least satisfactory he could imagine.

Saul was cold, stinking of the weed-rot of the fens, and terrified. And brave, painfully so. How he'd got through the last—however long it was, the period since his life had turned supernatural chaos— Randolph couldn't imagine, except that he'd seen the man's core already. Heart of oak, as the song said, enduring whatever might assail it.

Morally, at least. Saul wasn't equipped to fight off nightmares from the waterland, nor should he be. That was Randolph's job.

He looked around. The castle grounds were barely anything to normal eyes: a couple of ruined stone walls on a rectangular raised bit of ground. The edges rose a little where the foundations of defences had been, and dipped down to the vestiges of a moat. It had never been finished.

Randolph saw differently. He saw the great wooden stockades that kept the outside firmly out, the wide expanse of moat beyond it, the stone buildings rising around him. All of it limned in moon-silver, translucent, the spidery image of what once was or might have been.

They'd be safe here, probably. The monster whose legend haunted the fens had taken a mortal wound on this ground, and that couldn't be forgotten.

He'd taken a mortal wound, and been carried back to Temple Church and hung off a tree like a side of beef. Randolph would put money he'd been trapped that way, the Master of London's foul soul eternally enslaved to the city's good. He didn't approve of that sort of thing as a general rule, but de Mandeville had clearly had it coming.

The ghastly man had been Custodian of the Tower, too, all too close to another crucial protection. Randolph didn't like any of this, except the part that put Saul Lazenby right here next to him, barely clothed, breathing steadily.

He looked. He shouldn't, but he did, and saw Saul faintly silvered, as though his skin were luminous. Randolph could see the spidery webs and trails of his jacket, but he was only interested in the man under them. Long lean legs, dark-bright eyes, naked and glowing.

"I feel as though you're looking at me," Saul said.

"I am."

"Any reason?"

"You're worth looking at."

Saul gave a ghost of a laugh. "That's a ringing endorsement. All cats are grey in the dark."

"I can see," Randolph reminded him.

Pause. "That puts me at rather a disadvantage, no?"

"Only if I were planning to take advantage." And Christ, wouldn't he like to. "Are you all right?"

"I *think* so," Saul said seriously, as though assessing the state of some ancient artefact. "I'm entirely confused, and rather frightened, and hopelessly reliant on you, but—well, you're a good chap to rely on."

"I'm doing my best," Randolph said. "Let's say, you won't come to any harm that I can avert."

"I'm sure of that. Thank you."

After whatever Saul had endured in the war, the years of trying to get back on his feet, it could hardly be pleasant to be rendered helpless yet again. There wasn't much to be done about that now, although Randolph made a vengeful resolution to put an extra few nails in the coffin of whoever or whatever was behind this charade once he got it under control.

"May I ask," Saul said. "Why is the castle safe? In that we're not behind any walls that I saw."

"It's where our twelfth-century friend lost his last battle. I felt that if it was here at all, it would be standing against him."

"And we are still, er, east of the sun and west of the moon? What I mean is, when dawn comes, am I going to find myself bare-arsed on Burwell Castle's remains, and a lady antiquarian belabouring me with her parasol?"

"I can only pray you will. First, it would mean we were home, and second, I'd pay to see that."

"Yes, I've heard about you public-school sorts."

Randolph laughed aloud, throwing his head back. Saul was shaking silently in his arms, laughing in the dark, and Randolph found himself unreasonably delighted. "Arse. Where did you go to school?"

"The local grammar, then St. John's Oxford. You?"

"Eton, then St. John's Cambridge."

"Ha. Two John's men."

"That's not all we have in common," Randolph said. "I find myself in an invidious position. I can see in the dark, among other talents you don't share, and while I have no idea what's going on now, I'm used to this sort of thing in general. Whereas you are, for the moment, in a rather dependent situation."

"And therefore?"

Randolph took a deep breath. "And therefore it would be villainous of me to suggest any of the things I've had in mind more or less since setting eyes on you."

"Villainous is rather harsh," Saul said. "Ungentlemanly, perhaps. What things are those?"

"Villainous," Randolph said firmly. "You have my word I would take refusal with grace, needless to say, but we both know men are liars. Ah...a number of things but dear God, I'd like to find the places that make you moan. You seem to me a man who could be usefully lavished with attention, and also tongue."

"If I didn't feel I could trust you I'd have decided that already, based on your history of inexplicable arrivals and departures, and your habit of never answering questions. The crooks of my knees and elbows, would you believe, as well as the usual. I wouldn't recommend that until I've had a bath, though."

"I wouldn't normally make a fuss, but I don't like the idea of getting anything of this place in my mouth. Or yours."

"Not to worry," Saul said. "I'm sure we can make do."

Randolph closed his eyes. He wanted Saul, but he'd wanted plenty of men in his time. He hadn't previously felt this way: not precisely nervous about asking, but certainly as if there were a pressing reason to get it right. "Suppose I were sufficiently villainous to make any advances tonight...?"

"If you can see in the dark, you can presumably see me waiting for you to kiss me. I'd do it but I'd be guessing where your face is."

"Here," Randolph said, and twisted round.

Saul's face was shimmering silver, his lips slightly parted. He didn't look afraid. Randolph met his mouth, felt its welcome. Saul's lips were warm, his tongue gently flickering, his skin as clean-shaven as though no time at all had passed since the morning, as indeed it had not. He shifted awkwardly—blindly, even, *mustn't forget he can't bloody see*—and Randolph moved too, till they were face to face, body to body, breath to breath. Saul's hands roamed upwards, into Randolph's hair; Randolph let his roam down, and inside the jacket. He'd forgotten for a second Saul was naked under it; he was almost as shocked by the touch of fingers on bare skin as Saul was, judging by his intake of breath.

Randolph paused, letting his hands hover; Saul nodded against his mouth, his own hands sliding down the linen of Randolph's shirt, and tugging at it where it was tucked into his waistband.

It seemed only fair. Randolph allowed his own hands to roam as they kissed, enjoying the gentle movements of Saul's mouth, feeling the shape of shoulderblades, the dips of Saul's spine, the careful, methodical touch of fingers as Saul worked his way down the shirt buttons. He pulled the two sides of the garment apart, pushed the cloth off Randolph's shoulders and down his arms, and then his hands came up again and landed right over Randolph's shoulders.

Saul's fingers went rigid. He pulled his mouth away, and Randolph had to set his jaw not to jerk away himself at the touch. Thumbs on the scars under his collarbones, fingertips on the scars on his back.

"Randolph," Saul said. "What am I feeling?"

"Scars."

"Matching ones, on both sides, front and back?"

"Indeed."

"*Randolph.*"

"Believe me, you don't want to know," Randolph said. "It will do nothing for the mood."

"Nor will evasion. Why do you have— It feels as though something went straight through." He sounded incredulous, as well he might. "They're lined up."

"Hooks."

"Hooks," Saul repeated.

"I carry words the human mind is not equipped to contain. I see in the dark. I can command obedience to an extent. That sort of thing has a price, which was this."

"Hooks," Saul said again. "But—"

"Nine days and nights, suspended by hooks through my shoulders, hanging off a tree. If you suspect that was unpleasant, you're right."

Saul's hands moved up, cupping his face. "Randolph. My God. Who did that to you?"

"I did, of course. Well, my father, but it couldn't have been done without my cooperation. It's what I was born for."

"The devil it is," Saul said. "That's monstrous. Your *father*."

Randolph tried not to remember that. The ancient iron, the rigid look on his father's face, the pain. His own too-late desperate begging for it not to happen, for it to stop. Father hadn't begged when it had been his turn, he'd said, though Randolph always wondered, just as he'd wondered if his father's chilly lack of affection had been in part because he'd known what he'd have to do to his son.

"It's the family role," he repeated. "Father to son—or occasionally grandson or nephew. It has to be done, or the Words will be lost."

"And what about you?" Saul demanded. "Are you going to father a child and hang him off a tree by hooks?"

"I would have," Randolph said, the words bare in the darkness. "I was intended to marry my cousin Theresa, you see. It would have been a sham of course—on both our parts, I may add; she didn't care to stay with just one man for an evening, let alone for life. We're not a romantic family. But she was my dearest friend. It would have worked in its way. And she died at the second Great Summoning, screaming through blood and broken glass, and I wasn't with her."

Saul's hands, still on his shoulders, tightened, and Randolph felt himself tugged forward into warm arms. He resisted for a second, then gave in, loosening his rigid muscles by an effort of will. "I'm so sorry."

"So am I," Randolph said. "I'm sorry she's dead, and I'm sorry I can't do her job, and I'm sorry that I'm going to fail at everything because I can't—the idea of having a child, of doing that, explaining—I can't."

"Of course you can't." Saul's breath was warm against his scalp, his touch so comforting. "Good God, it's revolting. Does it have to be a Glyde? Surely to heaven you can find an adult volunteer, not breed a human to a purpose?"

"Oh, naturally. It's merely a matter of finding someone one can trust with that level of power and responsibility, who has not been educated to it for his or her entire life but can nevertheless cope. And of giving away a duty that has been my family's sole responsibility for twenty-three generations."

"I suppose that matters." Saul's tone suggested he didn't suppose anything of the sort.

"It mattered enough for my father to put the hooks in my shoulders, and for me to let him. It was unthinkable not to. And then everyone died, and I'm damned if I know what matters now."

"No." Saul's lips brushed his ear. "You poor swine."

"I don't need sympathy."

"How would you know? Have you had any?"

Randolph gave the ghost of a laugh. "Not a great deal. People have high expectations of my family."

Hands slid up to hold his face, warm and firm. "I have immensely high expectations of you," Saul told him, and leaned in for a kiss.

Randolph met it fiercely. They kissed in urgent silence, in the darkness with silver flaring in Randolph's vision, lips and tongues giving the only comfort they could, with an echo of wartime need. Randolph knew that feeling well, the desperate need for warmth and connection in the face of things too big and dreadful to comprehend. He had no doubt Saul knew it too.

This wasn't the almost angry biting and shoving of a wartime fuck, though. That wasn't Saul's nature, or what Randolph wanted of him. This was hands and skin, and simply being together in the dark.

Randolph was on his back now, Saul over him. Randolph would have liked to see him properly, not just with other sight, but at least he could feel. He skimmed his hands over a taut arse as Saul pressed against him, his hard arousal and Randolph's trapped together, separated only by cloth. He wanted to touch; he wanted to make Saul groan and writhe, he wanted to see his face when he climaxed. He was one of those men who'd look anguished when he came, Randolph thought, and raked his nails over Saul's back at the thought.

"God," Saul said against his mouth. "I wish I could see you. I wish I could see. Don't let go."

"Are you all right?"

"No." Hands fumbled at Randolph's waistband, pressed between bodies. "No, I'm not bloody all right. I can't see, I don't know where I am, and it feels like the end of the world." He worked a button open and his hand in. His fingers bumped against Randolph's hard prick, a clumsy touch that still made him gasp aloud. *"And the earth was without form, and void; and darkness was upon the face of the deep.* I'm trying not to think about it. For Christ's sake, distract me."

Randolph lifted his hips to work his trousers and drawers down. Saul used the movement to tug at him so that they rolled over, Saul landing on his back on the grass, where at least he'd be able to feel solid earth, Randolph over him, pressing close, wanting to touch every part of the man at once. He got his mouth to Saul's neck, licking and nipping where he was most sensitive himself. There was a slim chain around Saul's throat holding some heavy trinket or other that had fallen to the side; he worked around it, until Saul was squirming under him, groaning.

"What distraction would you like?" Randolph enquired at last.

"How do you feel about the sin of Sodom?" Saul asked with a silvery shadow of a smile in the darkness, and that effort to brave it out made Randolph's chest hurt.

"Dear boy, your Biblical exegesis is either terrible or superb."

"What?"

"The sin of Sodom was arrogance. Which I will freely grant describes me to a T. But if you want a fuck, that also suits."

"You really are the most exasperating— Fine. Fuck me arrogantly."

Randolph didn't feel arrogant; he'd rarely felt so humbled in his life. Saul was brave, and beautiful, and deserved so much better than a rough and ready screwing on the grass, but that was what he wanted, and indeed all Randolph had to offer.

He kicked off shoes and clothing, not moving from his position over Saul, letting one hand roam over his chest and up to his mouth. Saul caught his finger there and sucked, lips tight and close, tongue curling to wet it thoroughly.

"I want to taste your cock," Randolph rasped. "Which, as noted, would be a bad idea until you've washed, but if you could put it on my bill for later..."

Saul made a noise of assent, sucking harder on his finger. It might as well have been his prick; the sensation was ridiculously erotic. Randolph pulled away with reluctance, spat in his palm for additional lubrication, and moved his hand down to between Saul's legs. He saw Saul's mouth open, felt his body's tremor, heard his little gasp—

The scream erupted from behind them. A wet, phlegm-rattled, drowned gargle of a scream, a wave of fen-stench rolling over them like ancient damp rot, and then a chorus of echoing howls from all around.

"Jesus!" Saul yelled, convulsing under him as Randolph scrabbled backwards. "Randolph!"

"Here, I'm here." Randolph grabbed his hand. "I have you. I can see you."

"What else can you see?"

"I'm going to stand. Stay down." Randolph rose to his feet, and looked.

The ghostly castle was shimmering silver still, but there were clawing shapes rising against its walls, weed-ragged, needle-mouthed, lightless. A lot of shapes. Surrounding them.

"Shit."

"Don't you dare not tell me," Saul said through his teeth.

"There's about five hundred fen-grendels at the walls. I don't know if the defences will hold. I think perhaps they won't."

"On second thoughts, I didn't want to know." Saul stood, naked but for the jacket, fists clenched. "Can we fight?"

"Of course we can."

"Can we win?"

There was another bubbling scream, and a rending noise. Randolph looked over at the castle's silvery wall and saw the marks, the pressure of long scratches from the other side against the walls, and a night-coloured spot that suggested something had got a claw through. As he looked, the spot became a tear, slow and dreadfully sure. "That, I cannot promise."

Saul's head went back, chin up. Naked, helpless, sightless, and still not giving in. "Right. Well. Lead on, then."

"I hadn't finished," Randolph said. "I can't promise victory, but by God I intend it. I have something to say to the fen-grendels and whatever insane spirit of a long-dead lunatic may lie behind them. I have something to say to whoever has provoked this, and to every force keeping us here against our will. *My* will." He let his voice rise. "I am the Keeper of Wayland's Words, the Walker of Camlet Moat, a Green Man of the Green Men. I am Randolph Glyde, and I say *leoht*!"

The light flamed at his shout, rolling outward like silent thunder, a wave of green and yellow dappled sunshine, life in the dead land. It lit the castle, making the silvery not-there walls solid stone, sending the fen-weed man-things scrambling backwards in a chorus of yelps and howls. Randolph had just time to see Saul staring at him, face slack with astonishment and fear, before it faded away.

"Randolph?" Saul whispered. "Did it not work?"

Randolph grabbed his hand again. "That kind of light is a gift. If you want it to last, we have to make our own."

"Uh." Saul sounded tremulous. "I can see something. A bit. Like silver."

Randolph would be amazed if he couldn't. The castle walls were blazing in his own eyes from the power he'd called upon, towering in their strength. "That's all right."

"What about her?" Saul said hoarsely.

Randolph turned, fast, and saw. A woman's shape, walking towards them. She was made of silver and shadow, with curved lips, smiling eyes, hair cropped in the wartime style.

"*Theresa?*"

"Ran," she said, or at least her lips moved and the sound whispered around him. "Dearest. Walker, indeed."

"I had to. There's nobody else left. I'm sorry."

Theresa's form rippled like a silk scarf in the wind. "You are not the Walker."

"I know," Randolph said desperately. She was already fading, too fast, her eyes holes in the night. "Stay with me, Tee."

"They're coming back," Saul said by his side. "Randolph? I can hear them. The things are *coming back.*"

"Ran..." Theresa was a whisper on the wind, her form visibly dissipating.

"Leoht." He directed it at Theresa, ignoring the creatures clawing at the walls. The billow of light washed over her and left her solid. "Talk to me!"

"You are not the Walker," Theresa said again.

"I know, damn it! Tell me how to be!"

Theresa shook her head. "Not with the Words. You can't carry it all. It's a little arrogant to try."

"Then what?" Randolph could feel the pressure outside the walls. Not just the creatures, but a rising force, malignant, angry, very old, and very wronged. He suspected he knew what that was, or had been. "Who else is there?"

Theresa turned to Saul.

"No," Randolph said. *"No.* You cannot—"

"You cannot." Theresa was speaking to him, but her silver gaze was on Saul. "The veil is too thin. The defences are falling. The Moat needs a Walker. He drank."

"Not him," Randolph said urgently. "Don't. Please."

"Soldier?" She raised her arm, pointing one finger to Saul in a deliberate mimicry of the famous poster. "Your country needs you."

Saul looked as unlike a soldier as any man alive, naked under Randolph's jacket, but his back was straight. "What do you want me to do?"

"Wait," Randolph said. "At least he should understand—"

"No time. No choice. Your permission?" she asked Saul.

His eyes flickered to Randolph, and back to Theresa. "Yes, ma'am."

Theresa smiled, that glorious mischievous smile Randolph had missed so much. She was a translucent silver ghost, and her smile hadn't changed a bit. She took Saul's face in her hands, floated forward, and kissed him. He made a single startled noise.

"*Leoht*," Randolph said savagely, bracing his feet on the earth, locking his knees. His shoulders ached with the old familiar pain as he called the light again and again, so that it barely faltered between waves. "*Leoht.*"

Theresa was almost solid to his eyes, her face and hands nearly real, her mouth on Saul's. She was kissing him, or breathing into him, and Randolph's other sight could see the tendrils of ivy snaking from her ears and eyes and mouth and fingers, snaking into Saul.

If Saul wasn't screaming, it was only because he couldn't. Randolph's own mouth tasted of green leaves and green wood. And he couldn't stop this, wouldn't if he could, because Theresa knew her business, and Camlet Moat needed a Walker. No matter what that did to Saul, already chewed up and spat out by one war, being dragged into another, and both times by a kiss.

All Randolph could do for the woman he loved and the man he wanted was to make it work. So he brought the light until the marrow of his bones ached, until he could smell the ancient stone around him and the gibbering fen-things were fleeing from the barrage, until Theresa was nothing more than a faded wisp of fog over Saul's slack face.

"Tee?" he rasped. "Saul?"

Saul turned, or was turned, because it didn't look like his muscles were working, and for just a second as the light faded Randolph saw Theresa's eyes smiling from Saul's face. He took an urgent step forward, grasping Saul's arms, and Theresa leaned in and kissed him on the lips. The kiss they would have exchanged on their wedding day, the one he'd never given her.

Dearest, the wind breathed. *Good luck. Take care of him.*

And then she was gone, and it was dark except for the silver castle that blazed around them, and Randolph was kissing Saul. Holding him, or holding him up, and as he realised that, Saul slumped in his arms, unconscious.

CHAPTER NINE

Saul woke up in the light. White light, light all around him, with an odd feeling of heaviness, and a desperate, agonising thirst that was only matched by the equally desperate fullness of his bladder.

That urgency drove him to sit up as nothing else could have. The heavy sensation turned out to be a couple of quilts, and as his eyes adjusted, he saw he was in a room. A small whitewashed room with a rag rug, a dresser, an old-fashioned china commode. He stood cautiously, blinking at the dizziness that threatened to send him stumbling, hung onto the walls to work his way round to the necessary, propped himself up with one hand, and pissed like a horse.

He was wearing pyjamas, blue and white stripes, and he seemed to be clean judging by his feet. He last remembered them streaked with the dried remnants of fen-slime.

If that had happened.

There was a jug of water and a tumbler on the dresser. He poured himself a glass, downed it in two swallows, poured another, and ended up emptying the jug as his body clamoured for water.

He sat back on the bed once he'd finally finished and propped his head on his hand, trying to think.

He remembered meeting Randolph in the church, and walking along the road. Those things had happened, he was sure. After that, he remembered it all in a dreamlike way that would have persuaded him it wasn't real, except that it had been dreamlike as he'd lived it. The weird timelessness, or time running in fits and starts. The impossible landscape. The thing in the fens. The darkness.

Randolph kissing him. He could feel the sensation still: Randolph's lips, his oddly calloused hands. The feel of his finger in Saul's mouth, that blissful anticipatory thrill as his hand had moved to between Saul's legs. He'd been so afraid he could barely breathe and it had been all he could do to feign some sort of calm, and he'd wanted Randolph with a terrified world's-end desperation—

No, it was more than that. Far more. It was Randolph's kindness, which came wrapped like a pass-the-parcel in so many layers of irony that one might almost not realise it was there at all. It was his clear-sightedness; his sense of duty that demanded much and gave everything; his implacable grip as he dragged Saul away from horrors, and the burning-cold fury in his voice as he stood and fought.

Saul had wanted it all then, and he wanted it—wanted Randolph—now.

Sodding fen-grendels getting in the way. Apart from anything else, if Randolph had fucked him, he'd have unmistakable proof of the experience, considering they hadn't had anything to ease the way but spit. He hoicked up his pyjama leg where the marsh thing had clutched him and saw unmarked skin with what might have been a faint bruise, or might not.

He needed to know where he was—and indeed, where Randolph and Major Peabody were. "Unless they're both figments of my imagination," he said aloud. He also needed food, since, now his thirst was slaked, he was becoming aware of intense hunger. As though—

As though he hadn't eaten for a day or more.

There was a dressing gown hanging on the back of the door. Saul donned it, tried the door with a sudden qualm, and was relieved when it opened. It would not have been pleasant to discover he was locked in a sanatorium.

He found himself at the top of a narrow flight of stairs. He made his way down, and came to a landing with a large window, giving a good view of flat grey-green lands. The Fens. That, at least, was where he should be.

There was a throat-clearing cough. Saul turned sharply, and saw an elderly man in black offering him a slightly worried smile. "Ah, Mr. Lazenby, you're awake. My name is Herbert, and I'm the vicar here. Of Burwell, that is. St. Mary's. I imagine you're hungry, and probably rather confused?"

"Very," Saul said. "Both."

"Well, do come downstairs if you feel up to it," the Vicar said. "Let's deal with the first before we tackle the second."

"Wait. I'm not quite sure—how did I come here?"

"If you mean to this house, Randolph Glyde brought you yesterday morning. If you mean Burwell, you arrived with a gentleman from London on Monday."

Saul blinked. "What day is it?"

"Thursday. About eleven o'clock."

Saul had set off on that accursed walk on Tuesday morning. "Thursday? What the hell happened to Wednesday?" He caught himself, flushing. "I beg your pardon, sir. It's just that, uh, I seem to have lost a day."

"Time passes differently where you've been."

Mr. Herbert said that in such a tone of religious platitude that Saul didn't take in the meaning for a moment, and then he could only stare. The Vicar gave him a weary smile. "Yes, I did mean that. Do come down, Mr. Lazenby, I think we could both do with a cup of tea."

Saul followed him to a light, airy kitchen, where a plump woman in an apron gave him a surprised smile. "Nice to see you up and about, sir."

"Mrs. Allan, my housekeeper," the Vicar said. "I expect you're hungry? Mrs. Allan, perhaps breakfast?"

"Bacon and eggs?" Mrs. Allan suggested. Saul murmured thanks, with a sensation of profound dismay at the idea of waiting for food to be cooked. She gave him a shrewd look as she went to the larder, and returned with a loaf of bread, pat of butter, and plate piled with ham. "Help yourself while I put your breakfast on the stove, and I'll just get the kettle on."

Saul reached for the plate, and stopped himself. It all felt entirely real, entirely normal, but he was losing track of normal. Perhaps he had imagined being in fairyland, but what if he were in fairyland, imagining being home?

He glanced round to see if there was a clock in the kitchen. One hung on the wall behind him. It was ticking, a barely audible sound, and as he looked, the minute hand moved. He twisted back, feeling ridiculous, and saw the vicar's sympathetic expression.

"I understand your concern, Mr. Lazenby. Mr. Glyde explained a little of your experience. Let me assure you, you are safe here, and may eat without fear."

"Well, I should hope so," Mrs. Allan said, somewhat huffily.

Saul did, devouring two thick slices of bread laden with ham even before the tea was made. He stopped himself there, with reluctance, since the housekeeper was busy at the stove and the smells rising were delectably savoury. He took a sip of tea instead, and looked up at the Vicar who sat opposite.

"Thank you for your hospitality, sir. I have a number of questions." He glanced at Mrs. Allan's back.

"If you'd like to discuss anything, be my guest," the Vicar reassured him.

"Well, Randolph Glyde. You said he brought me here. Where is he?"

"He returned to London yesterday."

"I beg your pardon?" Saul said blankly. "He left me here?"

"He seemed to have urgent business," the Vicar said. "There's a letter for you. I'll get it once you've eaten," he added firmly as Saul made to rise.

"And what about Major Peabody?" Saul asked. "My employer. He and I were staying with the Abchurches."

"He returned to London the day after you arrived, I think."

"He what?" The Major was eccentric and obsessive, and Saul was used to being disregarded, but this was beyond anything. "I disappeared and he just went home? Where did he think I was? Did he call the police?"

"Not to my knowledge. He left after lunch on Tuesday, while for all anyone knew you were still taking a long walk."

"But we'd only just arrived. Why would he leave?"

"I couldn't say. I only know that he departed most abruptly, leaving a verbal message for you to join him in London. The Abchurches were rather put out, I think. I'm sure he will be most concerned by now."

Saul bloody hoped so. "What about my bag, do you happen to know?"

"Oh, we have that. I sent to the Abchurches yesterday."

"I should offer them my apologies for vanishing."

"If there's time, I dare say."

"How do you mean?"

"I'll get Mr. Glyde's letter."

Saul had to bite back a sharp remark—evidently all Randolph's acquaintance shared his reluctance to answer a damned question—but he waited patiently until the Vicar returned with a sealed envelope. He tore it open and scanned the note. Randolph had angular, slanted handwriting, more beautiful than legible, which didn't surprise Saul at all.

Saul

Apologies for leaving; you were reluctant to wake and events are pressing. Herbert will look after you; he is one of ours.

Come and find me.

Randolph

There was also one of Randolph's cards, on which he had written a second address: 166 Fetter Lane. Saul turned the card and note over and back, but there was nothing more.

He wasn't quite sure how he felt about this. Not that he'd expect Randolph to sit by his bedside—the man had work to do, after all. Merely, it would have been better if he'd been here, if Saul had been able to talk to him. But he wasn't, and one would just have to put up with that.

Come and find me. And another card, which, given what he'd said about the last card, seemed promising. Saul would have to find Major Peabody first and discover if he still had a job, but after that he would unquestionably pay a visit to Randolph.

Mrs. Allan said, "Now," in a businesslike way, and put a gigantic plate in front of him. Fried mushrooms flecked with parsley, a fried egg, sausages, bacon, two slabs of black pudding. It looked like more food than he usually ate in a day; he just about managed to murmur thanks before diving in. Mrs. Allan watched him eat with an expression of professional satisfaction, refilled the teapot, and departed.

"There," the Vicar said as Saul devoured the black pudding. It wasn't normally his favourite but the savoury richness was grounding, somehow, making him feel less like a confused, lost man in someone else's pyjamas. "You've got some colour back. I suppose you had rather a bad time of it."

"Rather, yes. Did Mr. Glyde tell you what happened?"

"Only in the loosest terms. It's not really my area, you know." He indicated his clerical collar. "It ought not be at all, I suppose, but St. Mary's is special. A responsibility. I'm too old for it, I fear. I have asked to be relieved of my duties, but there are so few of us now. The War, of course, and I quite understand we must all pull together now, but I'm an old man and I was never trained to this, merely chosen. I have asked for the cup to pass from my lips, and I shall be glad to retire. The world is changing, Mr. Lazenby, and we who are old must leave it for younger men to tackle."

Saul briefly considered pointing out that the younger generation had a fair bit on its plate already, thanks to the decisions of old men, but swallowed the thought along with a mouthful of bacon. The Vicar rambled on, rotating his teacup in his hands. "I have never been active in hidden matters. I am merely the custodian of the church, and its special features. This is a troubled area and St. Mary's is a bulwark. A bulwark and a beacon, Mr. Glyde's father observed to me once. Well. In any case, Mr. Glyde brought you here and asked me to ensure you were kept safe and well, and I have done that. Yes, I'm quite sure I have done my duty there." He gave a firm nod, apparently to himself.

"How did Mr. Glyde get me here?" Saul asked. "I remember falling in the water, and darkness."

"Oh, you'd have to ask him about that. He was carrying you—he looked exhausted, poor chap. Mrs. Allan has cleaned and pressed your jacket and trousers but I'm afraid you had no shoes, or indeed anything else. Shirt and so on. I don't envy the time you had."

"No."

"I do think it's best for this to be handled by those with knowledge," the Vicar said. "I'm simply not in a position to help, truth be told. Would that I could. Naturally, if there is any spiritual reassurance I can offer...?"

I'd like to know what happened to me between seeing a silver woman and waking up here, Saul thought, but it was evident the Vicar neither knew nor cared to know.

Once he'd finished eating, having cleared the heaped plate, he stood, feeling decidedly less wobbly. "Thank you, sir. Ah, my clothes?"

"Yes, yes. I'll ask Mrs. Allan to put them out."

"And I'd like to return to London as soon as is convenient," Saul added. "I don't know if there's a car that might take me to Cambridge station?" He'd have to check he had enough money for a ticket, he realised, and if not, to borrow some.

"Oh, there's no need to worry about that," the Vicar assured him. "I've arranged transport, which should be here within the hour."

"That is immensely kind. Thank you very much. Would it be possible for me to see the church before I leave?"

"Absolutely. I'd be delighted."

Saul's luggage and cleaned, pressed jacket and trousers were waiting in the room when he went up. No drawers, no vest, no shirt. He couldn't imagine how Randolph had wrestled him into those sodden clothes, or dragged him here, or got them both out of those dreadful castle grounds at all.

He'd passed out and Randolph had been left to defend him, alone for God knew how long in the darkness. Or not, of course, because Randolph could see in the dark, because he'd spent days and nights hanging off a tree in some kind of appalling ritual. The idea made Saul feel sick, and the thought of the night Randolph must have spent in the Fens, or wherever they'd been, made it worse.

Saul still couldn't remember why he'd passed out. He remembered Randolph's hands though, his lips, the desire. The noise of the fen-grendels and their stink, too. A wave of light; a silver woman walking through darkness; anguish in Randolph's voice.

There were toiletries set out for him. He washed and shaved, then dressed in what he had, his smart new shirt and black shoes that he'd worn for the evening along with his usual jacket and trousers. It felt better to be dressed and clean, and he ignored the slight feeling of dizziness that persisted. It was probably the effect of a couple of days without food, followed by a meal that would have done for three.

The Vicar indicated that he'd wait for Saul's lift and meet him in the church if Saul wasn't back by then, so he left the vicarage on his own and stood outside for a moment, breathing clean air. It was a beautiful day, the endless Fenland sky early-summer blue. It would have been a lovely day for a walk, if Saul had ever again intended to go for a walk in this countryside without carrying weapons. He checked he could see the sun just in case, blinked away the resulting spots on his vision, and went to the church.

He stopped in the porch to look at the stone arch, carved with three bands of monsters, the stonework indistinct with age. Before he'd probably have ignored the fen-grendels or seen them as wild men or shaggy demons. They looked very obvious now.

Inside the church was cool and dark, with green light spilling into it from above and glowing from the great window at the end, tinting the columns to give them the look of an avenue of trees. Saul went up to the pew where he'd found Randolph, wishing he were here now and wondering what he'd seen. He roamed up and down the aisle and along the walls, peering at the carvings and craning at the stonework, irritated he couldn't find it. The damn thing was around here somewhere, he was sure—

He was looking for something.

He'd come to the church to find it.

Saul gave himself a moment to let the panic subside, then he went up to the top of the centre aisle, where he was bathed in green light. He narrowed his eyes till all he could see was the blurred glow, and let himself think once more of Camlet Moat, as if he were there. The trees rising around him, the bright eyes in the leaves, the smell of cool well water and growing green things, a gust of laughter on the breeze.

He walked without thinking to the arch that stood some little way before the altar, and over to one side where the hard, dark, ancient oak stood. There was a shape carved there, a face. Deep eyes, a mouth pulled to rectangular by the leaves and branches that sprouted from it. A Green Man.

Saul stared at it, and saw again the fen-grendel with ivy bursting from its mouth and eyes, and then he remembered.

Her kiss on his lips. Her ivy twisting into him. Her silver, cold and pure as Camlet Moat's water, running through him. And the flood of knowledge that came with it all, like a book he'd read again and again in his childhood and somehow forgotten. Theresa Glyde, curling her tendrils into his heart, running her fingers through his mind, lighting up parts of him he hadn't known existed until he was blinded by green and silver and the smell of Camlet Moat, and that last whispered instruction rang deafeningly in his ears. *Green Man. Good luck. Take care of him.*

Green Man. Saul stared at the wooden face, and deep-set bright eyes looked back.

"Mr. Lazenby!"

Saul turned. The Vicar was hurrying through the church with two men at his heels, a tweedy chap in his late fifties and a younger, taller, thinner man in an excellent suit who seemed to have come straight from a London office. "Mr. Lazenby, here you are. This is Mr. Delingpole and Mr. Bracknell, of the Shadow Ministry—Whitehall, you know. I sent for them yesterday and they have come to take you back to London."

"The Shadow Ministry," Saul repeated.

"Is that a term you recognise?" Mr. Delingpole asked. He had a long face, thin lips, with a hard look.

"Not really. Why would Whitehall men want to give me a lift?"

Mr. Delingpole gave him a very perfunctory smile. "Let's not waste time, Mr. Lazenby. You're coming with us."

They caught the train from Cambridge, both Delingpole and Bracknell declining to answer any questions before then. The Shadow Ministry men secured a first-class compartment for the three of them, and sat together opposite Saul, giving him the unnerving impression of being under interrogation.

"Well," he said as the train moved off. "Are you able now to tell me what's going on?"

"I think it's for you to tell us that, Mr. Lazenby."

"You are asking the wrong person," Saul told them wholeheartedly.

"No, I don't think so," Delingpole said. "Saul Nathan Lazenby, of St. John's Oxford. Your war record makes interesting reading."

Saul kept his voice level. "And I served my sentence, and you won't find anything against my name since."

"What is your involvement with Randolph Glyde?"

"I've met him. I wouldn't say that constitutes an involvement."

"You've more than met him, haven't you?"

Keep calm, deny everything. "How do you mean?"

Bracknell gave him an incredulous look. "The Vicar, Mr. Herbert, assures me you went to the other side with him. What the devil's that if not an involvement?"

"It wasn't my idea or his. We just found ourselves there," Saul protested. "Look, am I allowed to talk about this? I don't want to speak about matters I shouldn't, and my understanding was that this sort of thing is not to be discussed widely."

"Very wise," Delingpole said. "But this is our business. I assure you, you may speak."

Saul nodded. "All right. But I can't imagine why you're talking to me and not Glyde if you want to know what happened because, to be quite honest, I don't have the foggiest."

He probably should be frank with these men, he knew. They were, after all, official, and he had no reason not to except Randolph's distrust. He still didn't want to.

Bracknell was scrutinising him. "I suppose you had to rely on Glyde a great deal."

"Entirely."

"I dare say he had a lot to say about Whitehall, too. About the conduct of the war, threats to the nation, and so on."

"Well, we talked," Saul hedged. "We were there for a while."

"Yes, it would be. This isn't your area, is it, Mr. Lazenby? There you are, in a most confusing situation, and of course you have to put your trust in Glyde—a very competent man, nobody would deny that. But if I may say so, you probably shouldn't take everything he says at face value. He had a hard war, damned hard, and, well, he has a bee in his bonnet."

"An obsession," Delingpole said.

"That's a little harsh," Bracknell said with a hint of rebuke. "He expresses himself strongly, but he remains one of the best we have. Nevertheless he—like many, let us be fair—he carries scars, and he chooses to blame his tragic losses on the conduct of the war. I think we can afford to be tolerant of that. The poor fellow lost his whole family, most of them in a single day and under circumstances which, I am sorry to say, reflect poorly on his own conduct. Naturally he feels a great deal of regret."

Delingpole inclined his head. Bracknell went on. "But the fact is, Glyde is running amok. Here we have some sort of event in the Fens, which Mr. Herbert summoned him to deal with; instead of doing so he takes you off to elsewhere—"

"He didn't take me," Saul objected. "We went for a walk and found ourselves trapped."

"Well, that is good to know," Mr. Delingpole said. "Excellent. The more you can tell us, Mr. Lazenby, the quicker we will clear all of this up."

"But why can't you ask Glyde?"

"He isn't inclined to talk to us," Mr. Bracknell said. "He is, I regret, rather too used to having it all his own way. That's been how things were for a very long time, but I fear he must learn, as so many ancient families have, that the world is changing. Tradition is all very well, but if there is some force operating in Cambridgeshire, it must be dealt with. Suppose a child had walked along that road instead of you? Suppose a child walks there again? Can you tell me that Glyde put a permanent stop to whatever trapped you on the road?"

"I don't know."

"Because if he did not, if it is still there, a threat lurking—"

"Yes. I understand."

"We need to know," Delingpole said. "We need Glyde's cooperation, and don't have it, so we need yours. We need to know if he is working in the best interests of the country; we need, urgently, to know if he is not. If you wish to serve those, you can help us now."

Saul looked between the two men, both regarding him intently. He had no idea what to say, or where to start. Perhaps he should tell them everything, up to Theresa Glyde's silvery shade breathing knowledge of Camlet Moat through him, and let the experts take action. They were, after all, official, and Saul didn't put any more stock in Randolph's elevated family and their sacred duty than these men seemed to. He could still feel those awful, sickening matched scars, front and back. Nothing that inflicted such a thing could be good.

Randolph had expressed the strongest possible opinion of the Shadow Ministry's worth; but Saul had kept secrets from officialdom for the sake of a lover before, and he knew where that led.

It's happening again, you damned fool. Don't make the same mistake.

It's not happening again, because Randolph is different.

Are you sure of that? asked the scarred, frightened part of Saul's mind. *Are you quite, quite sure?*

"Right," he said. "My employer, Major Peabody, is interested in Geoffrey de Mandeville." He recounted the trip up to Burwell and the events of the night at the Abchurch house, then meeting Randolph in St. Mary's. He allowed them to infer that Randolph had sought him out as a witness to the event of the previous night, and went on to the walk along the road.

"Whose idea was it to walk?" asked Mr. Bracknell.

"I don't recall. Mine, possibly. I like to walk and I wanted fresh air."

"You're sure Glyde didn't suggest it?"

Saul knew damned well he had, and had an unpleasant sense of a noose closing. "I can't say either way. Why would it make a difference?"

"Just trying to get to the root of the matter," Mr. Delingpole said. "Go on."

Saul did, at length. He had experience of being interrogated for every detail, however slight, so he gave it, and if that meant he wasn't asked about other things, well, that couldn't be helped. He reached their refuge in the castle and the renewed attack of fen-grendels, omitting how they had passed the time in between, and stopped.

"Then what?" demanded Bracknell. "What did he do?"

"It's impossible for me to say. There was light, he made light, in a sort of flash. It frightened them away, I think."

"And then?"

"I must have fainted. I don't remember any more."

"What did he do?"

"I don't know. I had fainted. I woke up in the vicarage."

"Something happened then. An upheaval. A disturbance."

"Maybe that was what made me faint. What sort of upheaval?"

"A potentially very serious one," Delingpole said crisply. "Whatever you remember, you must tell us, and at once."

Would Camlet Moat's guardianship count as serious? Saul wondered that, and if he should say something. But they'd ask what he knew, and the thought of telling them gave him a wave of revulsion. He had no right, none at all, to pass on what he'd been told. Theresa Glyde had given him the guardianship of the Moat and he'd felt her fade from the world with that kiss. How long had she held on, waiting for her moment to appoint a Walker?

Saul didn't have the least idea what to do, but that was not a trust he could betray.

"Mr. Lazenby? Have you remembered something?"

"No. No. I'm sorry, the experience in that place made me feel very unwell, and then I ate a large breakfast, and—excuse me." He put a hand to his mouth, working his throat, and saw the men turn away.

The rest of the train ride was repeated interrogation. Saul stuck to his story, for lack of better ideas, as they passed through town after town, and was relieved to see the ugly red brick and soot of London. "Once we arrive, I take it I am free to go?"

Bracknell glanced at Delingpole, who shook his head. "No. I don't think so."

"I beg your pardon?"

"I'm not satisfied, Mr. Lazenby. The fact is, some most peculiar things seem to have happened at once—the events in, or outside, Burwell, and a matter in London. I find it difficult to believe they are not connected given Glyde's involvement. I am quite sure you will remember more, given assistance."

"I've been assisted to remember things before," Saul said. "I still have the scars. May I remind you that I'm a British citizen who has committed no crime?"

"There's no need to be dramatic," said Delingpole. "And your protests have been noted. But the nature of the Ministry's work means that we have special powers granted by the Government. We require you to accompany us."

"I think I'd like to speak to a lawyer."

Delingpole gave a cold smile. "No."

"What? That's—"

"You have a record of collaborating with the enemies of this country in a peculiarly disgraceful manner, Mr. Lazenby," Delingpole said over him. "You will now co-operate with her protectors, whether you like it or not."

Saul leaned forward, resting his arms on his thighs, trying not to show the fear he felt. *They'll lock me up, they'll put me in a police station, in a cell...*

He was *not* going to panic. He opened his eyes, trying to display a bit of backbone, and saw something under his shoe.

It was an ivy leaf, fresh and smooth as though it had just been plucked. He leaned forward and picked it up. It must have been stuck to his shoe, except that he couldn't think of when he'd walked on greenery or how it had survived the journey from Burwell. He stroked the smooth surface, tracing the edge, sitting in silence as the train jolted on.

At last they pulled into the London terminal. The platform was crowded as they disembarked, Bracknell holding Saul's arm, not in a friendly way. Saul wondered about shaking him off and making a run for it, whether that would just make matters worse.

They headed for the ticket gates, which demanded passengers proceed in single file. Delingpole went through, followed by Saul, and as he came out someone grabbed his arm and pulled, hard.

Saul stumbled sideways, finding himself dragged along at speed. "What the—"

"Lazenby, yes? I'm from Randolph," said the man who held him, not slowing down. "He thought you might want a change of company. Come on, this way."

"How do I know you're from Randolph?"

"He said, I quote, 'I'd give you a visiting card but the blighter's had three of mine already.' I suppose that means something to you? It's certainly typical Randolph. Good afternoon, by the way. I'm Hugh Barnaby, call me Barney."

He was something under thirty, with the fairish hair and goodish looks of the typical young English squire, a well cut lounge suit, a friendly face. Saul guessed minor public school, rugby football, a junior officer, probably a good war carried out with courage if not brains. He seemed that sort in every respect apart from the fact that Randolph had sent him.

"Saul Lazenby. Er, the Ministry—"

"My man's dealing with them. They won't get past him."

"But am I not under arrest?"

"Oh, I shouldn't think so," Barney said without concern. "They aren't the police." He led the way through the station building and out onto the street, to where an Austin Seven waited. "That's my bus. Sling your bag in the back, we're just waiting for Isaacs."

"Just a moment," Saul said. "What is going on, please? Am I being rescued? Abducted? Given a lift?"

"Oh, the last of those, definitely," Barney assured him with a grin. "I shouldn't claim that Randolph wouldn't abduct you if he felt the need, the man's an absolute bandit. But those are not my orders, and you're welcome to pootle off if you'd rather, it's quite up to you. Ah, there he is. Chop chop, Isaacs." That was directed to an approaching man: smallish, dark, bright-eyed, with the unmistakable look of the city-bred. "Everything all right?"

"Well, I told 'em to piss off as per, sir, which they may or may not of done, so if it's convenient to scarper?"

"Righty-ho. In you get."

Saul took the back seat as indicated. Barney hopped behind the wheel, surprising Saul, who'd expected Isaacs to be the chauffeur. The engine roared and they shot off, taking the corner in such style that Saul grabbed for a handle to hang on to.

"Right," Barney said over the engine noise. "Now, Randolph asked us to deliver you to him. Is that all right with you?"

"Uh— I don't know. How the devil did you, or he, know I'd be on that train? Or who those men were? Who *are* you?"

"Hugh Barnaby, Max Isaacs. We work with Randolph in—well, his sort of business. You know. The occult." Barney gave his occupation with a sort of muttered embarrassment, much as if confessing to designing ladies' undergarments.

"You're like Randolph?"

"God, no, not at all. We're...well, we're *sui generis*, aren't we, Isaacs?"

"Pretty sure I seen 'er on stage at the Alhambra," Isaacs said. "Did a dance in feathers."

Barney snorted with laughter. Saul gathered up his patience. "All right, but how—"

"There's honestly no use asking me, old fellow." Barney overtook a Ford Model T with not nearly enough space. Saul shut his eyes. "Randolph's the expert; we just do what we can. I understand you've been caught up in something nasty recently? Yes, that was very much what happened to us. It's like one of those whatsits, those things, you get into them and you can't get out. What am I thinking of?"

"Chokey? Tar pits?" Isaacs suggested.

"No, not that. It's a sort of rat-catching device."

"Man traps?"

Barney removed a hand from the wheel to snap his fingers, causing the car to lurch. "That's it. Lobster pot."

"Notwithstanding which..." Saul said.

"What I'm getting at is, can't help you." Barney's voice held just a hint of a suggestion that it was time to stop asking questions. "If you want answers, Randolph will give them to you."

Isaacs made an indescribable noise. Barney looked round, grinning again. "All right, perhaps he won't. But I'll take you to him so he can fail to give them in person. All right?"

CHAPTER TEN

Randolph wouldn't have admitted he was waiting for a knock at the door. He was, however, hovering irritably in his sitting room not doing anything while the knock failed to come, and when it finally sounded he had to prevent himself from running. He checked his hair in the mirror instead, smoothing it to sleekness, and went to open the door.

Saul was there. He looked haunted, as well he might, and the dreadful thing was, it suited him, with his dark eyes, the fine, sensitive mouth. He looked vulnerable, which was a rotten thing to find attractive, and nervy too, which Randolph could permit himself to relish at the thought of making those nerve endings sing for him.

"Hello to you too," said Barney, as though Randolph ought to have noticed him beside Saul. "Sam says, sort out whatever it is and catch up at Fetter Lane tomorrow, could you? Cheerio, Lazenby, nice to meet you."

Randolph stepped back, letting Saul in. He was wearing the brown suit he'd had on in the Fens with black shoes of the kind one might wear for dinner. He shrugged at Randolph's examining look. "I lost my other shoes in the Fens. Which is a shame as I've doubtless lost my position as well."

"Have you?"

"Well, Major Peabody returned to London after my disappearance, and I've been AWOL for days. After which I was more or less placed under arrest by the Shadow Ministry, if that's what we must call them, and brought down here, then snatched away by the worst driver in London at your behest—"

"I do apologise for Barney. Would you care for a drink?"

"Yes, I bloody would."

"Will dry sherry do?"

"If it has alcohol in it."

Randolph led him into the lounge and gestured to him to take one of the pair of easy chairs by the fireplace, empty this warm afternoon. Saul sat, looking around, and Randolph wondered what the place might look like to him. It was large, light and bright, with pale cream walls and furniture chosen because otherwise the collection of leatherbound books and carved faces might have become rather overpowering.

"Green Men, I see." Saul nodded at the carvings, all foliage and deep pits for eyes, as Randolph handed him a glass. "I looked at one of those in the church at Burwell and I could have sworn it looked back at me. With eyes. I don't know whether to fear I'm going mad or to hope it."

"For good or ill, you're not going mad."

"It hardly matters. A sanatorium room, government detention, I'll still be in a cell."

"Nobody will lock you up. The Shadow Ministry has no authority over you, and they grossly overreached if they suggested they did. I'll have words for Delingpole, and for that fool Herbert too. I told him to look after you, not throw you to the wolves."

"Oh, I don't blame him," Saul said. "For one thing, he's old and afraid and obviously doesn't want whatever ghastly responsibility was foisted on him, and for another, he had no particular reason to want me on his hands. It wasn't him rolling around the grass with me before I got ravished into unconsciousness by a ghost."

"Right." Randolph took the other chair, feeling he'd need it. "I gather you're unhappy."

"I am, yes. I woke up wondering if I was in some sort of asylum to discover that you'd gone back to London and my employer is no longer interested in whether I live or die, and was promptly collected up by some sort of hush-hush Government organisation that appears to operate outside the law, and accused of things I don't understand, without so much as the right to a lawyer. I am *very* unhappy, in fact. Since you ask."

"I don't blame you," Randolph said. "Left to myself, I should have waited for you to wake up instead of leaving you to that bumbling coward of a vicar. But I was not left to myself, and you wouldn't wake up, and everything in London had gone to hell in a handcart."

"*What* went to hell?" Saul demanded. "Delingpole and Bracknell more or less implied that something you, or we, did in the Fens caused some disaster here."

"Did they? Yes, I dare say."

"What disaster?" Saul demanded, voice rising. "What did we do? What happened to me and why is it your fault, and what did it cause?"

"We did nothing, you and I," Randolph said. "And I rather think it was the other way around. It appears that at some point on Monday or Tuesday, while you were in the Fens, someone was playing silly buggers in Temple Church. It's shut up for renovation work at the moment so the damage wasn't immediately discovered, but what is unquestionable is that a solid stone effigy of Geoffrey de Mandeville crumbled to dust, presumably as a result. It appears to have been a large and complex event, but nobody knows who, why, or what actually happened."

"Good God."

"Mmm. Something destroyed de Mandeville's effigy, all hell broke loose in de Mandeville country, and it is known I was up there. Hence the Ministry's fishing expedition. If that pair could blame me for some calamity by commission or omission, that would be highly convenient for them. What did you tell them?"

"Roughly what happened. Omitting the private matters, and—her."

"You didn't tell them about Theresa, or Camlet Moat?"

"No."

"Thank you," Randolph said. "May I ask why not? It would have got you out of trouble at a stroke. Delingpole and Bracknell would be overjoyed to see that responsibility taken out of my family's hands."

"I didn't like them."

"Well, it is hard to."

Saul looked into his sherry, holding the cut crystal glass in both hands. Randolph watched his face, the little troubled frown. "And it didn't feel mine to tell. I don't know what happened that night, or what it means—"

"Don't you?"

Saul contemplated his drink a moment more, then looked up. "All right. I think your dead fiancée told me her secrets and gave me her duties. I don't know what they are but I can feel them, inside me. I think she, uh, she gave me a job."

"Theresa was the greatest Walker Camlet Moat has ever had. She knew the duty hadn't been passed on, that I couldn't, haven't done it. You're right. She gave it to you."

"*Why?*"

"Three reasons leap to mind," Randolph said. "Firstly, because you're worthy. If I'd wanted a layman in the role, and God knows I did not, you'd have been first on my list. Lord, it would be pleasant to have a few more intelligent people around. Secondly, you were there."

"Sorry?"

"It's not easy to return to this side of the veil. Most spirits are echoes, distortions, things that haven't ever left properly. We were in a borderland, where it was easier for her to meet us, and that chance wouldn't come twice. It was you or nobody. Which I appreciate is less flattering to you, but then again I wouldn't have taken a walk with Major Peabody in the first place. Theresa and England may be grateful I have good taste in companions."

"Because I was there," Saul said. "Marvellous."

"Right man, right place, right time. Yes. Although, thirdly, and this is where it becomes rather more awkward for me: you drank the water at Camlet Moat. I gave you the water, and you drank."

"But surely lots of people—"

"There isn't water all the time. You will probably understand it better than I now. I have drunk the water myself twice and I've given it to people three times. One of them lost part of his tongue."

"Well, he would," Saul said, and gave a startled twitch. Randolph sympathised. It was an unpleasant sensation to know something without knowing how.

"Yes. Well. I gave it to you and washed you and, I think, attracted the Moat's enemies to you as well as its friend. I'm afraid that may be why the spirit in the Fens took such exception to you, and why Theresa came to you. It's possible this is my fault."

Saul looked at him, sherry glass in his hands. Randolph looked back, refusing to drop his eyes.

"You didn't think this would happen, though. Did you?"

"I didn't have the faintest inkling. For all I knew, when I gave you the water it might have burned and mutilated you instead. It was entirely irresponsible."

"It wouldn't have burned me if I didn't deserve it," Saul said absently. "Are you expecting me to storm out in a rage because you did something that had unexpected consequences? Some people might consider that hypocritical on my part."

"I don't give a damn what some, or any, people think. I did this to you, or at least I put you in the position where it became inevitable, and I am profoundly sorry. Your life is going to change, not for the better; you may expect a great deal of unpleasantness from all sides; you will have to learn your duty if you aren't to neglect it—which I cannot permit you to do—and if you were hoping to have done with war, bad luck, because you've been conscripted into a larger and more complex one than you could have known."

"You seem to forget," Saul said. "She asked my permission. I volunteered."

"Without knowing what you were volunteering for. That's hardly a free choice."

"Free choice? Are you serious? When do you think I last had one of those?"

"You should."

"Says the man born to be hung off a tree with hooks."

"A cheap shot," Randolph said, because it was a very well-directed one. "Nevertheless, you should have had a choice, and you didn't, and you are now, I fear, stuck."

"Stuck with you."

"For work, yes. Like it or not."

Saul leaned over and put his glass down on the fireplace tiles. "And beyond work? No," he added, as Randolph opened his mouth. "Do *not*. I can see the evasive answer coming and I don't want it. I've enough incomprehensible situations on my plate. If you're no longer interested, or prefer not to mix business with pleasure, say so and have done."

He spoke with studied calm, as though they were discussing a game of cards, not hot skin and clutching fingers. Randolph knew the armour well: a casual pose and a light voice, making everything sound trivial. It wouldn't do to show yearning, to reveal weakness, to embarrass anyone.

Randolph knew it because it was his own armour, deflecting all feeling, leaving him protected and alone. He hated seeing it on Saul, who didn't even do it well.

"I shan't say I'm not interested. It would be an obvious lie. As for mixing business with pleasure—that, I think, has to be your choice, since you're the one finding his feet. If it were up to me..." Saul's eyes were fixed on him, so dark, so painfully vulnerable in a face set tight against self-betrayal, and Randolph gave up. "If it were up to me I should beg to discover—I think you said the crooks of your knees in particular? I'm fascinated by that. I want to see you in the light instead of the dark. I want to know how you look when you come. I imagine you look like an angel in pain, and I want quite desperately to see if I'm right." That got those dark eyes wide. "I should like to spend a great deal of time pleasing you in every possible way, but I shouldn't blame you if you'd rather not. In this at least, the choice is entirely yours."

Saul opened his mouth, appeared to search for words, and finally said, "So is this what you're like when you're not evading the question?"

"It's *why* I evade questions. Imagine if I told people what I really think."

"You may tell me whenever you like," Saul said. "For Christ's sake, fuck me."

They both moved at once, pushing themselves off the easy chairs, colliding before they stood and ending up kneeling on the rug, kissing wildly. Saul had his hands in Randolph's hair; Randolph got his under Saul's jacket, pushing against his shirt, wanting skin. Saul's mouth was hot and yearning and open, there for the taking, so Randolph took it, feeling Saul give way till he was on his back with Randolph over him, bodies pressing, tugging at clothes.

"God. Saul." Randolph bit at his ear and neck. "I want..."

"So do I. Do it."

"I didn't say what."

"I don't care."

"Get these off." Randolph pulled him up enough for Saul to shrug his jacket off. He took the shirt slowly though, unbuttoning with care, pushing the linen away to expose Saul's chest. Sinewy, lean, with dark hair over the pectorals and a very marked trail from his navel down. Randolph traced the lines of bone and muscle, tangled his fingers in the coarse curls above the waistband. "This looks promising. And—" He stopped.

"What?"

"You appear to be wearing a bullet around your neck."

"Oh. Yes." Saul's fingers came up, an automatic movement, and dropped.

It wasn't a cartridge, just a plain, shaped piece of lead, hanging on a thin chain. Randolph stared at it. "Why—"

"It doesn't matter."

"Is that the bullet they gave you? It is, isn't it?"

"Don't. Not now."

"Saul. *Why?*"

Saul exhaled. "When I decided not to use it, I thought I'd take it with me in case I changed my mind. And I couldn't throw it away."

"So you decided to wear it? Because otherwise you were in danger of forgetting about the whole business?"

"I'm not reminded more by wearing it. Can we drop the subject please?"

He leaned back on the words, pillowing his head with one arm, and gave a deliberate, lazy stretch. Randolph swallowed what he wanted to say, and let his fingers roam, acquainting himself with the skin he'd felt but not really seen, flicking at one dark nipple with first a fingertip and then his tongue.

Saul shifted under him with a low sound of pleasure, which served as a reminder.

"Shirt," he said. "Off. I want to find out about this elbow business."

"Are you always this dictatorial?" Saul sat up to pull off the open shirt, the movement pressing against Randolph as he sat astride him.

"Usually." Randolph caught Saul's bare arm before he could recline again so they were face to face, sitting up. Randolph turned the limb, still sun-browned to the upper arm, and leaned forward. He met the crook with his tongue, just tasting, then licked it deliberately, and felt Saul's body jerk. "Good God. Excuse me." He licked again, stroking, then digging his tongue into the flesh, kissing his way up and down the arm and returning to the crook until Saul was moaning aloud and his arm was shaking. He looked up, moving his hand to grasp Saul's elbow, kneading the inside of the joint with his thumb and noting with satisfaction that it worked just as well.

Saul was flushed, eyes shut. He looked transfigured, ecstatic and agonised at once.

"Christ, you're beautiful," Randolph said, voice catching with desire. "I want to do everything to you. Get your trousers off."

Saul leaned back, lifting his hips in silent surrender, kicking his shoes off. Randolph shifted off his thighs to strip him bare, working around the hard press of Saul's prick, which sprang free delightfully as he drew the drawers down. He skimmed his hands over the lean body exposed to him, running his nails down a long thigh, then drew them across the underside of Saul's knee and watched him jolt. "Oh, yes. Lovely."

"Why are you still dressed?"

Randolph stroked the curve of Saul's calf. "A better question is, how do I conveniently reach the backs of a man's knees. For some reason, the problem has never presented itself before. Why don't you lie on your front?"

Saul gave him a look, then rolled over, moving with some care to accommodate his rigid erection. Randolph inhaled sharply. His back should have been—was—lovely. The wings of shoulderblades, the curved line of the spine, the irresistible swell of arse, with that dip of muscle to either side that you found in men who used their legs as God intended—although, that said, surely God actually intended Saul's legs to be wrapped around Randolph's hips; he was positive they'd fit. It was a perfect back except for the thin diagonal white stripes of an old, cruel flogging, and Randolph had a sudden and overwhelming urge to throw up his duty. Let the bastards have their endless war, let them choke on it. He hoped it would hurt before they died.

He forced the rage back, and instead ran his finger down Saul's spine, feeling each vertebra, then, very lightly, along the cleft of his arse. Saul's breath hitched in a highly satisfactory manner. Randolph took his time, letting his hands roam, and finally arranged himself on the floor so he could get his mouth to the back of Saul's knees. The skin there was soft, quite hairless, and tasted of Saul, and Randolph nuzzled at it, feeling the flesh quiver under his ministrations.

"Christ," Saul said, muffled by the rug. "*Christ.*"

He was jerking under Randolph's mouth, muscles twitching, hips working. Randolph had sucked men off to less erotic effect. He didn't think any part of his body could reduce him to this whimpering helplessness, and he almost envied Saul's abandon.

Envied it, perhaps; certainly wanted to use it. He was over Saul's prone form now, licking at one knee and pushing at the other with his thumb in a thrusting motion that wasn't intended to be subtle. Saul's legs were spread and slack, and his groans of pleasure were everything Randolph had imagined.

"Quite extraordinary," he said, lifting his mouth away. "On your back."

Saul rolled over, sluggishly. His face was reddened from lying against the rug; he looked dizzied with arousal, and his prick was dark with the fill of blood. Randolph moved between his legs, pushing them up to bend a little, getting his thumbs back to work in the crooks of the knees. Saul whimpered.

"Why don't you stroke yourself," Randolph suggested. "On your back with me doing this."

Saul tipped his head back, hand moving like an automaton, taking hold of himself. On shameless display, entirely lost. Randolph watched, eyes flicking between the earthy pleasure of a fist on a cock, and the painful ecstasy of Saul's fine agonised features. "Yes. Sweet Jesus, you're lovely. I want to see you come. Harder. Work yourself more." He was digging his thumbs into Saul's knees. "I want to see you spill all over yourself. And to suck you and fuck you until you're a whimpering shell of a man, make no mistake, but first you're going to bring yourself off while I watch. Faster."

"I'll come."

"Good."

Saul's head went back. His face spasmed, the bone structure standing clear under the skin and he gave a strangled cry as he shot, two, three times, cream onto pale flat stomach, coating the dark hairs.

His head dropped back, the expression of anguish relaxing, and Randolph didn't think he'd ever been so hard in his life. "Dear God. That was something."

"I did say." Saul blinked his eyes open, a slightly hesitant smile curving his lips. "It's nice to be taken seriously."

"I shall pay the closest attention to any further advice."

"My best advice is to come here and kiss me. And take your shirt off first," Saul said. "I'd hate to cover you in spunk—what is it?"

Randolph didn't think he'd reacted at all. "Nothing."

Saul's brows went up. "Problem?"

"No."

"Is it the scars?"

Of course it was the scars. They were one of the many reasons Randolph liked to fuck fully clothed, standing up, preferably with men he didn't know. "No," he said and then, "Yes. They're ugly."

"I expect they are. My back was a vile sight for a long time, and I scar well. You obviously don't."

Saul had felt the lumpy mess, Randolph reminded himself; he knew something of what they'd be like. "No. Or, at least, in this case I didn't."

"And do you think I'm going to recoil from you in disgust? Are they so bad? Am I so feeble?"

Randolph exhaled. "No to all. Merely, I, ah—"

"You don't like to be imperfect."

"Does anyone?"

"Most of us come to terms with it. Would you please take your shirt off and stop playing silly buggers?"

Randolph pulled off his jacket. "I could have sworn *you* accused *me* of being dictatorial."

"You are," Saul said. "'Undress, turn over, bring yourself off.' Nothing but orders. Mine were, uh, courteous suggestions."

"They were nothing of the sort." The bickering helped distract him as he shrugged off his waistcoat and unbuttoned the shirt, so that all he had to do was pull open the two sides of the cloth, but he didn't.

Saul sat up, naked and intent. "May I?"

Randolph nodded. Saul shifted forward and very gently pulled his shirt off his shoulders.

He knew what it looked like. The scars were a good two inches in diameter, irregular, lumpen, blackish. He sometimes thought they looked more like reptile skin than human.

Saul had that frown between his eyes. "Do they hurt?"

"My shoulders ache in wet weather. Unfortunately, I live in England."

"Yes, I see where you went wrong. I'd like to touch them, unless you'd rather I didn't."

"Do you have a particular fondness for scars?"

"They're part of you." Saul skimmed his palms over the rough surface where Randolph could feel pressure, no real sensation. "Not pretty. Nor, I imagine, a terribly pleasant memory to carry around, and you don't have the choice."

"No."

"But still you, for good or ill. To answer your question, it's not that I have a fondness for scars as such. But I *do* like a good pair of shoulders to hang on to, scarred or otherwise, and I'm living in hope you might get around to fucking me before we both die of old age."

"Well, if you're in a hurry," Randolph said, and grabbed him.

There was a frantic period of kissing and fumbling at clothes, which ended with Randolph naked and on his back, Saul sitting over him, hands roaming. Randolph had Saul's arse in a firm grip; he kneaded the flesh, watching his partner's eyes. "About my dictatorial tendencies."

"Mmm?"

"Would you prefer me to mind my tongue?"

"Given what you can do with it? No."

"I'm serious," Randolph said. "I tend to give orders. You may not wish to be given orders, in which case I'll endeavour to stop."

Saul's hand moved down, fingers skimming Randolph's prick. "Is that just because you're habitually autocratic, or do you particularly like to be in charge?" His eyes narrowed slightly. "Or does it disturb you not to have control?"

"All of the above," Randolph told him as lightly as possible. Saul's eyes were intent and Randolph had an uncomfortable feeling they saw more than a mild preference and a habit of speech.

"Of course. Suppose you carry on as suits you, and I'll let you know if it doesn't suit me."

"Suppose you get your mouth to my cock, then."

Saul's eyes widened a fraction, then his lips curled. He moved down in silence and dipped his head. The touch of his lips was perfection, soft but sure, tongue flickering, then snaking around Randolph's shaft as Saul took him deeper. Randolph got a hand to his fine hair, fingers against his scalp and sliding down to feel the working of his jaw and cheek as he sucked. "Oh yes. Christ, you're good at that. All right, stop."

Saul pulled away just enough. "Really?"

"I thought you wanted fucking."

"Very much."

"On your back, then." It wasn't a huge leap, given Saul's remark about shoulders, enough that he felt happy to make it a command rather than a question. Something flared in Saul's eyes, and he moved deliberately to lie as instructed, pillowing his head on his arm again. "Stay there," Randolph added, and went to get the petroleum jelly from the bathroom. His appearance in the mirror was something of a shock. His usually sleek hair was everywhere, his face flushed, and he hadn't even known he was smiling.

Saul looked up at him as he returned, one brow raised in something between question, amusement, and challenge. Randolph dropped to his knees, unscrewing the lid of the jar. "Legs apart. Do you always prefer it this way?"

"Either or neither. I'm accommodating."

"So I see." Randolph insinuated a slick, probing finger as he spoke. Saul sucked in a breath. "Highly accommodating. I've *very* much pictured myself fucking you. I'm not sure I've ever known anyone want it so badly as you did back at the castle."

"I suppose you prefer to give than receive."

"You suppose correctly. Legs wider."

Saul shifted. He was hard again, and Randolph leaned forward, getting his mouth to the straining prick and taking it in slowly even as he worked his finger into Saul's body. Saul was making pleasingly incoherent noises. Randolph pinned his other arm with his free hand, running fingernails over the sensitive elbow crook, and elicited a yelp.

"Good?" he said, around his mouthful.

"Christ, yes."

"Excellent. If you're wondering why you're on your back, it's because I intend to make you come till your legs won't hold you up."

"No argument here," Saul said hoarsely, and then convulsed as Randolph's questing finger met the knot of nerve endings he'd been seeking. "Jesus. *God.*"

Randolph took him in his mouth again. Saul's heels thumped the floor. He was groaning, a hand tangled in Randolph's hair, holding on for dear life. Abandoned to pleasure, free from every thought, helplessly aroused, and entirely Randolph's in this moment.

He pulled his mouth away and knelt up to get a look at the ecstatic torment on Saul's face. "Dear God, you are beautiful beyond words. I need to see how you look when you're fucked."

Saul shifted his legs wordlessly, eyes flickering open. He watched as Randolph scooped out another fingerful of petroleum jelly and slid his hand along his own length. The smooth slide against hot, rigid skin was pleasant, but nothing to the look in Saul's eyes. Randolph wanted to give him everything—or to rid him of everything, to drive it all away and leave nothing but this, the two of them in a room, the world locked out.

His palms were slick with the grease. He took hold of Saul's hot prick, sliding his hands up and down, feeling it twitch, until Saul said, as one driven beyond endurance, *"Randolph."*

They moved together, Randolph crawling over him to position himself so they could be face to face. He needed that, and Saul's silent shift to give him access told its own story. His long legs wrapped around Randolph's back; his hands on Randolph's shoulders, over skin and scars, all of him ready and waiting.

"Now?"

"Just a second. Yes."

Randolph pushed in, and Saul's face in that moment of penetration, the second as the muscle loosened and his body gave way, was everything he could have dreamed.

"Christ. Oh Christ. Randolph."

"All right?"

"So good." His hands tightened. *"Please."*

"I'm going to fuck you insensible," Randolph told him hoarsely. Saul's feet were flat against his thighs, his fingers digging in, and Randolph rocked into him, carefully at first, then thrusting deeper. He wanted to root himself in Saul, to grow through him, the pair of them entwined forever. "Jesus, you're lovely. Your face." Mouth open, head tipped back, so willingly helpless under him. The thought made him dig his teeth savagely into his own lip, forcing himself not to spill too soon. "You feel superb."

"So do you," Saul said on a breath. "More. All of it." He pulled with hands and legs as Randolph pushed, flesh meeting flesh with an audible slap. *"Yes.* God. Hard, please."

"At your disposal," Randolph assured him. He had one arm behind Saul's head; he grabbed with his free hand for one of Saul's, pushing his hand against the floor, entwining their fingers. Thrusting, kissing, feeling the slide of Saul's cock against his belly, the slide of his own in the heat of Saul's body, watching his face contort. Harder, deeper, losing himself in the sheer joy of seeing Saul lost, driving upward to push him closer to the fall.

"Randolph," Saul gasped. "Please, God, I can't. I can't." He clutched harder at Randolph's hand and shoulder as he spoke, urging him on.

"Oh, you can," Randolph whispered. "You can and will." He released Saul's hand, pushed his own between their bellies. Saul gave a strangled yelp as Randolph's fingers met his prick and slid under it. "You'll come as I fuck you and I'm going to see you do it. Christ." He couldn't hold back much longer himself; the look on Saul's face was so naked, so perfect in its abandonment. They were lifting off the rug now, Saul arching to meet his thrusts, crying out, coming in pulses against Randolph's skin. Randolph let go then, driving into him as though fucking could make everything all right, and for a few seconds, as he shot and shuddered, it did.

They lay together, gasping, letting their breathing calm, sweaty and sticky. Randolph's thigh muscles felt like chewed string. He felt a kiss against the side of his head and managed to angle his neck sufficiently so that his lips met Saul's.

"Good God," Saul said at last. "You may give me orders any time. Great Scott, I wanted that."

"So did I." Randolph withdrew, with a grunt of effort, and collapsed back down over Saul with a show of perhaps more exhaustion than he felt.

He wasn't entirely sure of the etiquette here. He'd never actually had anyone come to his home for this purpose before, since he had too many reasons for privacy; and on the occasions he'd gone to other men's rooms, his concern had always been how to leave as quickly as possible, without any unwanted sentiment or awkward scenes.

Randolph didn't want Saul to leave, and had no idea how to ask him to stay.

"You look somewhat perplexed," Saul said.

"Merely drained. Are you, or might you become, hungry?"

"I'd say so."

"Well, we have a great deal to discuss," Randolph said. "Theresa's parting gift, the Ministry and so on. And it's nearly six. Suppose I order something brought up and we can get down to business?"

Saul blinked. "That would be very kind. I'd like a wash, if you don't mind."

"Of course, old chap. I'll look you out a towel." He sat up.

"Randolph?" Saul sat up too.

"Mmm?"

Saul took his face in both hands, one still a touch slippery with grease, and kissed him. It wasn't the hungry need of before, but a careful, serious kiss, deep and open, and Randolph leaned into it, taking what he was given with a deep, nameless relief.

Saul sat back at last, looking into his eyes, a little frown between his own. Randolph met the gaze, held it. He wasn't sure he knew what Saul was looking for; he didn't think he had the courage to ask, in case he found out.

Finally Saul released him, with a twitch of a smile. "You're an odd duck."

"Am I? Well, of course I am."

"The hanging off trees and making ivy grow out of monsters is the most comprehensible part. Quite seriously, have you ever had a lover, in a regular sort of way? I don't mean a convenient body. I mean someone for whom you care."

Randolph winced. "Is it so obvious?"

"I don't know if it's obvious. You seem so solitary, that's all. Well, to be honest, if you were the sort of chap who had lovers, you'd already have one, wouldn't you? You're not short of looks, or confidence, or a few bob if it comes to that."

"Thank you."

"You're welcome. What I'm getting at is, I'd far rather you were clear on what you want, out of bed as well as in, and I don't want you to spare my feelings, not that you've shown any inclination to do so. If all you want is to fuck, please say so now. I shan't be offended, and I would much rather know where I stand. I like you a great deal, but—well, I'm not the type to roll over, wipe off, and get straight back to work, that's all."

Randolph felt himself flush. "No. I beg your pardon."

"Not at all," Saul said, equally politely. "But if that's what we have—"

"Could we have more?" Randolph asked on a breath.

Saul's eyes were steady on him. "Such as?"

"I don't know. You are quite right; I've never had anyone I'd call a lover. I was meant to marry Theresa till Ypres, of course. And since then I've been too damned busy, and I've too much to hide, and I dislike most people intensely anyway. Sam Caldwell tells me I have no idea how to conduct normal human relations."

"Oh. Are you and he—"

"Good Lord, no, Sam's not that way. Or at least I assume not; I've never asked. One may infer that even if he were, I'm not his type."

"Well, I agree with his observation, but you're very much my type," Saul said. "If supercilious, cryptic, and devastatingly attractive is a type."

"I hope it is." Randolph had no idea what he wanted to ask for, or grope towards. *Something*, that was all. "Please stay for dinner. We do have to talk about the many and various problems, but that isn't why I ask. For God's sake give me a hand here; I'm damned if I know what I ought to say."

"You're doing awfully well, old chap," Saul assured him.

"Oh, sod you. Devastatingly attractive, was that?"

"Utterly."

"Well, that makes two of us." He took Saul's hand and raised it to his lips, brushing a kiss over the fingertips. "In addition to which you are courageous, intriguing, and quite remarkably tolerable."

"I think you mean tolerant."

"I mean both, and that *doesn't* make two of us. This business with the Moat will have me crawling all over your life, you know. That's unavoidable, and if you decide you need to make things purely professional now or later, I want your word you will say so with no more regard for my feelings than I have for yours." He waited for Saul's nod. "But if you *are* prepared to...let us say, to risk matters becoming complicated, I wish you would."

"I should love to complicate matters with you and see how we go," Saul said. "And dinner would be delightful. How about that wash?"

CHAPTER ELEVEN

Randolph's bathroom was absurd. Saul wasn't surprised by that—
he'd read about the luxuries of these new serviced flats, and it was
obvious that the man was rich—but he stood in the expanse of marble
fittings and gleaming glass and said, "For heaven's sake."

"What?"

Saul gestured at both of them in the huge gold-framed mirror. "I feel
as though we'll get your bathroom dirty rather than it getting us clean."

It was a fair observation. They were both naked, tousle-haired,
flushed from kissing, skin marked all over by fingers, lips, and teeth,
and Saul's chest and stomach hair was matted dark and glistening with
drying spunk. He looked a disgrace, and Randolph looked a thorough
bandit.

Saul grinned at him in the mirror. "Being less groomed suits you."

"I beg to differ. Do you want a shower bath?"

"You don't have— You *do*." Saul had never known a private
home to have such a thing. "Good heavens."

"All modern conveniences." Randolph showed him the operation
of the device, and left him to it, for which Saul was grateful. He had a
lot to wash off.

The shower bath sprayed water down with some heat and force, a
gloriously efficient luxury, sluicing him clean. Saul had no idea if the

water would last—probably it would, he didn't imagine Randolph tolerated cold showers—but he moved quickly anyway, more quickly than he'd have liked.

Perhaps he could use it another time.

Saul was almost afraid to think about that. He'd been so bitterly lonely for so long; he'd longed to feel alive, and longing led to self-delusion. He never again wanted to persuade himself he was loved when he was merely being fucked.

But Randolph was prepared to complicate matters, he'd said so, and if Saul was sure of one thing, it was that Randolph wouldn't hesitate to give a chap the brush-off. He wanted more than fucking. He'd told Saul he was beautiful, and perhaps talk was cheap, but the expression in his dappled eyes had been beyond price.

You are not going to fall at his feet, Saul told himself severely. *He's not a hearts-and-flowers fellow. Even if he didn't have a hell of a job on, he's not...* He thought of sleek, prowling, predatory Randolph, carrying the words and scars of an ancient god. *He's not domesticated*, Saul concluded, and nodded at his reflection with determination.

Nevertheless, he whistled as he towelled himself dry.

He emerged from the bathroom in a robe Randolph had dropped over the bath for him, and dressed while Randolph had a wash in his turn, then poked around the sitting room a bit. Randolph had a large collection of peculiar-looking books, a few of which Saul recognised from Major Peabody's library. He also had those Green Men heads, wood and stone, a couple looking as though they were especially carved pieces, the others apparently cut or chipped out of their original settings. That was a barbarism he doubted Randolph would commit, at least not without reason.

He was looking at the leaf from his pocket when Randolph came up behind him in black trousers, waistcoat, and shirtsleeves. "What have you there?"

"Just a leaf. It turned up, or I found it, on the train."

"May I?" Randolph rubbed the leaf lightly between thumb and forefinger, then returned it. "Well."

"What do you mean, well?"

"Merely those." Randolph jerked a thumb at the carvings.

"Was that an attempt at an answer? Needs more work."

"Theresa dragooned you into the Green Men when she made you Walker," Randolph said, as though explaining what should be obvious. "The leaves go with the territory."

"My understanding of the Green Man is, well, these things." Saul indicated the wall in his turn. "Foliate heads. Early church decorations harking back to pagan times."

"Yes. And also no."

Saul sighed. "I swear, no jury would convict me."

"There is the Green Man, the stone decoration. There is the Jack in the Green, the country custom of dressing up in foliage. And there is more. There is the face in the woods, the laughter in the trees, the spirit of old England and an older land before the name. The land of Wayland Smith, the maker, the word-giver."

"Your words?" Saul asked. "The ones you—" He touched his shoulder.

"He was not a kindly god. There is nothing kindly about the old land at all, but there have been Green Men—that is, people who work with the land and are permitted to borrow a little of its power—for as long as anyone knows and doubtless longer. When I say Green Men," Randolph added, "it should be taken to apply to both men and women. Theresa found the term most irritating. She was a suffragist, of course."

"Good for her," Saul said. "I'm not quite sure I understand yet. You said I...?" He didn't find himself quite able to say the words. It seemed obscenely presumptuous to claim the lineage Randolph had outlined.

"Yes, you. You're the Walker now; that puts you very much at the heart of these matters. Think of it this way: there is an ancient duty to protect the land and its people. The Green Men carry out that duty, and that role can't be taken, or given, at a whim. Theresa couldn't have brought you in if you didn't meet with approval."

"Whose approval?"

"Suppose we pretend you didn't ask that. Here it is, Saul: London, like certain other key places, stands for England, and Camlet Moat stands for London, and you now stand for Camlet Moat. You will, I think, find yourself able to do so. Not easily or lightly, but you wouldn't have been chosen if you weren't capable. And you may fail, you may fall, but— well, I'll do my best to catch you. That's what you need to know now; I imagine the rest will make itself apparent. These things usually do."

"Right. I was rather hoping for a handbook."

"Wouldn't that be nice? Don't worry about not being born to it," Randolph added, with a slightly uncomfortable perceptiveness. "Sam Caldwell was only brought in three years ago, after the War, when it was imperative to make up the numbers. He is quite the most urban Green Man one can imagine, the occult equivalent of Coram's Fields, but it seems to work. You look alarmed."

"I am alarmed," Saul said. "I still have only the vaguest idea what you're talking about, and none what I'm meant to do." He remembered the church, though, the rising need to find the carved head, its bright eyes. "Are there many of you—us?"

"Never many, now far too few," Randolph said. "We fight on. Meanwhile, I rather thought we might go out to eat tonight. Somewhere decent. I think we deserve it."

Saul accepted the change of subject, mostly because he was famished again. "I'm hardly dressed to dine out."

"You have the right shoes, and you're as close to my size as makes no odds. I have plenty of evening clothes. Borrow something."

Saul raised a brow. Randolph gave a superbly casual shrug. "If we went out, we wouldn't talk any more about work."

"Don't we have to talk about work?"

"Of course. You've been given a duty. You've also been given a rotten time of it and I am absolutely sure that, were Theresa here, she would instruct me to take you out for dinner as a first step. Dancing, even, if you like that."

"Dancing?"

"There are places, dear boy. Not places I generally frequent, admittedly, but they exist. The point is, we need you in good shape because you'll have a lot on your plate. You deserve time to recuperate, and we deserve an evening to ourselves. Or, at least, I should like an evening in which I have you to myself, so we're going to take one. Tomorrow, you and I will see if Major Peabody's back, and discover whence came the book that set him on his trail and tackle Camlet Moat and all the rest. But let's have tonight first."

Saul felt he should say *What about the Shadow Ministry?* and *Ought not we—?* He didn't. He wanted more time with Randolph, to forget about threats to the world, the country, the city, and himself. Tomorrow he'd probably be jobless; he'd still have a headful of someone else's memories and the smell of ivy in his nose; he'd have to find out what duty he'd blundered into and how on earth he was meant to perform it. Tonight, he wanted to go to dinner in a decent set of clothes with the man who'd just fucked him into incoherence and talk about something else.

"Evening clothes, you say."

"Come through."

Randolph's bedroom was as large as might be expected—this flat had about half the floor space of the entirety of Saul's lodging house— with two brightly coloured canvases of extremely peculiar type on the walls. Saul blinked. "Those are very...avant garde."

"Severini, of the Italian Futurist school. Do you like them?"

Saul contemplated the garish colours and broken or flattened shapes. "No. Not at all. They're ghastly."

"Thank God for that. I can't stand them either."

"So why—?"

"Theresa gave them to me, and by that I mean nailed in the hooks herself while I was out. Birthday present. She said I needed to buck up my ideas."

"She took a lot on herself, I gather."

"You've no idea. I keep them as a reminder that I ought not to let my thoughts ossify. And because I'm used to them, I suppose, although that rather defeats the purpose now I think of it. Here." He handed Saul a hanger with a black coat and trousers. "Let's see how you look."

How he looked was...rather good, in the end. Saul hadn't worn evening dress in years, not since Oxford. He'd forgotten how flattering a well-cut dinner jacket could be, and this one was, even if it had been well cut for someone else. The fact wasn't obvious as he contemplated himself in the full-length mirror, Randolph beside him.

"That," Randolph said, "will do nicely. I thought the Cafe Royal."

"Wherever you choose. I should probably point out I don't have a penny in my pocket."

"I invited you, dear chap, my shout. I am aware of your circumstances, but can we add that to the list of things to discuss tomorrow? I find money desperately dull as a topic, and I'm well aware that's a privilege afforded only to the rich, but since I *am* rich, let's avail ourselves of all the benefits thereto."

"Good Lord, how is it you're not a lawyer?"

"There's no need to be rude." Randolph stepped closer to tweak Saul's lapel, like the world's most gentlemanly gentleman's gentleman, studying the set of the coat with a little frown that melted away as he looked up to meet Saul's eyes, and Saul was lost. He leaned to meet Randolph's lips, tasting toothpowder, felt Randolph's hand curl down around his hip and arse as though it belonged there. Randolph's mouth was open to his, in long, blissful kisses that said all the things two lonely, hoping men were afraid to put in words.

Saul curled a leg around Randolph's, pushing hips together. He very much doubted he was up to another round quite yet, but he could feel the solid bulge of Randolph's arousal. He rubbed up against him deliberately, heard the intake of breath, and slid to his knees.

"What are you doing?" Randolph enquired.

Saul reached for his waistband. "Not to state the obvious, I thought I might suck you off. Call it an aperitif."

Randolph choked, but didn't protest. They were still in front of the mirror. Saul concentrated on unfastening buttons, drawing out his prick with a thrill of power, and only then glanced up to the glass to see Randolph watching him, eyes intent.

"God, you look good on your knees," he said softly. "Go on."

Saul ran his tongue over and round Randolph's prick, tasting its faint savour of soap, taking time to get acquainted. It was straight and slender, like the man himself; long enough to make taking the whole thing a challenge, but then Saul liked a challenge. He leaned forward, sliding his lips down the length, and felt as well as heard Randolph's deep groan.

"Beautiful. You should always wear evening dress to suck me off. I may have to fuck you in that. Take you to one of those clubs I mentioned, bend you over a table and make you whimper for it. Or just have you on your knees like this. Sweet Jesus."

He did love to talk. Saul had never had that knack, and was generally happy to screw in silence, but then he'd never met anyone who used his mouth like Randolph. That light, filthy drawl was going straight to Saul's previously exhausted prick, and he could very happily get used to this.

He ran a hand between Randolph's legs, cupping his balls, looking up. "Tell me what you want me to do. Since you're so keen on giving orders."

Randolph's lips curled. "For a start, get your mouth back on my cock. Deeper. I want you taking all of it. Christ, yes. And watch yourself. I want to see you watch yourself."

Saul was; he couldn't look away. They looked like strangers in the mirror: one elegant man in evening dress, on his knees fellating another. He'd once bought a collection of photographs in a furtive sort of shop on Holywell Street, all of them showing supposedly aristocratic men at play; this could have been one of those.

"I could swear you're hard again," Randolph rasped. "Well, if it gives you pleasure to have your mouth fucked..." He was thrusting gently, hand in Saul's hair, and Saul's mouth tasted of soap and a tang that suggested Randolph would be coming soon, and ivy. He made an urgent noise. Randolph responded to that, thrusting harder, finally wordless, and Saul just held on as he spent, loving every gasp.

He swallowed the viscous, salty-sweet mouthful as Randolph braced himself with a hand against the mirror.

"Sweet God. I had no idea how much I wanted you to do that."

"I've wanted to do that for some time," Saul said. "To be honest, you could have had me at that blasted burning tree and saved us all a lot of trouble."

"Then we have time to make up. May I—?"

"God, not yet, I couldn't." Saul hauled himself to his feet. "Or rather, probably I could but it would take a while and I'm hungry as a hunter."

"Well, you can't blame me for that," Randolph pointed out. "As you please. Tidy yourself up, though, you look like you've been sucking cock."

Saul had no idea why that was even funny, but he doubled over, howling. Randolph caught his hilarity, shoulders shaking with that odd silent laugh of his, and the two of them were still spluttering as they left the flat.

The Cafe Royal was on Piccadilly, and it was glittering. Men in black and white, women with shingled hair in shimmering dresses. Saul had been eating alone in Lyons Coffee Houses for years, a solitary watcher of the chattering crowds. It felt peculiar to be one of them, but not wrong. He was dressed for it, and Randolph's casual superiority was a passport to anywhere he chose.

The menu was in French, and the prices astounding. Randolph glanced at him. "I suppose you're better at Arab food. The sweetbreads and the turbot are particularly good here."

"I'll trust your judgement," Saul said, with some relief, since his French extended only to comparing the garden of his uncle to the pen of his aunt.

Randolph crooked a finger, and a waiter appeared. He ordered for them both, and added a bottle of champagne, which arrived within seconds, with two gleaming flutes. Randolph raised his glass. "Shall we say, to making the best of complications?"

"I'll drink to that." Saul raised his glass in salute. The golden wine sparkled against his lips. It tasted of nothing so much as sweet biscuits. "So this is how the other half live?"

"Fewer than half, but indeed."

"Family money?"

"Quite a lot of it over the years, yes. Various gifts and grants from grateful monarchs and governments. And only me left to spend it."

"But no titles?"

"Many offered, but we turn them down. It's better to have the country obliged to you than vice versa. We talk a great deal about my family; what about yours?"

Saul sipped champagne. "I'm from Tring, in Hertfordshire. It isn't terribly noteworthy. I've—I had—a brother and a sister. My father was a solicitor. That's about it."

"All gone?" Randolph asked with a frown.

"As far as I'm aware they are all very well, but they, uh, they disowned me after the war. I attempt to respect that."

"You're a better man than I, then, since I can't sufficiently convey my contempt. My family history includes a number of catastrophic errors and some shockingly black sheep—wolves in black sheep's clothing, even—but we never pretended they weren't ours. Disowning, indeed. How bourgeois."

Saul wasn't sure whether to be amused or offended. "Well, that's a country solicitor for you. What did your family do with your black sheep, if not disowning?"

"Killed them, mostly."

"Oh, that's much better."

Randolph gave his slanted smile. "In our line of work, when people go bad they go spectacularly bad. Power corrupts and all that. It's why I am very conscious of the distinction between making a pig's ear of things and deliberate wrongdoing."

"So if I'd been in your family—"

"We'd have removed you from gaol first, and then gone after the gentlemen who entrapped you. One wouldn't want them to feel they could exploit one of our own and live to tell the tale. No indeed. And there would have been a great deal of shouting and unpleasantness, naturally, but that's only to be expected."

"Even under those circumstances?"

"We've weathered worse, believe me."

"I see. Uh, did your family know you're—" Saul twiddled a finger to indicate *queer*.

"Undoubtedly. I never made any effort to pretend otherwise. I'm sure it contributed to my father's dislike of me, which was ongoing and entirely mutual, but nobody else gave a damn so long as Theresa and I did our duty by the family."

"I always got on with my parents." Saul twisted his glass, contemplating the bubbles in the golden wine. "It never really occurred to me that we might ever fall out. That they would turn on me. I didn't spend a lot of time at home after I went to university but I thought they'd always be there."

"I couldn't stand most of mine, and spent far too long with them. I thought they'd always be there too."

Their eyes met. After a moment Saul managed a smile. Randolph didn't, but he tilted his glass again. "Lost things."

"Lost and found," Saul amended. "We're still on our feet, aren't we? Or occasionally knees, of course."

Now Randolph smiled. "I will definitely drink to that."

Food came, superbly cooked in wine and butter. Delicate flavours, delicate textures. They talked about books and plays and trivial memories, a rambling conversation for no more purpose than listening to one another talk, watching one another eat. Randolph ate with care, paying the food due but not excessive attention. Saul, consuming possibly the best-cooked meal of his life and certainly the best in seven years, was amazed how easy he found it to forget the food with Randolph's glinting eyes and half-smile across the table. His eyes, his smile, his wry humour, his love for unreadable eighteenth-century poetry and, entirely unexpectedly, Gothic novels. That led them onto the Casebooks of Simon Feximal, about which Saul was still fascinated.

"We, my siblings and I, grew up terrifying ourselves on them and M.R. James," he said. "My parents tutted and called them nonsense, and read the *Strand* when we went to bed. I still can't believe you knew Simon Feximal."

"Not well. He was remote, and mildly terrifying, and of course a tradesman."

"A what?"

"We aristocratic arcanists rather look down on ghost-hunters," Randolph said with a self-mocking drawl. "Gentlemen and players, you know. Feximal helped people, and got his hands dirty doing it in a way my father preferred not to."

"You admired him?"

"Not at the time. I took my guidance from my father, whether I knew it or not. But I've been working with Sam, his adoptive son, for a few years now, and it's impossible not to respect him, or Feximal as seen through his eyes. I doubt most people would respect my father seen through mine." Saul gave an acknowledging tilt of the head, having long concluded Randolph's father had been a first-class arsehole. "I'm glad of it. Sorry I didn't learn sooner. Everyone bemoans the changing world, you know, but there was a lot overdue for change."

"True enough. Why is he Sam Caldwell if he was Feximal's adoptive son?"

"Well, Caldwell adopted him as a matter of law, but Sam regards both of them in the same parental, or avuncular, light." Randolph hesitated, toying with his glass, then added, "They were together, Caldwell and Feximal. A couple."

"You're joking."

"No. Twenty-three years, I'm told."

"Great Scott." Saul took that in. "That's...rather marvellous." It was huge, and he wasn't sure why. He'd loved the stories, but that wasn't it. It was the possibility; the knowledge that men like him had found each other for whole lives, not stolen hours. He had to clear his throat to repeat, "Marvellous. Thank you for telling me. Er, was that common knowledge in your circles?"

"Good God, no. Sam knew of course. They were lost at Passchendaele, the pair of them, but they went together."

Saul raised his glass in silent tribute. Randolph tapped it with his own, the crystal ringing pure and clear like a bell.

He insisted that Saul try the soufflé, which was magnificent. Saul declined coffee, but accepted a cigar and a brandy. The chatter and laughter rose and fell around them, diners coming and going, heedless youth and people old enough to know better, off to dance at jazz clubs and nightclubs. Frenetic pursuit of pleasure under artificial light, while he and Randolph smoked, and talked, and watched each other.

Randolph called for the bill, paying with what looked like about two months' rent. That evidently didn't bother him; Saul decided he wasn't going to worry about it either. Randolph left the waiter a generous tip, exhaled smoke, and carefully extinguished his cigar. "It's later than I realised. Will you come back with me? We shan't be interrupted and I'd prefer the night not to end quite yet."

So would Saul. It would be back to work tomorrow, discovering what had happened to his old life, and what shape his new one might take. He didn't want this charmed evening to end with a long trudge back to Mornington Crescent and his cold, lonely, bare room. "If you think that's safe, I'd love to."

It was a mile or so from Randolph's rooms in the Albany to Major Peabody's house on Berners Street. Saul set off around ten the next morning in a positive frame of mind. At one point he found himself whistling.

Why not? It was a beautiful May morning, with a light breeze cutting through London's permanent smoke-haze. He'd woken in Randolph's bed and stayed there for some time, as sleepy kisses moved to a more energetic waking. Randolph had fucked him Oxford style, between the thighs, then sucked him off, leaving Saul once again flattened by sensation as by a juggernaut. Randolph seemed to enjoy giving pleasure more than taking it, his chief aim being reducing his partner to a whimpering mass of nerve endings. Saul felt he could get used to that.

They'd fucked, and breakfasted together, and Randolph had suggested Saul leave his bag in the Albany rather than drag it to Major Peabody's, in a casual assumption that he would be returning. So he was whistling, and if it hadn't been for everything else he'd have wanted to sing.

Everything else loomed large, though Saul chose not to think of that quite yet. He'd learned in gaol how to protect moments of happiness from thoughts of the inevitable and unpleasant future, and he'd take this sunny, satisfied saunter as the gift it was. Work would begin when he reached his possibly-erstwhile employer and tried to find out what was going on; until then he would think of Randolph. His hands, his mouth, his hard-edged understanding which meant more because it came not from a kindly nature, but from bitter experience.

Heaven knew where this might lead, if anywhere. Saul didn't know how to think about it. He'd lost his past, and that had made it impossible to consider the future: he'd simply eked out a daily existence ever since, and trudged on because there was no choice. The prospect of Randolph wanting him, shared smiles and touches, desire grounded in friendship and trust...that was more than he could take in. More, he knew, than he could afford to lose, and that was frightening, no less so for the sense that Randolph was as afraid to hope as he.

No castles in the air, he told himself. He'd enjoy this time day by day, and not wonder how many days there might be.

He switched his thoughts to work as he approached Major Peabody's house, going over phrasing in his head. In their brief conversation on the topic, over fried sausages and mushrooms, Randolph had advised him to claim an accident and temporary memory loss. The last thing they needed, he'd said, was that fumbling amateur getting further in the way. Saul was to see if he still had a job, and find out all he could about what had put the Major onto Geoffrey de Mandeville in the first place.

That was the plan. He knocked, therefore, at Major Peabody's door and waited for several minutes. No answer came. He knocked again, and heard nothing.

Where had the Major gone? Had he come home at all? Saul had taken the Vicar's word for it that Major Peabody had left the Fens; he hadn't spoken to the Abchurches or sent a message. If the Vicar had deceived him on behalf of the Shadow Ministry, Major Peabody might still be kicking his heels in Cambridgeshire.

The thought was appalling. Saul turned from the door with the intention of finding a telegraph office as quickly as possible, and almost collided with a large man right behind him.

"Excuse me," he said, and made to step around.

The large man grasped his arm. Saul attempted to wrench it away and failed. "Hoi! What are you playing at?"

"Saul Lazenby?"

He wasn't wearing a uniform, only a brown suit and bowler. Saul jerked angrily at the grip once more. "Yes, and you may get your hand off me. What the devil's this?"

"I'd like you to come with us, sir."

Us. Saul registered another man standing further back. "Why? And who are you?"

"We'll deal with that later, sir."

"We'll deal with it now, thank you. Again, who are you and what's your authority?"

"Department of Special Affairs," said the other man, approaching. "Shadow Ministry to you. We're answerable to Mr. Delingpole, and he wants a word with you, so you, Mr. Lazenby, are coming with us like it or not."

They took him to an anonymous building on William IV Street. It had a blandly official look to it, and heavy doors with heavy doormen. He was brought in and conducted to a small bare room, its one window high up and barred.

"This appears to be a cell," Saul said. "I've done nothing wrong. I'm not under arrest, am I? Why are you putting me in a cell?"

"Just get in, sir."

"No." Saul could feel the panic clawing at his throat. "I'm not going in there. If your Mr. Delingpole wants to speak to me he can do it in an office like a civilised man. I demand to speak to him at once."

His captors exchanged glances. Then there was an unexpected hard shove, which sent Saul stumbling over a foot neatly placed by his ankle, into the cell. The door slammed, a lock scraped, and he was trapped.

He looked around, frantic. The room held a chair, a long bench suspended from the wall by chains, and a toilet in the corner. Nothing else. It wasn't like his Mesopotamian army cell—sanitation, no obvious crawling things, no sobbing from other cells as yet—but he was locked in and helpless against a gaoler's cruelty or whim, and he had to get his head between his knees and shut his eyes before the fear stopped his breath.

This is a misunderstanding, he told himself. *Or a piece of bullying. They're trying to soften you up. You've done nothing wrong.* Only he had, of course, he'd lied through his teeth to Bracknell and Delingpole, to the authorities in their persons. He'd made his allegiance to Randolph clear, and please God nobody could know or guess it was more than allegiance. If the Shadow Ministry wanted to find a way to get at the inconveniently resistant last Glyde, Saul was a crack in his defences. And he couldn't do a damn thing about it, didn't know what to say or not say, and was having trouble getting air into his lungs because the walls were closing in.

Breathe, he told himself, and then imagined Randolph saying it in that drily authoritative tone he used in the bedroom. *Suppose you breathe. Really, dear chap, it's what your lungs are for.*

He tried that, against the constriction of his chest, and it helped a little. Not enough. Perhaps he ought to get up and shout, demand a lawyer? But the Shadow Ministry evidently had a limited regard for legal niceties, and he risked betraying himself and perhaps Randolph. He needed to get himself under control before he spoke to anyone.

He tested the bench then lay on it, trying to stretch his ribcage against the invisible fist crushing the breath out of it. *Camlet Moat*, he told himself. The sunlight in the trees, the cool water in his throat, sluicing through him, washing the panic away. He built up the picture until he could smell greenery and feel the slight give of mulch underfoot as he wandered through the trees, up to an oak so thickly wound with glossy ivy that he feared the tree might fall.

Bright eyes opened wide in the leaves, staring at him. Saul stumbled away with a yelp of shock and found himself on his back on the bench in the cell, disoriented and dizzy.

He felt sick, too. He sat up, which didn't help, and had to lie down again, with his heart pounding and waves of nausea passing through him. Christ, this couldn't just be fear-induced. Was he actually ill? He'd had plenty of gut-rot in gaol, thanks to the foul slop that had passed for rations, and he knew the feeling well. It seemed unjust that a superb and expensive restaurant in Piccadilly could have poisoned him.

He shut his eyes again, which made his brain lurch in his skull. This was unspeakable. He wanted to call for help now, felt a terror it would be ignored, and had a sudden vision of himself lying face down on the floor of the cell. He'd been feverish after the flogging, and the fearful misery of that memory crowded in.

He wasn't in his bloody cell, and this wasn't the bloody Army. He was in England, held by some Whitehall department albeit an unaccountable one, and he was not going to panic. He told himself that as the dizziness shuddered through him, again and again.

He might have slept, or at least dozed, because the next thing he knew was a rough hand on his shoulder. "Oi. Sit up. Up."

Saul muttered protest. The electric light of the cell was bright against his closed eyelids and he didn't want to move.

"Get him on his feet," Mr. Delingpole's cold voice said. Saul found himself jerked violently vertical, onto legs that wouldn't hold him. He leaned forward and retched over the floor and over a set of shiny patent leather shoes topped by well-creased trousers.

"For God's sake!" Mr. Delingpole yelped, leaping back. "What's wrong with him?"

"He looks ill."

"Give him some water. You, Lazenby! Oh, this is no use, he's barely seeing me."

"Should we get a doctor, sir?"

"Looks like a bad head," Mr. Delingpole said. "He was carousing with Glyde half the night, I'm told. Let him sleep it off, we have more to worry about."

"Sir, are you—"

"Check back in an hour."

Saul folded back onto the bench, vaguely aware he should have demanded a doctor, a lawyer, Randolph. He couldn't. He'd never felt so ill in his life. It felt like he had a lump of corruption in his stomach, something so old and foul it tasted of spiderwebs and grave rot. How could he have eaten anything so poisonous and not tasted it? He wanted help; he wanted Randolph; he wanted water. Most of all he wanted to vomit it all up, but the idea of standing was very nearly as bad as the idea of lying here letting the vileness churn inside him.

He slid off the bench in the end, and crawled to the lavatory where he threw up for what seemed like hours, until his stomach was cramping with pain, his throat burning. It didn't give even a momentary relief. He stayed there, kneeling on the floor and gripping the bowl, till his spasming stomach calmed and he was sure he had nothing left to vomit, then he crawled back to haul himself onto the bench. He managed to drink a little water from the jug, washing away some of the taste, then curled up on his side, shuddering with cold. He jammed his icy hands under his armpits, which were unpleasantly sweaty, then into his jacket pockets, where his fingers met something. A leaf, he realised, the ivy leaf from the train. He crumpled it in his palm and shut his eyes, unable to do anything but wait for this to be over.

Eventually, he dreamed.

CHAPTER TWELVE

Randolph stalked up William IV Street to the Shadow Ministry building, where a doorman stood, looking sturdy and immovable.

"Help you, sir?" the man asked.

"Open the fucking door or I'll put you through it."

"Mr. Randolph Glyde would like to be admitted," Sam translated from beside him. "There's a good chap."

"Uh—" The doorman looked from one to another of them.

"Randolph Glyde," Sam repeated. "I'm quite sure you're not paid enough for this."

"I'll go and, um..." The man opened the door, apparently intending to slip inside. Randolph, Sam, Barney, and Isaacs moved simultaneously, with at least one of them adding a kick to swing the door wide, ignoring the cry of protest.

It was past five in the evening, but the Ministry building still had plenty of pinstriped people sticking heads out of offices, and retreating as quickly. Randolph was darkly glad of that. *Be afraid*, he thought. *You should be.*

"You," he said, grabbing a passing clerk at random. "Saul Lazenby. Brought in this morning. Where is he?"

"I don't know!" the man said, with some affront.

"Then find out." Randolph shoved him away.

"In the cells." Sam emerged from the reception office, which would have been a more logical place to start, but Randolph wasn't feeling logical. "Delingpole's authority. Bracknell ordered him brought in."

"Get Delingpole," Randolph told him. "Isaacs, with me. Barney, take Bracknell."

"Sir," the other three chorused with varying levels of sarcasm, to none of which Randolph paid the slightest attention. He marched through the corridors, daring anyone who passed not to get the hell out of his way, to the corridor of cells, and hurried down the row, glancing through the barred hatches. All the rooms were empty till the fourth, where a dark-haired man was curled on a bench. It smelled sour and rank, like vomit.

"Christ," Randolph said, peering in. "Saul? What the— Saul!"

"There's some people coming," Isaacs remarked. "You want to get him and I'll deal with 'em?"

"Thank you." Isaacs might even be better at dealing with the door, but he could hold off any number of interfering officials, and Randolph needed to get to Saul. He put his hands against the door. It was solid wood, old and dry and painted.

Breathe in. Breathe out.

He let the ivy wind up through him, through muscles and veins, around sinews and bones, until it thrust under his skin, at his eyes and ears; until his mouth was bitter with the taste of leaves and his vision was dappled green and his shoulders hurt. Then he flattened his tendrils against the door and demanded, *"Forthlaede."*

The ivy burst from his hands. It ripped through the door in a cloud of splinters with a loud rending noise, tearing the wood away from the lock and handle and hinges. The door collapsed inwards in three parts and a pile of greenery, over which Randolph took a long stride. Out of his trance, he could hear the sound of Isaacs in energetic discussion up the corridor.

Saul had pushed himself up, leaning on his hands. He was sallow-faced and haggard. "Randolph?"

"What the *hell*?"

"Sick," Saul mumbled.

"Can you walk?"

Saul nodded, swung his legs down, and almost fell off the bench. Randolph scooped him up, staggering slightly under his weight. "Right, we're leaving." He lugged Saul out of the cell, over the heap of debris, and down the corridor, turned the corner, and stopped.

There were six men, arcanists and officials, strung in a semicircle around Isaacs that would have been more intimidating if they weren't keeping a nervous and substantial distance. As it was, it looked very much as though he was intimidating them. One of them glanced past him to Randolph and said, plaintively, "Oh God."

Randolph snarled, not bothering to articulate a threat. All of the men moved back a step.

"Er, Glyde," began a fresh-faced someone. Randolph had forgotten his name; his elder brother had died in France.

"You're in the wrong place," he informed the group. "Immediately, and generally. The Ministry has exceeded its authority; if I were you I'd rethink my allegiances."

"*You* are exceeding your authority!" Delingpole rapped. He was hurrying up the corridor with Sam behind him. "That man is a—"

Randolph let Saul's feet slip to the ground so he could brace the slumped body and hold his face up, and also because he was too damned heavy. "Look at him. A layman, left in the cells without attention. What the devil are you playing at, you damned irresponsible fool?"

"What's wrong with him?" Sam asked, brow furrowing as he came to give Saul his shoulder, supporting his other arm. He could feel it too, Randolph knew, a deep and growing sense of wrongness. "This is not good."

"I'm going to find out. Give me a hand. No, Delingpole, you have no right to detain him or any other innocent civilian. I will have *words* for you on this."

"The Ministry has authority to procure information—"

"You and your information," Isaacs said. "Mr. G, whyn't you get on? Me and the Captain can handle this."

"Good idea," Randolph said. "Don't feel obliged to leave anything standing."

Saul muttered something. He was taking his weight on his feet now that Sam and Randolph both had him, and Randolph could feel the push of greenery, the drive upward to the sun. Saul was calling on the Green Men, know it or not. He needed to get out of here.

"Come on, Sam." He pulled Saul forward.

Delingpole planted himself in their way. "I said, no. You may consider yourself above the law—"

"I'm not the one unlawfully detaining citizens."

"I have the authority of the Government!"

"I have that of the Crown. I have letters patent of monarchs from the Virgin onwards, including his majesty who now graces the throne, and none of them matter a damn. I serve England."

Delingpole leaned in. "You seem to think you live in a medieval system where your orders go unquestioned." His lip curled, a menacing sneer. "You do not."

"The medievals are Johnny-come-latelies. I am of the old land. Get out of my way, bureaucrat, or I'll burn your paper castle to the ground."

He headed forward, he and Sam with Saul between them. The other men—it was all men, the Ministry didn't employ women arcanists—retreated. Delingpole didn't. "The world is changing, Glyde. You need to understand that."

He stood as though his pinstripes and position made him untouchable. One saw that a great deal with those who had found employment in sending other people to war; they hadn't had the civilisation trained out of them. Randolph simply shouldered him out of the way, and the man went staggering back.

"Some of you, stop him!" Delingpole snapped, regaining his balance.

"You could try," Isaacs said. He was walking behind them, backwards, in the manner of a rear guard. "I wouldn't if I was you."

Isaacs was spoiling for a fight, and the atmosphere boiling off him was raising the hairs on Randolph's neck. Everyone around them clearly felt the same strong disinclination to get any closer, and the Green Men moved into the main hall unmolested. Saul was more or less walking by this point, his hand gripping Randolph's shoulder.

"It's all right, old chap. I have you," Randolph told him quietly. "We'll get you home."

"Camlet Moat," Saul rasped.

Randolph's stride faltered. "Did you say—"

"The Moat. Now. Please."

"Hell," Randolph said under his breath. "Isaacs, get the front door, then find Barney and meet us at Camlet Moat. Up past Cockfosters, in a place called Trent Park. Quick smart."

"Got yer." Isaacs nipped round them and trotted up to the doorman, who was nearly a foot taller than him. By the time Sam and Randolph had got Saul to the door, it stood wide and unobstructed, and they made their way into the evening air. Saul took a shuddering breath.

"That was fun," Sam said. "I suppose you realise we've more or less declared war. We certainly will have done by the time Barney and Max are finished in there."

"It's about time. This was a personal attack on me as well as a gross overstepping of all civilised bounds. Thank you."

"What was that last bit?"

"Thank you for standing by me," Randolph amplified. "That was above and beyond, from you and from the others, and I appreciate it. You're a damned good ally—friend—to have."

"Are you planning to go over the top or something?" Sam asked cautiously. "Farewell speech, sort of thing?"

"I was trying to express human feelings as requested. Christ, you're fussy. Taxi!"

"Should we not take him home?" Sam suggested.

"Camlet Moat," Saul repeated, more strongly.

"Trent Park, cabbie," Randolph ordered. "Up past Cockfosters. You know it? Good." He climbed into the back of the cab after Sam and Saul, and pulled the partition across. Goodness knew how long this journey might take with all central London to cross, but at least they'd be private.

"Right," Sam said. "I think I've been remarkably patient. What's going on?"

"Saul first." His head was back, eyes shut, but his hand was groping. Randolph took it, feeling the flesh cold and clammy, and sucked in a breath. "Oof. Grab his hand, would you?"

Sam did so, and muffled a Navy expression. "Gah. Leaves."

"He's calling on us."

"I thought you said he wasn't involved in our business. This is your jack-in-the-box fellow Lazenby, yes?"

"Yes. Things have become complicated, I fear." Randolph had barely seen Sam since his return to London. "He turned up in the Fens when I was dragged up there the other day. We had quite a time." He gave Sam a brief summary. "And that was where we encountered my cousin Theresa."

"Your dead cousin Theresa?"

"Indeed. She made Saul the Walker of Camlet Moat."

Sam assimilated that for a moment. "Right. Well, that's that issue dealt with. Or not. You're sure it was her, not some trick?"

"Entirely."

"And we now have the Walker of Camlet Moat between us, looking sick as a dog and demanding to be taken there. Oh God. Give me the entire story, from the beginning, in detail."

Randolph did, with as much concision as possible. Sam heard him out in silence. "So the Ministry want him as a witness to the upheaval in the Fens. Because they think he could testify to your wrongdoing or failures?"

"I think so. Delingpole and Bracknell are keen to be rid of me."

"And could he bear witness? What actually happened up there?"

"I'm not sure. It seems that something to do with Geoffrey de bloody Mandeville triggered it all, but whether that was to do with Camlet Moat, or Saul's presence, or the Temple Church business, damned if I know."

"Will he not know?" Sam indicated Saul.

"I hope so. I haven't discussed any of this with him. We need to sit down and talk, but—well, there hasn't been an opportunity."

"Balls," Sam said flatly. "Barney told me he dropped Lazenby off at your rooms yesterday afternoon. Delingpole said you were wining and dining him at some fancy restaurant all evening. How did you not make time to discuss the small matter of Camlet Moat?"

"The poor bastard was dragged east of the sun, attacked by a fen-grendel, and had Theresa inside his head," Randolph snapped. "I thought he deserved an evening off."

"So you of all men took one too?" Sam demanded, sitting forward and twisting round to glare at him. "Come off it, Randolph. And don't lie to me, I can tell when you're hiding something. Actually, I'm damned if I know what you look like when you're not. Why on earth would you—" He stopped dead, then said, more quietly, "Ah."

"What?" Randolph returned, and realised that Sam was looking down to where he was still holding Saul's hand. Loose on his lap, fingers interlinked, perhaps a little warmer now.

"Right," Sam said. "Got you. Sorry, old man. So you had an evening off; then what happened?"

"Saul left—this morning," Randolph said deliberately, "to go and find out what put his employer, the idiot Peabody, onto de Mandeville. I assume the Ministry picked him up at some point. It's all circling round him and Peabody and de Mandeville and I don't understand why. I am well aware I probably shouldn't have taken the evening off, in case you're wondering."

"You've had about six in the three years I've known you, while Bracknell and the others all go home to the wife and children every night. What is this de Mandeville business?"

"He was the lord of Camlet Moat," Saul said, eyes shut, something a little odd in his tone. It was pitched lighter than usual, with a clear musical note to it that wasn't his warm tenor at all, and there was a very faint silvery sheen to his skin through Randolph's other sight. "Master of London. Custodian of the Tower. Dying in the Fens, begging for life. Hung like meat from a tree for a year and a day, encased in lead. Suspended between life and death, and taken back to where he began in service of the city."

Randolph hissed. "Hell's teeth."

"He swore to guard London," Saul said, or at least the words came from his lips. "He made a vow, and the vow would be kept so long as the lead should hold him."

There was a moment's silence, which Sam broke when it was clear there wouldn't be more. "Someone explain."

"You know about blood sacrifice?" Randolph said. "Buildings mortared with human blood, people buried under foundations?"

"Uncle Robert told me about an awful case of it he saw, involving murdered children."

"Well, I suspect this is what we're looking at, but I rather have the impression de Mandeville wasn't dead."

"You mean he was buried alive?" Sam asked.

"I am wondering if he stayed alive," Randolph said grimly. "The tree, the hanging man, the lead. Lead is Saturn's metal. It means death and rebirth, creation and destruction. Betwixt and between."

"Whether buried or not buried, damned or saved, I do not know; I cannot tell," Saul whispered.

Sam made a face. "Nasty for him. What does it mean for us?"

"Good question."

"Randolph!"

"Well, it depends. Dead or alive or neither, he was taken to Camlet Moat to fulfil his duty to London forever. Which may explain the nastiness in the Fens. Saul drank the Camlet Moat water, washed in it, benefited from the blessing de Mandeville was obliged to provide. That must have seemed provocative."

"Could de Mandeville's spirit be bound in London and free in the Fens at the same time? That's surely not possible."

"If he's not fully dead, anything's possible. Or it might have been a particularly powerful spirit of place. I don't know. Saul and Peabody went up there to look at a collection of de Mandeville artefacts; that was what Peabody was doing when Saul and I took that ill-fated walk. I wonder what he found. Saul!" He turned and gave his lover a shake. "Saul. I need you to wake up and talk to me."

Saul grunted, eyes flickering open. "Randolph?"

"Did you see Peabody this morning?"

Saul took a second to work through the question in his head. "Uh, no. Wasn't in. Those men—" He blinked, then straightened, as if waking. "Those men took me to some prison in an office. What happened? What the devil's going on?"

Randolph squinted out of the window. They were somewhere in the region of Kentish Town, the taxi chugging along towards Camlet Moat. The shadows were long now, the light beginning to fade. "What do you remember? Oh, this is Sam Caldwell, by the way. Saul is a great admirer of your Uncle Robert's writing, Sam."

"Good taste. Pleased to meet you, Saul. Go on."

"I went to see Major Peabody this morning, but he wasn't there. A couple of Shadow Ministry men turned up there as I waited. They refused to tell me what it was about, just hauled me off to their office, where I was thrown in a cell. And then I fell ill."

"Ill," Randolph repeated. "What sort of ill?"

"Food poisoning," Saul said, and then, more doubtfully, "At least, I think it was. We ate the same thing last night, didn't we? But I was sick to my stomach. And..." He paused, then delved in his pocket and produced a wrinkled brown leaf. "Well."

The leaf from the train, if Randolph didn't miss his guess. "Hmm."

"It wasn't dried this morning," Saul said, rather hopelessly. "I don't know much more, I'm sorry. I felt appalling, and I tried to sleep, and then after what seemed an age you arrived."

"Did you imagine yourself in Camlet Moat, at all?"

"I did at first. I, uh, I don't like being in cells much, you see." He didn't look at Sam. "I was in rather a funk. I tried to calm myself down. You know. And I saw a face, a Green Man, with living eyes."

"I expect that was me," Randolph said. "I saw you too, it's how I knew to come after you, though it took half the damned day to track you down."

"You saw— Right. And that was when I got sick. Nothing personal."

"You thought of Camlet Moat, and the sickness came on," Randolph repeated. "And now what?"

"Well, we have to go there," Saul said with certainty, and blinked. "Uh..."

"My uncle Robert gets—got that sort of thing quite often," Sam said. "Apparently it's best to say what you know and not worry about how you know it."

"Easier said than done," Saul muttered.

"Isn't it all. Why are we going to Camlet Moat?"

"Because— I don't know. It's important. Something's not right." Saul crushed the leaf between his fingers. "Not right at all."

"Tell me more about Peabody," Randolph said. "What did you go to the Fens to see?"

"Mr. Abchurch has a collection relating to de Mandeville. I never saw it—we were to take a look after I'd stretched my legs that morning, but then you and I found ourselves on that blasted road. I don't know what he had."

Randolph made a face. "Can you speak about what happened with Theresa?"

Saul was silent for a few moments. Finally he said, "I'm very reluctant to. I'm sorry. I feel as if I shouldn't."

Sam nodded. "Fair enough."

Randolph didn't respond. He was struggling with an unfamiliar sensation, something contemptibly like jealousy. That Theresa's last efforts had been for someone else; that she'd put her mark on Saul; that this was between the two of them alone.

Which was absurd. What was there for Randolph to envy in that contact? Only that it was private and secret and he wanted to be part of it, not excluded by silence. He'd wanted to protect Saul from the stain of shadows, then and now. He wanted, ludicrously enough, to be Saul's knight in shining armour, a role for which he was unfitted by ability or temperament even if Saul needed one.

He'd unquestionably needed help earlier today, though, and in the course of providing it Randolph had let loose the ancient strength of the Green Man in the middle of a building, unleashed Barney and Isaacs, and kicked away the last pretences of rapprochement with the Shadow Ministry, all without the slightest compunction.

"Oh my God," he said aloud.

"What is it?" Sam asked.

"Nothing. Nothing that need concern you, at least."

"*Randolph.*"

"Entirely private. Forget I spoke."

Sam made an irritated noise. Randolph sat back as the taxi-cab chugged on through the evening streets, letting his thoughts curl carefully around his feelings like a cat nudging kittens into order.

He'd never thought of more than casual encounters even before the War; he hadn't really been aware that was a possibility and in truth he hadn't cared to find out. He had been very happy with the idea of a cousin-marriage, decoupling trust and companionship from sordid bodily need and the vulgarity of violent feeling. It had seemed perfect. And now here he was, seething with jealousy of his dead cousin for an entirely necessary claim on the attention of the lover for whom he'd abandoned duty and restraint without even thinking, because the idea of some bastard hurting Saul had gone from unacceptable to unbearable.

You've spent one night with him, you fool. Two if you count the one where he was unconscious for half of it.

Except it was worse than that, because he'd felt like this when he'd kissed Saul on the road. He wasn't cockstruck, he was sure of that: he was far too old to be led by his prick. He was...taken with him, that was the term for it. Intrigued. Charmed, even. He liked Saul very much; he trusted him; he valued his friendship, delighted in his company, wanted to talk to him, ached for his body, needed the smile in those dark eyes to remind him why he bothered to keep on.

Randolph had a feeling that "taken with" wasn't actually the term for it at all.

Trent Park was closed to the public for the evening, its gates locked. Randolph directed the cabbie to leave them at the north side, nearest to Camlet Moat, then contemplated the high brick wall with disgust. Sam rolled his eyes, found a point with an overhanging branch, and shinned up the wall without effort. Saul followed, being apparently equally familiar with illegal entries, and they both leaned down to give Randolph a hand.

That undignified scrabble done with, they jumped down one at a time into the woodland that ringed the park. It was sunset now and would be dark soon, and the trees cut out what little light there was.

"Hold on," Sam said, searching in his ever-present satchel. "I've a flashlight in here."

"Dig it out, then," Randolph said with a touch of impatience. Other people's inability to see in the dark was always tiresome. "I doubt Saul—" He glanced round. "Oh, hell. Saul?"

Saul was swaying on his feet, face ghastly. "No," he whispered. "No, no, no!"

He was off and running then, stumbling over the uneven ground, dodging through trees. Randolph sprinted after him, Sam at their heels. They were heading for Camlet Moat, of course. Randolph had lost all sense of connection to the place, he realised—if there was something wrong there, he wasn't feeling it at all. He could only hope Saul would find the way, and that the Moat was amenable to being found.

Saul was hurdling obstacles, running desperately through the wood, over a path, and that in itself worried Randolph if they were heading for the Moat. Which they were, because he saw the dim green of the algae-coated water through the trees, and other shapes, too. Something big and angular that didn't, couldn't make sense. Not here, not on bloody Camlet Moat—

"Is that a mechanical excavator?" Sam asked, as they came to a stumbling stop. "It is, isn't it?"

"Oh no, no," Randolph said. "Don't tell me."

"Mother of God." Saul put out a shaking hand, pointing. "I think they've dug him up."

CHAPTER THIRTEEN

The bridge was covered in heavy wide planks, ones evidently designed to make a reliable path for the mechanical excavator to be driven on and off again. It was parked on the land side, along with a wheelbarrow full of spades. There was no sign of any men.

"The damned fools," Randolph said. "Let's see the damage, shall we?"

"We need to get these things off the bridge first," Saul said. The planks were an irritant like a splinter, forcing an entrance that should only be requested.

Neither Sam nor Randolph argued. The three of them carried the planks off, piling them to the side of the bridge, until there was only the dark semi-rotten wood once more, very low in the water. It was nearly dark by the time they'd done.

Sam flicked on his flashlight and turned to Saul. "When you're ready."

They were expecting him to lead. He nodded, and set out over the bridge, onto Camlet Moat.

It looked small. It *felt* small, like a little moated bit of land in the middle of a park, just an ordinary place. It was hard to see whatever damage had been done, but he could feel the wrongness.

The bridge was in the middle of one side of the Moat; the well was on the far side, in the left-hand corner. Saul headed that way, remembering the tales of treasure hunters and dreading what he'd find.

"Damnation," Randolph said as they approached. "Damn."

There was a great dip in the ground, perhaps eight feet deep at the lowest point, and a vast pile of earth and stones behind it. The cloutie tree sprawled some way away where it had been tossed, roots bare, offering cloths dangling in the dirt. The shaft of the well descended from the centre of the pit, dark and dead. Sam's torch beam played on that, and then moved sideways to illuminate a shape on the ground. A man's body, face down, not moving.

"That's not good," he said.

Saul scrambled down into the pit, loose earth sliding underfoot, to where the body lay. A shortish, plump form in a Norfolk jacket, hatless, grey hair matted dark with blood.

He moved around so as not to obstruct the beam of light, braced himself, and turned the body over.

Dull horror ignited into vivid revulsion and he scrambled back, unable to tear his eyes from the slack dead face, spectacles broken, open mouth half-filled with earth. "Oh God, no. It's the Major."

"Peabody?" Randolph asked from above. "Hell's teeth. The silly bastard."

"He was a decent man," Saul said, feeling he ought to offer something to the dead. "He didn't deserve this."

"If he dug up Camlet Moat, I hope he rots." Randolph lowered himself into the pit to join Saul, and bent to examine the body.

"Human, animal, other?" Sam asked from above.

"Head stoved in, one big dent. Not animal, so I'd guess human."

"Why?" Saul asked hopelessly. "Why would someone do this?"

Randolph blew out a breath. "He comes here to dig, presumably for relics, or treasure—"

"You can't excavate an ancient site with a mechanical digger!"

"Did he know that? Would he care?"

Saul opened his mouth, and closed it. Major Peabody hadn't been a scholar, or trained in any way. He'd wanted to prove his theories to be true, rather than to discover the truth. And he'd wanted to find something wonderful so very much.

"If he'd had reason to believe there was something here... Maybe not."

"And his pet archaeologist had vanished. So he came here, spurred by his fanaticism—alone?"

"With help. I very much doubt he could operate a digger, and there were several spades."

"With other people," Randolph agreed. "And then, well, either he didn't find what he was after, or he did. If he didn't, perhaps the other party knocked him on the head in a fit of justified annoyance and left. But if he did..."

"They took it off him, and stopped his mouth," Sam said from above. "Was someone hiding behind Peabody? Using him to get to the well?"

"Why would they?"

"Because I'd kill anyone buggering around at Camlet Moat," Randolph said. "I'd have been up here at the first spadeful of earth if it had happened last week, and buried the bodies in their own pit. But I didn't know this was happening, because Theresa made you the Walker, and you didn't know what was going on because you've been dropped into this mess as ignorant as a newborn babe, and I couldn't help you through it because that fucking fool Delingpole had locked you up. What a shambles."

"This is my fault," Saul said, a great hollow feeling spreading through him. "She gave me the responsibility, and *this*—"

"Is their fault, whoever *they* are," Randolph said. "We don't have time for guilt. What did they take?"

"I don't know."

"Yes, you do. Theresa told you the deep secrets. What's happening here?"

"I don't *know*." Saul's head was spinning.

"What were they digging for?" Randolph demanded. "What were they after? What did they take? All right, start with this: did they let de Mandeville out?"

The dark closed in on Saul. Utter darkness, impenetrably black. Pain in his head, an odd sweet metallic taste in his mouth, and through it all, the acid burn of wanting. He wanted to live, he wanted to die, he wanted to kill, and kill, and kill again. He wanted everything, all of it. To have empresses and prelates begging for his favour; to make the walls weep blood as he passed for fear of him. He would be the master of city and country and king, *had* to be, because nothing yet had been enough to satisfy the great raging hungry pit inside him, and he would throw broken bodies and ruined lives into it again and again until it was filled at last, if he could only get out of the soft enclosing metal and the *dark*—

"Saul!" Randolph had him by the arm. "Saul?"

"De, de— Him." Saul might have fallen except for Randolph's grip. "In lead. They wrapped him in lead and he was still alive, or at least, something of him was, and it was *dark*."

"Rotten for him," Randolph said, with no trace of sympathy. "And?"

"I don't know. I just felt him. Grotesque, vile. Greed beyond belief, greed well past the point of madness. He had a hole where his heart should be, and—the lead, the lead kept him in, and... Something's missing." He could feel it, the enclosing prison around a hateful soul, and the dawning awareness that somewhere a door had opened. "Oh God. I think whatever they took might have been keeping him there, in the dark. I think he's waking up."

"Well," Randolph said. "Shit."

"How bad is this likely to be?" Sam asked.

"If he's been at the heart of Camlet Moat for eight centuries? That old, that angry, and the sworn Master of London?"

"We'd better put him back to sleep then," Sam said. "Any idea how?"

"What did they take, Saul?" Randolph gave his arm a shake. "Think."

"I don't *know*. It was keeping him in, it was—it was in the well."

Randolph scrambled down the slope of the pit, towards the black hole of the well shaft. "They took out the lining stones. Piled them up, there. Were they looking for something set in the wall?"

"Can you see anything?" Sam slid into the pit, joining Saul. The flashlight was a comfort.

"Not to make out. It's all absolutely buggered. Wait a moment, what's that?" Randolph knelt in the loose, sloping soil, and leaned forward cautiously.

"Don't fall in," Sam said.

"Thank you, I shall try not— *Run!*"

That was a savage bark, as Randolph hurled himself away from the pit, landing on his arse. Saul started towards him instinctively. Sam grabbed his arm, shouting, "He said run!" as Randolph scrambled backwards, trying to get his footing. He was still on the ground when a great long dark shape emerged from the mouth of the well.

It looked in the beam of light like the waving frond of a river-plant or the ragged limb of some great spider, and Saul stared in blank horror as it moved. It fixed itself in the earth, a second one came out, and the head and shoulders of a long-armed fen-grendel rose out of Camlet Moat's holy well.

"*Forthlaede!*" Randolph bellowed, and ivy ripped out of the ground. "Run, you stupid sods!"

"Get on, then!" Sam shouted back, shoving Saul up the slope. Loose earth slipped and slid under his fingers and the toes of his shoes. "Get *up*, Saul! Take the torch!"

Saul rolled onto the edge of the pit, reaching for the torch with one hand, offering the other to Sam, who ignored it and vaulted up. Randolph was edging towards them, not taking his eyes from the mouth of the well, which was looped with greenery. Saul thought he could see it heave, as though the unnatural growth of ivy were a web and the thing struggling under it a huge insect.

"Get up here," he snapped at Randolph. "Come on!" He reached out. Randolph took his hand and scrambled inelegantly up and out. "Now what? Can you keep it in?"

"Unfortunately, dear boy, it's not an *it*. It's a *them*. Hence my alarm."

"Oh God," Sam said. "How many?"

"All of them."

There was a cracking sound from the well, the splintering of green wood. Saul trained the flashlight on the well mouth, revealing a tangled mass of greenery and long, clawed limbs scrabbling at every crack.

"That's the Master of London's horde," Randolph said. "Murder, torture, and rapine a speciality, and they go all the way down. We need to plug that hole."

As if on cue, the net of ivy heaved and split. Dark forms heaved, clambering out, and marsh-stink rolled over the watching men.

"*Leoht*," Randolph ordered, but the light was far less bright than Saul remembered from the castle, and the fen-grendels gibbered, but didn't flee.

"*Forthlaede!*" Sam barked at the same time, and green exploded from a single shaggy fen-thing's face. "Balls," he added. "This won't be enough. Saaamaaa Ritual?"

Randolph shook his head. "No use. They're native. They're *here*."

"And they're still coming out," Saul said.

"So use your words!" Sam snapped.

Randolph spoke. The words shuddered and clanged in Saul's brain, making his skull vibrate, each of them a hammer blow of iron. He reeled sideways, Sam dropped to a knee for balance, the fen-grendels shrieked cacophonously. And the world *lurched*, a dreadful thump like a huge heartbeat.

"Jesus wept," Sam said, rather loudly, as though he'd been deafened. "*Don't* do that again."

"Not planning to." Randolph sounded somewhat ragged. "That wasn't a good idea. Fighting fire with fire when what I need is water."

Sam shone the torch into the pit. The fen-grendels were all hunched over in apparent pain or shock, but they were unquestionably alive, and as Saul watched they started rising to their feet. "They'll be out of there any moment. And there's nothing to stop them strolling into London, all teeth and claws. How the devil do we stop that many of them?"

"They'll have to cross the bridge first," Saul said.

"They're amphibious," Randolph said irritably. "I'm fairly sure they can manage the moat."

He was still wearing his hat. Saul snatched it off his head, scrambled down the edge of the bank to the moat's edge, and scooped up as much of the algae-covered water as he could. It seemed to glow faintly. He returned to the edge of the pit, Sam lighting his way with the torchbeam, thought *Please be right*, and tossed the pint of brackish moat-water over the creatures below.

The scream that erupted was appalling. The fen-grendels heaved and fought to get away as though the water were acid, a movement that urged the seething crowd of them toward the sloping side of the pit furthest from Saul. One of them fell onto the slope, and started to climb with a gibbering cry.

"*Forthlaede*," Randolph commanded, and it writhed and screamed as ivy burst from its face, but there were more climbing now. "All right, point made, now stop ruining my hats."

"The water doesn't like them," Sam said. "That's something. So the Moat will hold them in as long as we can stop them crossing the bridge."

"At least until Johnny-in-the-well wakes up," Randolph said. "At which point all bets are off. Where are our reinforcements?"

"Do we have some?" Saul asked, with a flicker of hope.

"Probably lost in the fucking dark," Randolph said, and then his legs were jerked violently from under him. He crashed downwards into the pit with a scream, and disappeared into the mass of fen-grendels.

Sam bellowed, dropping the torch and hurling himself forward. Saul leapt to where the beam of light shone over the edge of the pit. He couldn't see anything except heaving bodies and flailing parts—claws, limbs, branches shooting up—and he couldn't do a damn thing to help Randolph, lost under shrieking devils. Everything was screaming, in pain or triumph or hatred, and he could hear the horrible low chuckling again, around or under him, as the terrible wrongness slowly pulled Camlet Moat apart.

This was his fault, his appalling failure. He'd been the Walker of Camlet Moat for two days and presided only over its death, and now it had taken Randolph too.

Walker, said a silvery breeze by his ear, quiet as the rustle of a leaf, as though he could hear such a thing over the shrieks.

Saul knelt, digging his fingers into the earth, calling on the image of the Moat as it should be in his head. The great ancient power of the endless forest, the purity of the water, the sacred cathedral of trees pierced with dappled sunlight, the bright eyes in the leaves. There had to be something that the Moat could do and he was its Walker, he would be, he *was*.

He was only sure of one word so he said, whispering it, "*Leoht*."

The light was blinding. It was more than day: it was desert light, so bright it hurt, blasting through the ravaged soil. The fen-grendels shrieked and clamoured, scrabbling at the earth as though trying to bury themselves back under the ground. There were, Saul now saw, an awful lot of them. And there were a number *not* scrabbling or moving, because they seemed to be impaled on wooden stakes. Leafy ones, rising straight and tall in a tiny grove just big enough to hold a man.

"Randolph!" he shouted desperately.

Sam appeared from the other side of the sapling grove with blood running down his face, eyes screwed up against the glare. He wrenched and shouldered the slender branches aside, and bent to haul a long body out from between them.

"No," Saul whispered, a dreadful fear curling through him. "Please. Please, no. *Randolph!*"

"Keep that light on," Sam called up. "Good work. He's fine."

Randolph struggled free and rolled away, shoving himself to his knees. "I'm not fucking fine," he said, extremely testily. "Can we get out of this hole?"

He emerged from the pit in a way that suggested Sam had given him a shove to get him over the edge. His clothes were filthy and ripped, blood seeping through; his face was masked with blood from a vicious tear across his scalp; he was muddy and ichor-stained. He'd never looked better.

"I thought you were a goner," Saul said. His lips felt numb.

"I thought you were a clever man, and I was right." Randolph gave him a quick grin. There was blood outlining his teeth. "*The unenlightened man brings light,* indeed. Can you keep that up?"

"I don't know."

The laughter came again, a deep mad throbbing sound, as Sam clambered out of the pit. The light had faded to normal intensity now, as though it were merely day. Saul wasn't sure if he could do it again. His mouth was bitter with green leaves, his fingers cramping in the abused soil, and he could feel a debilitating weakness through his muscles. Apparently this power had a price.

"Of course he can't, after the day he's had. Come to that, I can't do much more greenery and nor can you, Randolph," Sam said. "We're retreating to the bridge. Up you get, Saul."

"Will the light stop if I do?"

The fen-grendels were moving with purpose now, not pain. There was a surge of movement like the sway of waterweed, and a wave of them tumbled up the other side of the pit, just as reaching claws scratched the ground on Saul's side, and caught, and held.

"Let's risk it," Randolph said. "Up."

Saul grabbed two fistfuls of earth and allowed himself to be pulled to his feet. The three of them retreated, backing toward the bridge as the first of the fen-grendels gained its footing and stood straight.

It was about six feet tall, its arms hanging to its knees, great hands twice the size they should have been and tipped with curving claws. It was bedraggled green-brown, wet and stinking, and when it looked at Saul and opened its mouth in a long hiss, he saw all the teeth in the world.

There were about a hundred of them in the pit, and more coming, endlessly more. He could feel it, as though the well tunnel became a gullet, into the belly of something foul and ancient and stirring.

"Bastard's waking up," Randolph said. "You're the Walker. Can we break the bridge?"

"Not from the other side," Saul said, realising the truth of that as he spoke, as though reciting a long-ago lesson. "Nothing could. It's made to last. I—rather think I could close it off from here, though."

"No," Randolph said, "because that leaves you on the wrong fucking side. Saul—"

Saul stared at the pit. There were more fen-grendels climbing out, and those on the ground were spreading, forming a line with rudimentary military cunning. They wouldn't attack in single file to be picked off; it would take just one rush. "You go."

"No."

"They're *coming*. If they cross the bridge—" He imagined the marshweed things with needle teeth crawling London's streets, lurking in gutters and ditches, infesting the river, spreading, spreading everywhere, with the malevolent intelligence of the Master of London rising up behind them. "Go!"

"Sod your heroics." Randolph's hand landed on Saul's shoulder. "I got you into this. Clear off, Sam, we'll handle it. And thank you. It's been a pleasure."

"Randolph, no." There was anguish in Sam's voice. "We need you on this side."

"But I need to be on this one," Randolph said. "Shift yourself. Saul, break the bridge, whatever it takes. Now."

The unnatural day was twilight now, fading fast. The fen-grendels were slinking forward, wary, menacing, growing in number and confidence. Saul dropped to one knee, putting his hand to the earth, feeling Randolph's touch on his shoulder, steadfast and steadying.

He would break the bridge, cut Camlet Moat off east of the sun, and for all he knew be trapped on this little patch of land for the rest of his life, which he hoped would be numbered in seconds rather than minutes. Trapped with the fen-grendels, and the frustrated Master of London, and Randolph.

"You should go," he managed.

"Don't be silly." Randolph's fingers tightened. "Finish it."

"There you are! Sorry we're late," announced a cheerful, vaguely familiar voice from the other side of bridge. "Not a cab to be had for ages, then we couldn't find— Good Lord, what are those things?"

Randolph hauled Saul up one-handed, so hard he was lifted off the ground, and pushed him away with a shove that sent him stumbling. "Get up a tree! You two hold the bridge, the water's deadly, *go!*"

Sam sprinted back across the bridge and past Saul, hurling himself up into the branches of an oak like a monkey, clamping his legs around a branch and swinging upside down as Saul clambered up. He was offering a hand to Randolph: naturally the upper-crust sod couldn't climb a tree. Saul scrambled to the same branch in a couple of movements, and between them they hauled Randolph up, kicking wildly. Saul gasped, "What—"

"Reinforcements," Sam said. "About time, too."

"There's only two of them!" Saul could see them in the remnants of the light: Barney, the cheery junior officer type who'd given him a lift to Randolph's flat; Max Isaacs, his Cockney manservant. They were standing on the bridge, chatting casually to one another as each stripped off hat and coat and tossed them to the planks of the bridge. They didn't even have weapons, Saul saw with bewildered horror. Just two men standing in shirtsleeves and braces as the fen-grendels rose from their stalking crouch and moved as one in a wave of marshweed hair, teeth and claws and limbs that surged to the bridge like doom.

Isaacs swung his arm out with a slicing gesture. A draggled, sharp-toothed head flew like a football, hit the ground under the tree, and bounced. Randolph grabbed Saul's arm as he recoiled, so he didn't fall out of the tree.

He could have sworn they hadn't carried weapons, but Isaacs now seemed to be wielding two whips, each apparently studded with razors, because as he swung, they severed anything they touched. Barney held some sort of—Saul couldn't make it out, some dark angled thing that jack-knifed out and cut—

Isaacs' whip snaked around a fen-grendel's neck, lifted the creature above the pack, swung it around like the arm of a crane, and dropped it in the water. It screamed as the green algae rose to meet it, but only briefly. The whip curled back on itself, hovered over the melee for a second, then stiffened to a rigid spear and stabbed savagely down, at which point Saul's eyes gave up their effort to tell him a plausible lie.

"He's got fucking tentacles!" he shouted at Randolph. "Look at them! Who the hell are they? *What* are they?"

"Military-occult experiment." Randolph spoke loudly over the screams. "The Government wanted a battalion of abominations, and you can see why. Perhaps fifty men were put through hell in the process, by arcanists including, I'm ashamed to say, my cousin Vernon. Only that pair survived what was done to them. Those responsible should have swung."

"They'd all died," Sam pointed out.

"Typical Vernon. Suppose we tackle the rest of the problem while our abominations hold the bridge?"

"Just a moment. Wait." Saul gripped the branch, struggling to breathe. He'd been prepared to trap himself on an island with monsters and end it there, settling his debt to society in a single act. He hadn't wanted to die, least of all now life had started to take on meaning once more, but there had seemed an inevitability to it, and he'd felt entirely serene in that flawless moment when Randolph had stood with him to make their atonement together. Finding himself up a tree instead, watching two not-quite-men go through monsters like a threshing machine, was confusing.

"All right?" Randolph enquired, leaning close to speak at a reasonable volume.

"You were going to stay." The light faded out like a sigh. Saul was glad; he didn't want to see Randolph's face, or to have his seen. "I was going to— And you stayed."

"Did you think I'd leave?"

Saul couldn't find an answer. Randolph exhaled, a warm breath on his ear. "Ah, Saul. I will object to any further heroism on your part; it's a terribly bad habit to get into. Suppose we nail dear old Manders back into the coffin where he belongs, and continue this conversation at a more convenient time?"

Saul choked. "We were about to *die*. How can you be so—so—"

"Facetious? Years of practice." Randolph's fingers met Saul's against the tree bark. "I'd far rather be itemising the ways in which I adore you, but I've Sam squashed up against me which is really not a sensual experience I've ever aspired to, not to mention the dead prick in the well. Duty calls, Walker. Sam, old chap?"

"Here," Sam said. "Not deaf, either, and may I say you're no prize. Are those blasted things still climbing out of that hole?"

Randolph twisted to look. "They are, which suggests our friend is still in it for now. But clearly something that held him down has been removed. We need to lock him back in."

"Good-oh. How?"

"Asking you again, Saul," Randolph said. "You were ready to die for the Moat; now live for it. It's still holding our friend back, poisoning the waters against him. How may we help? What was stolen? What must we return, or replace, to keep him in? Think. You needn't tell us if it's a deep secret, but we need to know what to do, and I don't have a clue."

Saul looked around. His eyes were adjusting to the night—there was some moon, behind scudding clouds, the dull glow of London in the air. Enough to see the rise of trees around him, the heaving murderous chaos beneath. Barney and Isaacs were foursquare on the bridge, planted side by side, a distinct gap between their strangely shaped silhouettes and the ragweed things that gibbered and darted. The fen-grendels didn't want to die either, it seemed.

"I'll try," he said. "Make sure I don't fall?"

"Always." Randolph's arm came around his waist, fingers splaying. It was a firm hold and didn't feel at all like a grip for security.

Saul shut his eyes. He didn't want to think about the mechanical digger's blade biting into the well—he thought he might vomit again if he did—so instead he tried to imagine the well as it should have been, a stone-lined shaft, cool and deep and mysterious. It had held treasure, according to Major Peabody, the poor, stupid Major, whose body must lie trampled and disregarded, and he'd been wrong anyway. The well had held...

He could taste metal on his tongue again, dull and sweet and somehow soft. He could feel the weight, too, not crushing but confining. Lead, Saturn's metal, the stuff of transfiguration and doorways, death and rebirth and something in between.

De Mandeville was neither buried nor unburied; shot and hanged and drowned but not dead. Held in between life and death, his rotten heart seething with hate, but still fulfilling his vow as Master of London. Turncoat murderer, eternal protector.

"It's a balance," Saul said softly, or felt the words whispered through him. "And one thing shifted." Like scales, he realised, like a finely calibrated balance, when a dribble of sand could destroy the equilibrium. The weight on the Master under the water had become just a little less, not quite enough. "It was lead."

"Are you sure?" Randolph said sharply.

"Yes. Just enough weight. It was—" He felt the dull metal, cold and ridged in his hand, wedged into a crevice between the stones to keep the well. It had weighed just a few ounces, or if you considered its real weight, it had been heavier than any church.

"We need to weigh him down more," he said desperately. "With lead. *Heavy* lead. Not metal, but meaning, do you understand?" *Please understand*, he thought, *because I bloody don't*. "A sacrifice. They made a lead sacrifice, over him, and that was what held him."

"A lead sacrifice," Sam said. "What the devil does that mean? I don't mind seeing if I can nick some off a church roof, if you think—"

"Not needed," Randolph said. "We have to get to the well right now. Chop chop, no time to lose."

"How?" Saul demanded. "The island is seething with grendels, and your friends are busy on the bridge!"

"You can't use Wayland's words again," Sam said, warning in his voice.

"I don't need to. Saul's the Walker. He'll walk."

"*What?*" Saul demanded. "Can you not see them?"

"We're going to walk to the well, you and I," Randolph said. "Come on. Do you happen to have anything handy in that bag, Sam?"

He took something Sam offered, then squirmed on the branch, turning. Saul said, "Wait. I can't—!"

Randolph grinned bloodily at him. "Light my way."

He dropped to the ground. Howls erupted from multiple throats. Saul said, desperately, "*Leoht!*"

The light came—fainter, though, much fainter. His own failure, or Camlet Moat losing strength as the sleeper woke? No time to tell. Randolph had both hands out in a fighting stance, and a blade gleaming in one. He lunged at a fen-grendel in a way that suggested his war hadn't been entirely occult, and another dropped at the same time, vines sprouting from its mouth.

Saul swung himself down to land on the welcoming earth, Sam right behind him. "How do I do the leaves?"

"Focus on the light," Randolph said. "Claim your ground, ignore interruptions. Lead on, Walker, we're with you."

Saul walked. It ought to have been a few steps to the pit and the ravaged well, but he could feel the stretch of time and place in his mind. Camlet Moat was still there, wounded but living under his feet, and Saul breathed into it. *I'm here. I'm with you. We stand.*

Randolph and Sam were a green presence beside and behind him. Saul didn't look round, fixing his gaze on the path to the well, but he had the impression of bright eyes, leafy faces in the corner of his vision. Jacks in the Green, Green Men, part of a deep knowledge so ingrained he'd never known he had it. He walked in the yellow-green dappled light and ignored the thumps, shouts, and occasional bubbling scream.

Then they were at the pit, staring down into the endless black hole of the well, and Saul woke up.

It stank here, of fen-mud and weed and ancient dry rot, and the earth felt as though it were holding its breath, held in tension by the malevolent force under the water. It was gathering strength, and soon it would break its bonds and spring.

The discarded flashlight still lay on the ground, beaming white light. Sam picked it up, shone it onto a fen-grendel crawling over the side of the pit, and used it to hit the creature an extremely solid blow on the head. He clobbered it twice more before it fell back in; he slid down after it, shouting a word that sprayed earth and made the grendel scream. "Come on!"

Saul followed, slithering and slipping down the loose earth. There was another fen-thing emerging from the well mouth; Randolph took a long stride forward, dodged a flailing claw, and stabbed it in the eye with disturbing competence. "Right, Saul. Quick!"

"What?" Saul said desperately. "I don't know what to do!"

"Lead sacrifice. Your bullet. Throw it in."

Saul's hand went up to his neck. "But—"

"*No gun will save you.* We don't need a gun for that bullet. It's lead, and it's hung between life and death if ever metal has. And don't tell me it's not heavy, I've never felt a heavier thing. That's your sacrifice, Walker. Give it to the Moat, and hold the bastard down while we put this right."

Saul reached for the clasp. His fingers were shaking. He couldn't even remember how it worked; he'd never taken the chain off. He twined two fingers in the metal links and pulled.

"Any time you like," Sam said calmly. "Only there's rather a lot of them gathering round the edges."

Saul tugged again and this time the chain broke. He looked at the lump of lead in his hand. It meant death and shame and failure, loss and betrayal, unspeakable, unbearable grief which he'd lived in order to carry.

Randolph was right. It was so heavy he could barely lift it.

"I hope it nails you," he whispered to Geoffrey de Mandeville, and dropped it into the well.

The scream came from everywhere at once. It ripped through Saul's head, and blood, and hair, and he dropped to the ground as though his tendons had been cut, curling into a ball, vaguely aware he was dangerously near the well mouth but unable to move. The sound shrieked from below and above and around and through, the whole of Camlet Moat convulsing with agony as sky and earth shook with the impact of the single bullet.

And then it stopped.

Saul uncurled, eardrums throbbing, and looked up to see the baffled, distorted face of a fen-grendel shaking its head about a foot away. He yelled and hurled himself back, and a knife buried itself in the creature's skull with a meaty thud. The grendel fell sideways, and then Randolph was there, on his knees by Saul. "Saul. Dear one. Are you all right?"

"I think so."

"Good man. Stay out of the way while we mop up the stragglers." Randolph leaned over to retrieve the knife with a tug and a squelch. "And when we have time, remind me to tell you that you're marvellous."

He stalked off, knife in hand. Saul looked after him, bewildered, and saw Sam holding the flashlight and rubbing at his ear.

"That was loud. Well done, old chap. It seems you did the trick."

"For now."

"That's all we can usually hope for." Sam extended a hand. Saul took it and regained his feet. "I suggest you and I stay here in case anything else comes up through that well. Barney and Max can do all the mayhem required up there, if there's a finite number of the damn things."

"What about Randolph?"

"I'd let him relieve his feelings a bit. It'll do him a power of good."

"And what about Major Peabody?" Saul asked. "Where on earth— I can't see his body."

Sam ran the flashlight beam over the churned earth, and made a face. "It's possible they ate him. Poor old chap. Bloody fool."

"Yes." Saul looked around at the fallen tree, the churned earth, the well mouth. "And the Moat? That is—well, what happens now?"

Sam shrugged. "I don't know, Walker. You tell me."

CHAPTER FOURTEEN

"So this room will be yours," Sam said. "I'm at the front of the house on this floor. Barney and Max are both upstairs, but I wouldn't go wandering up willy-nilly. And if you do go up and their doors are bolted, do *not* let them out." Saul blinked. Sam gave him a rueful grin. "Just in case. Anyway, I hope it suits. Feel free to put up shelves or pictures or what-have-you, or to claim furniture from the unused rooms. We have a lot."

The bedroom was a larger and more comfortable room than any Saul had slept in for years, barring that one night in the Albany with Randolph. This wasn't comparable, of course, but it was good-sized, plainly decorated, and solidly furnished with inexpensive pieces from the middle of the previous century. A desk, a couple of old but comfortable-looking armchairs by the fire, and a large iron-framed double bed.

"Thanks," he said, feeling the word's inadequacy. "I can't help feeling I'm imposing horribly."

"Not at all. It's much easier having us all together, and you're one of us, like it or not."

"It's an honour," Saul said. "However— Look, I'm afraid we haven't discussed rent. Randolph rather dragooned me here and what with all the upheaval, I didn't think."

He couldn't have declined the invitation to move to Fetter Lane even had he wished. Major Peabody was dead; Saul had no savings, no prospects, no job in any conventional sense, and no time to do one even if he could get such a thing due to the weight of responsibility that had descended on him. Camlet Moat had to be repaired, the stolen thing reclaimed. Finding the rent was, Randolph had decided for him, an unnecessary distraction.

"Oh, don't worry about that," Sam said. "Randolph's rich as Croesus, all the family money for umpteen generations—"

"Randolph does not pay for me," Saul said rather crisply.

"Hold your horses. As I was saying: Randolph is rolling in it, and this is what he does. He supports the Green Men in London because it's a full-time job now and we all need to eat and dress. The house belongs to Jo, my sibling, so no need to fret about rent, and there's a monthly stipend for everybody. Including Barney and Max although they aren't Green Men as such, and including you because you are. Good luck finding time to spend it." He gave Saul a wry smile. "You're the Walker of Camlet Moat; you don't need any additional difficulties. Er, on which subject..."

"Yes?" Saul said cautiously.

"Well, just that nobody will give a damn if Randolph's here for breakfast, or indeed if you're not. What I mean is, feel free to conduct your personal business as you choose. Obviously one can't invite just anyone back here, as a matter of everyone's privacy, not to mention the stuff that tends to be lying around, so guests need to be chosen with care. But amongst us, it's Liberty Hall. Is that all right?"

"Uh, yes. Perfectly." Saul knew his face was scarlet. "That's extremely decent of you."

"I'd call it the bare minimum. Anyway, we'd all like to see Randolph happy, if only because he doesn't half spread it around when he's not."

Saul choked. "I believe you. Thanks, Sam."

"Thank me the first time you run into Max or Barney having an episode. I'll need to talk you through what to do about that. Oh, and if you see the ghost of a stout elderly man with a smashed head, let me know. I've sent him packing a dozen times but the swine will not leave."

"Are you serious?"

"Sadly, yes," Sam said. "Welcome to Fetter Lane. I suspect you'll fit right in."

Once his few things were unpacked, Saul joined the others gathered in the sitting room to wait for Randolph, who was expected back in the late afternoon. He wasn't sure what he expected—talk of supernatural matters, perhaps, or to be initiated into some course of peculiar study—but as he came in, Max Isaacs looked him up and down with a shrewd, penetrating gaze and said, "Afternoon. You any good with the cards?"

"You mean the Tarot?"

"Don't be a berk. How about whist?"

They decided on gin rummy, played at the single large table. Barney declared himself to be an utter duffer at cards, an assessment with which Max didn't argue, and instead settled on the sofa with *The Mysterious Affair at Styles*, which Saul made a mental note to borrow in due course. Sam put his feet up with a sheaf of papers.

And there they were, four chaps at home in their shared lodgings, passing a few idle hours in companionable quiet. Saul was disgraced, Barney and Max were apparently monsters, God knew what Sam might be; and it seemed that none of those things mattered. It was trivial, casual, quite unremarkable, and the most wonderful afternoon Saul had spent in years.

He had no idea what fresh horrors his bizarre new life might hold, but whatever the price would be, he'd pay it. For acceptance and perhaps even friendship; for a place to fill and a job to do; for time with Randolph.

Saul was ahead on points but losing a hand in spectacular fashion when there was the noise of arrival in the hall, and an aristocratic voice yelled, "Shop!"

"In here!" Sam and Barney chorused.

Max rolled his eyes, rapped the table, and put down his cards. "Gin. All right, let's see what his worship's got."

Randolph was elegantly dressed as ever, hair slicked back, appearance only slightly marred by the sticking plaster over the cut on his head. He'd undeniably taken the largest part of the damage. Barney and Max had looked battered that night but, Saul couldn't help observing, had both seemed entirely unscathed the next day.

Randolph took one of the armchairs. "God, that was a dull journey. The train was held at Peterborough for half an hour with a broken signal."

"Shocking," Sam said. "Was that the most noteworthy part of your trip?"

"There were a few other matters that might interest you." He'd been in Cambridge, Saul knew, interrogating Mr. Abchurch as to what he knew about the whole business, and what Major Peabody had done up in the Fens. "For a start, it seems fairly clear that Abchurch wasn't an active participant in this shambles. Major Peabody initiated contact, letter out of the blue saying that he'd been given Abchurch's name as a de Mandeville expert. Abchurch was flattered, but also confused, because he hasn't published a thing. He's been working on a monograph for ten years or so but with no urgency; had a couple of letters in historical journals but none recently. He did not feel that, if one asked around for an authority on de Mandeville, his name would be first, or even tenth."

"So how and why did Peabody choose him?" Sam asked.

"This is the question. In Peabody's initial approach, he claimed to have been given Abchurch's name by 'a correspondent'. Abchurch asked about that when they met, and says Peabody declined to answer, claiming he was acting under a promise of secrecy and could not give a name."

"That's the kind of thing he always said," Saul put in. "Which doesn't stop it being true, I suppose. He insisted all along that the de Mandeville book had been sent to him anonymously."

"Ah yes. The famous book. We'll come back to that."

Max had broken into the Major's house the previous day so Saul could search his papers, and everything on de Mandeville had gone. The study hadn't seemed ransacked, or even disturbed, and nothing else had been missing that Saul could see, but there was no sign at all of the book, notes, or any correspondence. Whether Major Peabody had taken it with him or someone else had come to get it first was impossible to say.

"Do you believe Abchurch?" Sam asked.

Randolph shrugged. "I had no sense he was lying to me, and he produced Peabody's letter as evidence. Let me tell this in order. I asked Abchurch if he'd had any approaches or visits or unexpected correspondence recently, and that was where it became interesting. It seems he recently received a single page from a fourteenth-century work, apparently sent on approval from a noted dealer, but without documentation or price. However, when he wrote to query this, the dealer denied all knowledge and wouldn't accept either payment or return. He insisted, in fact, that he had never possessed such a thing, let alone sent it to Abchurch."

"Well," Sam said. "Well, well."

"Quite. Abchurch kept the page, for lack of any idea what to do with it. He said it appeared to be extremely old and he believed it genuine."

Sam was sitting forward. "What was on this page?"

"A map of 'Camelot Moat'," Randolph said. "Camlet Moat when the buildings still stood, and with the well marked as the location of, I quote, *crux antica regis*. The ancient cross of the king."

Saul remembered the feel of the lead thing on his palm, the hard straightish edges. "That was what was in the well? A cross?"

"A king's cross," Barney repeated thoughtfully. "Which king? Hang on, hang on. *Camelot*?"

"Christ, don't you start."

"Did you get hold of this paper?" Sam demanded.

"I did not," Randolph said, "because Peabody did. He offered Abchurch a large sum for it, which that rather decent gentleman refused since it wasn't his to sell. Whereupon I regret to say that Peabody concealed it in his luggage and departed. That was why he abandoned you to the Fens, Saul; he was making away with the loot. He saw his chance for a great discovery, and he took it."

Sam steepled his fingers, frowning. "This sounds awfully convenient, doesn't it? He happens to receive a book about de Mandeville and a lead to Abchurch, who happens to have received a peculiar and untraceable document?"

"If you were going to tailor a trap for him, it would look just like this," Saul said. "An anonymous correspondent, someone taking him seriously. A rare and mysterious book. Proof of its truth when the Southcott Oak burned—"

"If someone set fire to the Oak purely in order to lure Peabrain, I am going to do violence."

"And after that, he was ready to listen to anything that supported his ideas," Saul went on. "He'd follow any path on which this marvellous anonymous correspondent chose to lead him—particularly one that led to the Fens, of course. And if he then saw some ancient treasure map linking de Mandeville to his Arthurian fantasies— You're right, Sam, it's far too convenient. Someone wound him up, and set him off." He remembered the dead face, despoiled earth in the slack mouth. "God. Why?"

Sam made a face. "We have to assume, to get their hands on what was in the well. The cross, if that's what it was. If someone wanted to find it while hiding their tracks—well, Peabody was easily hid behind. I've had the Trent Park people looking into it while you've been away, Randolph. It seems that Peabody bribed a couple of their groundsmen to do the work off the books, the damned fools."

"Do they know anything more?"

"No. Isaacs and I had a chat with them this morning," Barney said. "They'd have told us more if they could. People usually do."

Max grinned mirthlessly. "It's the Captain's natural charm what does it."

"So our theory is that some blighter set up Peabody to raid the Moat, then took the cross off him," Sam said. "What about the business in the Fens with you two? How does that fit?"

"Something stirred up de Mandeville in the Fens the first night Saul was there," Randolph said. "Herbert, the Vicar, panicked, as usual. He's never been up to the job. My father always used to hold his hand, but he's dead so Herbert called me."

"Some bugger was up to something in Temple Church. That set off a fuss in the Fens, and you trotted up and got caught," Max said. "Doesn't sound like chance, does it? They set you up too, Mr. G."

"That's really quite irritating." Randolph's drawl was casual, ironic, and held just a slight promise of burning buildings and ground sown with salt.

"Although they didn't quite manage to get you out of the way," Sam pointed out.

"But nearly. You know what it's like: we could have been gone for weeks or months, or not have returned at all. They took a chance, a daring one. And it worked, thanks to those imbeciles at the Ministry arresting Saul at precisely the wrong time."

"Are we worried about that?"

"They didn't know he was the Walker. If they had, it would suggest collusion, but I can't see any way they *can* have. And their efforts to get in my way were no greater than usual. It is possible that was simply a stroke of luck for our thieving friends. Regarding whom..." Randolph grimaced. "I suppose we all realise what this means."

"I don't," Barney said.

"It's someone in the know." Sam's voice was flat. "Someone who knew about Camlet Moat, even knew there was something in the well, and that seems to be a deep secret so far as we can tell from Saul. Someone who knew Randolph had to be got out of the way, and was able to summon up that business in the Fens. This isn't an enthusiastic treasure-hunter blundering in. This is the arcane equivalent of a cashier robbing the bank."

"Any occultist who knew all that would know the importance of Camlet Moat," Randolph said. "It's a cornerstone of London's protections, and someone ripped it apart to get their hands on treasure? Christ, I hate people."

"You sure it's that way round?" Max asked.

"Meaning?"

"Camlet Moat's like a machine-gun nest for London, right? What if this was someone trying to take it out? They didn't rip the Moat apart to get the cross; they took the cross to rip the Moat apart." Max shrugged. "Just a thought."

"Treachery." Something in the timbre of Barney's voice sent a decided and unpleasant crawling sensation down Saul's spine. "*A fool and a knave may do what an emperor could not.* Peabody was a fool. Who's the knave?"

Sam massaged his temples. "I don't suppose anyone has any bright ideas?"

"Not so far," Randolph said. "We'd better find out. Saul and I will be putting the Moat back together, insofar as that's possible, and I am going to go through the Ministry like a particularly nasty dose of clap. I've an appointment with Sir Ranjit tomorrow to stir him out of his torpor, and I will see Delingpole and Bracknell hung out to dry, and dig out any malicious intent while I'm at it. After which, gentlemen, we are going to find this cross or whatever it is, and the thieves or traitors who took it, and make them regret this. All the while keeping London ticking over, naturally. Any questions?"

They ate together—Max was quartermaster of the household—talking out the problem until the clock struck nine.

"Enough of today, I was up at five," Randolph said with a yawn. "Coming, Saul?"

Saul followed him out, feeling his face heat. He cast Randolph a look in the hall, and received a tilted brow in return. "Problem?"

"You weren't terribly subtle."

"We don't have to be," Randolph said. "Isaacs doesn't comment, Sam doesn't care, and Barney doesn't notice. This is a safe house, my dear, and you may do as you please. I rather wondered if we could have a word about that."

Saul led the way up to his room, waving Randolph to a chair. He couldn't help the twitch of nerves, despite everything said and done; he made himself sit, and wait.

"This is pleasant," Randolph said, looking around. "In its way. A little Spartan, perhaps. Can I offer you a Futurist painting to liven it up?"

"No, you cannot. It's a lovely room. You're just a sybarite."

"And proud of it. Saul, I wanted to speak to you. We rather fell into each other's arms at a fairly vile time. Well, it's been fairly vile for years. And I felt that I ought to raise the question of, let us say, the heightened emotions, the natural reaction to danger and so on—"

"Yes," Saul said, stifled. "Of course."

"Except that we were safe as houses dining in the Cafe Royal, and I will treasure that evening all my life." Randolph gave him a crooked smile. "I am not going to assume anything, my dear. You've had a hell of a time and, as Sam so rightly observes, I'm no prize. But Jo Caldwell was on the button about you. You bring light, you have brought me more light than I had thought would ever be possible. I didn't know there could be someone like you, I had no idea at all, and if you should choose to be rid of me tomorrow I shall nevertheless and always be bloody glad we met."

"And if I don't choose to be rid of you, tomorrow or later?"

"Well, that would be significantly better."

"I'm not sure how you think I could," Saul said. "The way you've stood by me, the way you're just—just *there*—" He couldn't find words for Randolph's unsentimental generosity, his acceptance, as strong and supple and steadfast as a blade. He'd looked past everything, and seen a light that Saul had thought gone out for good.

"I feel like myself again, with you," Saul managed. "I feel as though you gave me back myself."

"That would be a rare gift indeed, because you are quite exceptional. May I stay?"

"I hope you will."

"May I continue to stay?"

Saul smiled into his eyes. "As long as you like."

"Does the bed creak?"

"Let's find out."

There was no palaver with clothing this time. Randolph stripped off his shirt, perhaps with a fractional hesitation but not enough to need comment. He straddled Saul, supine on the quilt, with a meaningful expression, splaying his hard hands over Saul's chest as though he wanted to own everything within.

"My God, you're beautiful." He leaned forward for a kiss, and Saul met his lips, wrapping his legs around Randolph's waist, pulling him close. "I believe I promised to tell you all the ways in which I adore you. It may take some time."

Saul looked up into his dappled hazel eyes. Randolph looked back, and for once there was no irony, no tilted brow. He seemed raw, almost vulnerable. "I dare say it's absurd. We haven't known each other very long and so on and so forth. But I refuse to fuck under false pretences. I have a sinking feeling, based on no prior experience whatsoever, that I love you, you damned inconvenient turner-up in all the wrong places, and it's only right you should know, and—well, good luck with that. Ah, you aren't obliged to reciprocate," Randolph added. "I just thought I'd mention it."

"For heaven's sake," Saul said. "You've devastated me in the best possible way from the moment we met, and if you don't know that, you haven't been paying attention."

"I've been busy." Randolph pulled him close, burying his face in Saul's neck. "Saul, my Saul, my lightbearer. I sincerely hope this can survive us working together."

"You're intolerable," Saul assured him. "On the other hand, my most recent point of professional comparison is Major Peabody."

"Thank God for low standards." Randolph pushed himself up on his elbows. "Great Scott, I worship you. Let me see, where were we?

I'm fairly sure I intended to make love to you till you're hopelessly enslaved to my erotic wiles, and also can't walk straight. Suppose you turn over and I get on with that?"

"That sounds all right to me," Saul said. "Suppose you do."

The Green Men series

England, 1923. The Great War is over, the Twenties are roaring in, the Bright Young Things hold ever more extravagant parties. It seems as though the world has changed for good. But some far older forces are still at work, and some wars never end.

The occult battles fought in the War Beneath the War have torn the veil protecting our world from what lies outside. With most of the country's arcanists dead, and the Government unwilling to face the truth of the damage done, a small group pledged to an ancient duty must protect England from supernatural threat.

Set in the world of KJ Charles' award-winning *The Secret Casebook of Simon Feximal*, the Green Men series covers a motley crew of occult experts, jobbing ghost-hunters, and walking military experiments as they fight supernatural and human threats, save the land, and fall in love.

The story continues in *Last Couple in Hell*.

Last Couple in Hell

Green Men book 2

Theresa Glyde was once a Green Man, guardian of one of England's crucial magical sites. Now she's dead, but that's no excuse for lazing about. She has vital work to do, if only she can get back to the right side of reality. And that means finding someone she can use—with a willing body, a suitable mind, and an awful lot of nerve.

Joanie Robey has a London deity's blood in her veins, and a lifelong acquaintance with the strange, the unnatural, and the scary. She also has a perfectly good job as an artists' model and no interest in being possessed by a ghost. Particularly not an upper-class party girl who's having far too much fun being in a body again.

But the Green Men are dangerously overstretched. The veil that protects reality is slowly, steadily tearing, and now something is mounting an attack on London's occult protections. Joanie and Theresa must learn to cope with their forced intimacy–and their growing attraction to each other. Because the fragile bond between the goddess and the ghost may be England's last line of defence.

The Secret Casebook of Simon Feximal

A note to the Editor

Dear Henry,

I have been Simon Feximal's companion, assistant and chronicler for twenty years now, and during that time my Casebooks of Feximal the Ghost-Hunter have spread the reputation of this most accomplished of ghost-hunters far and wide.

You have asked me often for the tale of our first meeting, and how my association with Feximal came about. I have always declined, because it is a story too private to be truthfully recounted, and a memory too precious to be falsified. But none knows better than I that stories must be told.

So here is it, Henry, a full and accurate account of how I met Simon Feximal, which I shall leave with my solicitor to pass to you after my death.

I dare say it may not be quite what you expect.

Robert Caldwell
September 1914

More Books by KJ Charles

A Charm of Magpies series
The Magpie Lord
A Case of Possession
Flight of Magpies
Jackdaw
A Queer Trade
Rag and Bone

Society of Gentlemen series
The Ruin of Gabriel Ashleigh
A Fashionable Indulgence
A Seditious Affair
A Gentleman's Position

Sins of the Cities series
An Unseen Attraction
An Unnatural Vice
An Unsuitable Heir

Green Men series
Spectred Isle
Last Couple in Hell
Damned Young Things

Standalone books
Think of England
The Secret Casebook of Simon Feximal
Wanted, a Gentleman

About the Author

KJ Charles is a writer and editor. She lives in London with her husband, two kids, a garden with quite enough prickly things, and a cat with murder management issues.

Find her at www.kjcharleswriter.com for book info and blogging, on Twitter @kj_charles for daily timewasting and the odd rant, or in her Facebook group, KJ Charles Chat, for sneak peeks and special extras.